GOD ONLY
KNOWS

GOD ONLY KNOWS

BY

ELIZABETH REVILL

Author's Acknowledgements

My thanks to all my family and friends who have supported me throughout the creative process and most especially my husband, Andrew Spear, my dad, my son Ben Fielder, now a writer in his own right, and my dear friend Hayley Raistrick-Episkopos who never fails to cheer my spirits and with whom I share the greatest gift of all - laughter.

I always thought that God Only Knows would be the last in this particular series but I have received numerous requests for another and after so long I am ready to write another. So my next project will be one more in the lives of DCI Allison and Sergeant Stringer. It will continue where number three leaves off.

Finally, I must thank my amazing publishers Belvedere for all their wonderful encouragement and insight. Publishers don't get better than this.

Onwards and upwards and here's to the next!

Dedication

For Dad,

Who was always a great inspiration and a great man. You are so sorely missed by all who love you especially me.

1
With a little help from my friends

Rosie Partridge tossed her luxuriant, chestnut tresses with its fiery lights as she elegantly walked down her path to the front door of the flats. She didn't see the face from the bushes across the street devouring her every move. She didn't see the click of the zoom lens camera as several shots of her were taken in quick succession. She didn't see the look of satisfaction glint in the cameraman's eye, nor the cruel smile, which curled on his lips. He watched for a moment more until she had disappeared indoors and then walked nonchalantly past her house, his camera swinging like some snap happy tourist.

He paused momentarily at the bottom of the path and looked up at the window of her flat. The copper in Rosie's hair caught the midday sunlight as she moved past her living room window. He stirred himself and proceeded down the road to the church at the end of the street where he took several more photographs before moving onto the telephone booth at the corner of the road.

He dialled.

The telephone rang in Rosie's house.

She answered in a cheery tone, "Hello? ..."

Nothing.

Puzzled she replaced the receiver, pulled a face and marched into the kitchen to fill the kettle. The phone interrupted again.

This time Rosie gingerly picked up the receiver and listened. No one spoke. The receiver went 'click'.

She disconnected the call and dialled 1471. An official female voice came down the line, "You were called today, at twelve thirteen. The caller withheld their number. Please replace your set."

Rosie put down the phone and thought for a moment. She activated her answer phone and returned to the kitchen. She snapped on the radio, whilst waiting for the kettle to boil, although the blare of music brought her little comfort. She shivered.

That was the fourth time this week.

*

Vencat eyed himself in the mirror, adjusted his tie and smiled. His pearl white teeth glinted. They seemed to sparkle with that star of confidence from the toothpaste commercials. He looked good and he knew it.

His appearance had been altered just enough. He no longer resembled the flyers, which adorned the walls of Interpol and British police stations.

"You've done a grand job," he said appreciatively to the white-coated surgeon who stood at his side. "You've earned a nice, fat bonus."

Vencat removed a manila envelope containing what seemed to be a wad of notes from his inside jacket pocket and passed it to the eminent surgeon.

"Right, Riley, take him home."

Vencat's bodyguard who looked like he'd escaped from the set of Conan the Barbarian aped forward and ushered the doctor from the room.

The door closed softly behind them. Vencat gathered his papers together, checked his new passport in the name of Bartlett Sharma, and tossed them into the briefcase. He stopped briefly before rolling the combination locks. The satisfying clap of a pistol shot came from the room next door.

Vencat's usually slow smile spread quickly and readily across his remodelled features, which made him look, he believed, even more handsome than before. He picked up his case and swept from the room by the back door.

He paced down the dirt drive to his waiting Chevy and turned the key. The car began to roll down the track; he braked and stopped once he had reached a safe distance. Reaching into the glove compartment he took out a small black detonating device and flicked the switch. He turned fractionally in his seat to view the building he had just left and was rewarded with an explosion and fireball that both excited and contented him. Satisfied there would be no evidence left, he stepped on the gas, burst into song and drove off in a haze of dust for the airport.

*

Detective Chief Inspector Allison opened his desk drawer and looked longingly at the cocoa brown wrapper with passionate red writing, which read Mars Bar. Today was the day, the big day. Today he was to test his chocolate food sensitivity. He had spent months deprived of his vice. The vice, which had helped him conquer many a difficult case. Reduced as he was now, to carob bars he was convinced his thinking wasn't as clear as when he enjoyed the tempting delights of his beloved Mars Bars.

He had been stoic in his denial; religious in his keeping of a food diary and now the doctor had decided he was to test himself on some of the foods, which had previously triggered his migraines. Red wine, another culprit was now back on the menu, bananas however, were not. Now was the moment. He savoured it. Allison picked up the chunky bar. It felt good in his hands. He tore feverishly at the paper jealously guarding the mouth watering silky smooth chocolate. He felt his taste buds salivating with the promise of ecstasy and plunged his teeth into the yielding heaven. The caramel strands stretched from his lips and his tongue quickly retrieved all that he had missed and he chewed and swallowed. He looked at his watch and checked the time. It was bliss. Another four voracious bites and it was gone. Greg waited... Nothing. No flashing lights, no pounding pressure in his head, no rushing of blood in his ears. He hardly dared to believe it. Time would tell. The paper wrapper scrunched satisfyingly in his hand and dropped into the waste bin. The kinesiology that his daughter Cally had recommended had worked wonders. He flicked the intercom.

"Tea please, Maddie. And bring in the PM report on the Friel killing. Hurst promised it would be with me by three today."

"It's just been delivered. I'll get your tea."

Allison grunted softly and sat back in his chair. Things were looking better already. Grace Clifton was on remand awaiting trial. It was just her son, Tony Clifton who now posed major problems for the police. Allison had arranged to have him watched. He was convinced Clifton was a dangerous serial killer, despite evidence to the contrary and he was not going to allow the streets of Birmingham to run in fear once more.

Clifton had been secure for a number of months, residing at a voluntary, residential rehabilitation centre. But now.... now, he was on the move. He was going home. Young David Taylor who had transferred to CID was on the surveillance team with Pooley and with Beck, a newcomer to the West Midlands force. Allison was sure Clifton couldn't sneeze without him knowing. That in itself was reassuring.

There was a tap on the door, which opened at Greg's instruction.

Detective Sergeant Stringer presented himself before Allison.

"Well?" came the gruff tones of the DCI.

"I've got the results of the interviews in Handsworth. It's as you thought, there's a war on. Racial tension is running high."

"After the riots and the looting we made eighteen arrests. That should have calmed things down, I would have thought," remarked Allison.

"A temporary lull, I'm afraid, Sir. The youth of the Asian community are after revenge and they are not too particular who gets in the way. Simpson believes things are running out of control."

"Simpson?"

"Youth worker assigned to the patch. Has the ears and trust of the locals, black and white."

"I'll need to talk to him."

"He's coming in at three.... any word on Clifton?"

"He's being released today. Pooley's leading a surveillance team. We won't let him out of our sight."

*

Tony Clifton paid the taxi and stood at the front gate of his mother's house. He looked at the walk way littered with debris from the trees and the streets.

The path was no longer cleanly swept nor was the brass

4

letterbox gleaming. He caught his breath. He felt able to cope now and ready to return home. Didn't he? But could he return to Golden Hillock Road that was now devoid of his mother, who was imprisoned for his crimes as well as her own? He took a gulp of air and began the walk towards the front door. The curtains twitched briefly of the house next door. Lehmber Singh's face noted Tony's arrival then, the neighbour disappeared back into the recesses of the room.

Tony fumbled with the keys on his chain before finding the one to give him admittance to the family home. He pushed open the door with difficulty where junk mail and bills had piled up on the mat. He squinted in the dull light and tried the hall lamp. The electricity was off. Grumbling to himself he steered his way through the afternoon gloom to the main fuse box hidden behind the coat stand and flicked the switch. The fairy lights, around the old wooden cross on the wall, in the hall, blinked furiously, dazzling him. A roar of anguish erupted from his stomach. He snatched at the plain brown crucifix and the surrounding lights flashing on and off ripping them from their hangings. He stood there in the semi-gloom gazing at the desecration of wires, wood and lights and began to whimper like a small child as he closed the door against prying eyes. Tony retreated to the safety of the sitting room and sobbed.

There he remained until the escaping light of the afternoon had faded into a shadowy dusk.

*

Allison scratched his grizzled head. Mark Stringer was at his side and Simpson was in full flow.

"So you see, it's impossible to keep a lid on it. The white youths are roaming in gangs and now the Asians are doing the same. I can't say I blame them. They've turned the other cheek for far too long, but now.... now they are acting like Commancheros. It's getting out of hand."

"Do you know who they are?" Asked Allison.

"Some of them. A couple of the white bully boys are known National Front members, cause rumbles at football matches and so on. The Asian lads... I'm not so sure. As I said they're forming gangs and patrolling what they feel is

5

their territory and anyone who wanders in there by mistake is getting hammered, innocent or not. At least that is what I'm told. I have no proof except there is a marked increase in gang related graffiti on the street signs and walls."

"Who's handling this our end, Mark?"

"I believe Woodward is the liaising officer, Sir."

"Fix up a meeting with him and Simpson and let them take it from there. He's a good man, Woodward. He'll keep me informed."

*

Vencat sat comfortably in the first class cabin and stretched out his legs. He sipped his champagne. He almost laughed aloud as he inwardly toasted himself on his ingenuity, his new face, his new name and the fact that there was no one, no one left who could possibly identify him. His network was intact. Except that he, Bartlett Sharma, was now acting on behalf of Vencat but there could be one or two problems. The farmer in North Devon wouldn't recognise his voice. He was sure of that; they had only met the once. But Stuart Allen in Birmingham could be tricky. Stuart knew him very well and although faces change, mannerisms do not. He would have to be careful, very careful.

*

The black strap of night stretched before the silhouetted figure as he left his hideaway. Dressed in combat fatigues and a black balaclava he looked a formidable figure. His eyes burned with lust and longing as he took a last look at the snapshot of Rosie Partridge, which he held in his latex gloved hands.

"Soon, my darling. Soon," he huskily promised the glossy image. He stuffed the photo in his pocket, closed his front door and headed for his car.

He selected his route and unobserved he drove through the impersonal streets where no one knew anyone else and no one cared.

Once in the safety of an anonymous multi-storey car park, he removed the picture once again and stared at Rosie's image. It seemed to exhilarate him and give him a feeling of power. He pulled back the balaclava, to reveal his face, so as not to arouse suspicions from passers-by. Then, he slipped from his vehicle and made his way as unobtrusively as possible to the road where Rosie lived.

Few people were out. Cars that cruised the night rolled by intent on their own journies. No one paid him any attention. They were all wrapped up in their own worlds and their eyes saw nothing.

It was quiet in Saint Augustine's Road. It was quiet and dark. He settled himself by the red brick wall encasing the house opposite the small block of flats and looked up at her window. All was still. The curtains were closed. Her living quarters were engulfed in blackness.

The flame from his cigarette lighter dented the dark as he carefully singed the white edges of her picture. He took out a red pen and circled her head in a heart and inserted the photo into a self-seal envelope. Swiftly, he crossed the road and strode up the path where he deposited the envelope labelled with her name through the letterbox. There was a satisfying clunk as it hit the sides of the empty metal box. He checked his watch. It was 2:30 a.m. and he made his way to the phone booth on the corner.

He dialled Rosie's number.

*

Lehmber Singh awoke with a start. His wife Harpal clutched at him.

"Good gracious, Lehmber. Whatever is that noise?"

Their daughter and son came running in and tugged at their parents' bedclothes.

"Daddy, I'm scared," cried Harjinder

"Me, too," admitted Mohinder. "What's happening?"

The family huddled together and listened.

"Do you think we should call the police?" asked Harpal in a frightened tone.

"I don't know... I don't know. Let me think."

There was a terrifying, frenzied crashing and splintering of wood echoing through the walls. It was as if the house was being pounded by a demolition, wrecker's ball.

Next door, Tony was in a fit of fury. He swept his mother's precious hand carved box containing the tiny scrolls

7

of the verses of the Scriptures; each carefully wrapped in a red ribbon. He ripped down the benevolent pictures of Christ, which adorned the room. The incense and joss sticks were flung from their resting places. The small statuette of Madonna and child shattered in the hearth. Tony tore at the sign above the dining table heralding Christ as the unseen guest at every meal and he battered the model of the nativity on the dresser with a heavy glass ashtray. In his head he could hear his mother's reedy tones, with her thick Birmingham accent, spouting her truths from the Bible. He could see his mother's face, her thread veined cheeks and pale lips. Her cobra hooded eyes seemed to revolve in her head and rest on him. He wanted to stop her accusing stare. He yearned to crush her leering mouth, to shut her up. He smashed down the ashtray and ground it into the model until his hands, cut by the splinters of glass, were streaming with blood.

Tony let out a bellow, a roar of rage, which rose to a crescendo and died into a whimpering wail. He collapsed onto the floor amidst the debris and broken furniture and shuddered to a stop.

The doorbell rang.

*

"Would all passengers return to their places, fasten their safety belts and make sure their seats are in the upright position ready for landing."

Vencat, alias Bartlett Sharma, tossed his newspaper to the floor and altered his chair from recline. He swallowed the last of his champagne, glanced out of the porthole window and gazed down at the dark blanket of cloud beneath him, masking the lights of the control towers and runways of Gatwick airport. Now, would come the crucial test. Security in Columbia was slack. Not so in London. Would his passport and papers survive the acid test of a UK inspection?

He smiled confidently.

He was sure they would.

*

Tony reluctantly dragged himself off the floor and ventured towards the front door.

"Yes?" he enquired without opening it.

8

"Police. Mr. Clifton. We've had a report of a disturbance. May we come in?"

"Just a minute." Tony looked at the electrical mess of wiring, the broken lights and cross on the floor. He kicked at it with his foot towards the coat stand before opening the door.

The street light's muddy hues stretched into the hallway. Sergeant Pooley, together with young WPC Beck stepped across the threshold into the house in Golden Hillock Road.

Tony, if somewhat shaken did not show this and ushered the police into the hallway and through into the front room, avoiding the passageway to the parlour with its wreckage of religious artefacts. He switched on the light.

"Please sit down. Disturbance you say?"

Pooley and Beck gingerly seated themselves on the settee and Tony's well-cultured tones conveyed concern.

"I'm so sorry. I have just returned home and found the electricity was switched off. I'm afraid I blundered about a bit before finding the main switch. It must have sounded like a demolition derby when the dresser toppled over. Smashed most of my mother's blue willow china, it seems. I expect the neighbours thought I was wrecking the joint."

"Is that how you cut your hand?" queried WPC Beck in her lilting Dublin tones.

Tony hurriedly replaced his bloodied hand in his coat pocket.

"I must have done it picking up the broken glass and pottery fragments," he affirmed.

"I should get that looked at if I were you... it could get infected," she added.

"Thank you for your concern," he muttered and Tony's electric blue eyes held the gaze of the young WPC.

"Do you mind if we take a look around?" asked Pooley.

"Be my guest," replied Tony. "I expect this is something I will have to get used to..."

"Meaning?" questioned Pooley as he walked down the passage towards the parlour.

"You tell me... I'm newly released. Is this to be my future... constant surveillance?"

"Just a precaution, Mr. Clifton. Just a precaution." Pooley

stopped as he reached the parlour and surveyed the wreckage in the room.

"You certainly did blunder about..."

"I told you it was dark and there was no electricity." Tony's eyes held the gaze of the copper, "Now, if that is all, I would like to clear up this mess and get to bed. It's been a tiring day."

"Certainly, certainly... as long as that's it?" The question was left hanging in the air as the police walked back to the front door. Tony's eyes ranged over the WPC's shapely legs and he licked his lips.

The door opened to the street and with a flood of relief, Tony closed the door on the night and the police.

*

It was easy! No questions, no suspicious looks, no nothing. Vencat was home and dry. He smiled his perfect smile at the British Airways ground staff officer and moved out into the airport where people stood holding welcome cards and names. He soon spotted his driver, a sandy haired weasily looking man, holding a clipboard reading, "Mr. Sharma, Birmingham." Vencat crossed to the man. They exchanged a few words and Vencat followed the cabbie to the car park. He didn't notice the lean faced observer seemingly absorbed in a crossword seated near the automatic doors, who dialled out on his mobile phone as Vencat made contact with his driver. The anonymous shadow removed his glasses and hurried after the two men to the car park where his own vehicle was waiting.

*

Rosie Partridge was shaking. This was the first time he'd spoken. His voice was husky, low and threatening. She was sure it was disguised with some sort of voice changer gadget. And his laugh, his laugh had sent chill fingers of fear tracing down her spine. She reached for the light and fumbled with the switch in the pressing dark. Her heart was pounding. Her eyes twinged painfully at the flood of light and she screwed her face away from the lamp's glare. It was two thirty a.m. She listened to the small sounds of the night, imagining each creak of wood to be heralding the arrival of an intruder.

"Don't be ridiculous!" she told herself. "You're safe. No one can get in." Rosie swung her legs out of bed and pulled on her dressing gown. All remnants of sleep were now chased away. She checked each room. The windows were securely shut. The curtains were tightly closed against the prying eyes of the night. The safety door to the fire escape was firmly locked and bolted. Rosie paused. There was her front door and stairs to the flats' main door. Did she need to check there? No. The light on the stairwell, although dim, would allow those outside to see in whilst shielding trespassers from her view. She carefully put the chain on the door. The hallway could stay until morning. Rosie stepped softly into her kitchen and put the kettle on. A cup of tea would ease her troubled mind. She was just squeezing out the tea bag in her mug when the phone jangled for attention. Rosie froze. Impatiently the phone continued to ring, demanding to be answered. Rosie caught sight of her frightened face as she moved to the hall table and lifted the receiver.

"Awake, Rosie?" the voice asked. "Silly, both of us being up. If you can't sleep then why not make a cup of tea? Tell you what ... make a pot for two and I'll be round."

"Who is this? Why are you doing this? ... Leave me alone!"

"Now, that's not very friendly is it? Especially as I've been so concerned about you... There are things between us, Rosie. Things you can't possibly imagine... But the time will come..."

Rosie didn't wait to hear anymore. She slammed down the phone and then picked it up to dial the police but the call wasn't disengaged... he spoke again, "Now that wasn't a very nice thing to do was it?"

Rosie dropped the receiver into its cradle and ran into the lounge. She hunted frantically through her handbag for her mobile phone and rang the emergency services.

*

Holly awoke with a gasp. She sat up in bed. Paul grumbled softly in his sleep and placed a protective arm around her. He felt her trembling and forced himself awake.

11

"Holly? Holly what's wrong?"

"Cold! Oh, so cold." She shivered.

"What's happening? Not again?"

Holly began to cry, softly at first, gentle intakes of breath, which graduated into shuddering sobs. Paul cradled her in his arms, soothing her, gently kissing her face. He was worried. Was it happening again?

Holly struggled free from his loving embrace and sat bolt upright.

"It's her.... she won't let me be.... she wants me!" The tears began to flow once more.

Paul glanced at the bedside radio alarm 2:30 am. There had to be something he could do... something someone could do, anything to rid Holly of this recurring nightmare. Paul resolved to call their friend, criminal psychologist, Colin Brady, first thing in the morning. If anyone could help, he could. He had in the past.

*

Allison grimaced; the morning coffee was bitter and too hot. He flicked the intercom.

"What's wrong with the coffee this morning, Maddie?" he asked in his gravel tones.

"Sorry, Chief. I didn't make it. The new WPC did... She used the extra strong rather than your preferred fine blend."

"Well, get me another and pour this stuff away... and Maddie?"

"Sir?"

"Don't let her make it again."

Allison rummaged in his drawer and grabbed his Mars Bar. He was ecstatic. His beloved chocolate treat was back on the menu. The bin could have the remaining carob bars. It was bliss. Now, he felt he would be much better at coping with his workload. The phone rang.

"Yes?"

"Simpson here. Thought you ought to know the situation in Handsworth has been defused for the time being, except..."

"Well?"

"One house seems to be targeted by the bully boys, a small shop at the end of City Road."

"And?"

"Usual stuff, graffiti, and smashing windows, phone calls."

"What can we do?"

"I'm keeping an eye on things at the moment and working closely with the community policeman from Handsworth. The Asian youths are in check... just, but I don't know for how long. We need to stop this harassment of Darleston's."

"Darleston's?"

"The shop run by Jarnail Kumar. He kept the old name. Thought it would help them settle into the neighbourhood."

"Oh, I see. Thanks for the update."

"Anything new and I'll ring."

Allison replaced the phone just as Stringer walked in to the office.

"Busy night by all accounts, Sir."

"So, I understand," replied Allison. "Simpson's been on the phone. Something about harassment of a corner shop. Woodward should be onto it. See that he makes regular reports. We don't want a recurrence of the riots from two weeks ago. Anything else?"

"Mm. I think you'll find this interesting, Sir. Clifton trashed his house last night. The police were called out."

"Did he now? Any idea why?" asked Allison.

Stringer shook his head. "No. But if he puts a foot wrong we'll know about it. If he so much as blinks out of turn we'll be on him like a ton of bricks."

"Have you seen Brand's report?"

"No."

"It's there on the desk. It seems one of Vencat's men involved in the bogus meat packing plant at Bristol has served his time and turned driver. He picked up a rather elegant looking Asian from the airport and drove him to an address in Birmingham."

"Vencat?"

"No. But it's likely to be someone acting for him. Brand's been on his tail since he arrived in the city. It's a multi operational thing. Everything is reported back to the Met. They have a vested interest in anything that goes down."

"Because of Friel?"

"You can't kill an undercover cop and get away with it.... The Met want Vencat's blood in any shape or form."

"Anything for me?"

"Yes.... it could be nothing, or it could be something more sinister. See what you can find out about Rosie Partridge. Maybe pay her a visit."

"Rosie Partridge?"

"Yes, she rang here in the early hours absolutely terrified. Said she was being stalked."

"Why are you interested? That's usually something left to uniform to sort out."

"Rosie's a friend of my daughter, Cally, they went to school together. I remember her quite well. Not someone prone to flights of fancy... so, I thought we'd just keep an eye out. Maybe, I'll come with you. In fact, I will. Get a car. I'll meet you outside." Allison flicked his intercom, "Maddie hold all calls and cancel my morning appointments. There's something I want to check out."

"Yes, Sir." Maddie affirmed, "Also, Mrs. Allison rang to remind you about tonight. Said can you remember to pick up a couple of bottles of dry white wine on the way home, Frascati if you can get it and two red, preferably Blossom Hill."

"Right," Allison sighed, he had forgotten the dinner party. He supposed his sergeant, Mark had as well, but he was wrong.

"Don't worry about the red. Debbie has got some really smooth Classico Chianti and I'm sure David and Judy will bring some as well."

Allison grunted. Mary was such a fusspot when it came to wine. It had to be dry. The number of times he'd had to take back glasses of medium poured by mistake. He raised an eyebrow, "You remembered then? I must admit it had slipped my mind... other people's wedding anniversaries never figure very highly in my life, I have enough trouble remembering my own."

PC David Taylor had become involved with a talented artist who had been left for dead. She had suffered amnesia.

He was working on a case of antique fraud and the two had become involved and eventually married. It was their first wedding anniversary.

*

Criminal Psychologist Colin Brady spoke gently to his clairvoyant friend Holly, "There's a few avenues we can go down. You say it's not like the last time?"

"No, I'm not seeing murders or anything like that... just a persistent taunting in my head... like ...she wants me to see her... then it will stop."

"And maybe it will. We've already established that Grace Clifton is a powerful psychic force."

"Then, surely seeing her will only strengthen that link?" Holly's frightened eyes gazed at them both.

"I have to agree with Holly. There must be a way round this without her having to face her grandmother?" asserted Paul.

"Maybe.... Or maybe meeting her will have the opposite effect and leave her better able to deal with the situation," urged Colin.

"I don't know if I want Holly to risk that. The woman is insane," Paul continued.

"That surely has to be Holly's choice. She and only she can decide on that," said Colin.

"True, but what other options does she have?" queried Paul.

"I thought you said there were a number of avenues I could go down? interrupted Holly, "Tell me something that doesn't involve me seeing her?"

Colin went silent.

"You mean, all choices involve her?" stuttered Paul incredulously.

"Then I'll have to put up with the nightmares," decided Holly.

"Just a minute, you can't keep going through that torment... hear me out... please," pleaded Colin. "Let me follow up on Grace Clifton by going through the proper channels. Then we'll talk again. In the meantime, try and involve yourself in something that will take your mind off things. Can you get away for a few days? Take a short break somewhere?"

"We're overdue a visit to my Dad's in Cornwall. It would be good to give my sister some respite, if Holly doesn't mind?" Paul looked questioningly at her.

"I'm not the world's best when it comes to old people... but if you think it will help...?" Holly trailed off.

"That's a great idea. Arrange it," said Colin decisively, but Holly didn't look convinced.

No one noticed the breeze, which disturbed the net curtains and lifted the hem of the heavier velvet drapes or the chill that seemed to settle in the air around them.

*

Rosie Partridge hadn't gone into work that morning. Still shaken by the telephone calls from the night before, she had called in sick.

The bell rang; she peered out from her living room window and saw her usual postman holding a bundle of letters and a box. She opened the window.

"Parcel for you, Rosie. I can't leave it on the step and it's too big to fit through the letterbox. Can you come down?"

Rosie nodded, and ran down the stairs to the hall foyer. She opened the door to receive the mail. The postman smiled and nodded his thanks and set off back down the driveway.

Rosie turned the letters over in her hand and stooped down to pick the hand addressed envelope sitting on the coconut matting with no stamp or postmark. She placed the letters, which weren't for her on the communal hall table and ran lightly back up the stairs to her flat. Once inside she closed the door and refastened the safety chain. Her heart beating wildly, she placed the box and morning's post on the kitchen table and filled the kettle. A hot cup of tea would help her start the day and chase the panic and fears away. She tried to busy herself with the teapot but her eyes were constantly drawn to the box. Rosie left the tea to brew. Discarding the red ribbon and cellophane she was just about to open it when her flat bell rang. She peered out of her window.

"Yes?"

"Police, Miss Partridge relating to last night."

"Any identification?"

"If you'd care to come down you can verify it through the glass door," offered Mark.

"Surely, you remember me, Rosie?" added Allison's gruff tones.

"Popsie? Popsie! It *is* you. I'll be right down."

Mark suppressed a chuckle and looked at his chief with a questioning grin. "Popsie?" he queried.

"Don't ask," warned the chief.

Mark struggled to keep his face straight as Rosie appeared at the foot of the stairs. She beamed at Greg as she opened the door. As soon as they had crossed the threshold she threw her arms around his neck and hugged him.

"How lovely to see you. I just wish it were in better circumstances. Come on up." She trounced up the stairs, her glossy chestnut hair bouncing with each step.

"Cup of tea? I've just made a pot," she offered as soon as they were settled. The coppers gladly accepted and made themselves comfortable in her living room, while Rosie went to fetch the tea. Greg's eyes roamed over the wall by the cabinet littered with a mosaic of photos. He picked out snaps of his daughter Cally, with Rosie, the two of them together brandishing their hockey sticks and another of Rosie on Cally's back standing on a rock close to a foaming sea. Greg was about to launch into one of his reminiscences when Rosie screamed with horror. Stringer was on his feet and dashed into the kitchen closely followed by Allison. Rosie stood shaking over an open box in which was a lidless light balsa wood coffin housing three dead roses and a mess of peat and detritus. In and out of the withered blooms crawled a huge centipede, which had been feasting on a globule of wriggling white maggots attached to a rancid lump of raw meat. At the foot of the roses was a picture of a headstone it read, 'Here lies Rosie Partridge as lovely in death as she was in life'.

Mark ushered her to a seat and using his handkerchief removed the offending box, firmly replacing the lid and putting it out of sight.

Greg poured her tea and amidst her protests added a teaspoon of sugar and made her drink it.

"Good for shock," was all he said.

Rosie's panicked breathing settled down and she gazed at Greg with tear filled eyes. "Why would anyone want to do this.... it's so horrible."

"There are some sick people in this world, Rosie. Tell us what you can and we'll try and help".

They returned to the sitting room with their tea and Rosie began. "I don't know really, it started about a month ago, phone calls but no one there. Ringing my flat doorbell. At first I thought it was kids but then I started to get letters and last night he spoke to me. It should all be in the report I made to the police last night."

"I realise that... but I'd prefer to hear it from you," coaxed Greg gently.

So Rosie began again, reliving the events of the past month.

"Have you checked the rest of the post?" asked Greg Allison.

"No. I only opened the box."

"Mark get the rest of her mail and careful how you handle it," ordered the chief. "Have you got any rubber gloves? Freezer bags?"

"In the drawer under the sink. The post's all on the kitchen table... but surely, there won't be anything else?"

"Just playing safe."

Mark returned wearing yellow Marigolds carrying a fistful of junk mail and the letter from the coconut mat

Rosie looked at it with distaste.

"Delivered by hand," observed Mark.

Rosie looked pleadingly at Allison, "Would you open it please?"

Allison gingerly took the letter with his hankie and slipped his pen under the flap and opened it. He shook out a singed photo of Rosie with a big red heart scrawled around her head. He turned it over. There was one word etched on the back.... 'Soon!'

Rosie burst into tears.

2
A hard day's night

The tables in the Rainbow Casino, in Edgbaston were buzzing. A young Chinese man had just won £25,000 pounds in a single bet. Vencat watched the hangers on crowd around him. He saw the over attentive girls, eager for tips, surround him. He watched and waited; then moved across to Chrissy's Black Jack table and laid out two stakes.

"Deal."

The cards glided out of the shoe. Chrissy dealt her own hand, an ace, the ace of spades.

"Hope you're not superstitious," she smiled.

Vencat lit a cigarette, menthol with a gold band, and smiled.

"St. Moritz? I've not seen anyone smoke those in quite a while." She dealt two more. Vencat folded one hand, and tapped, she dealt again. He tapped again, and held. She dealt her own hand, five of diamonds, eight of hearts, four of clubs.

"Pay nineteens".

She waited while he turned his cards over, twenty and nineteen. The winning chips were pushed across. He nodded for her to deal again.

"You know you remind me of someone.... have you been here before?"

"No. I'm new in town."

"Then maybe you have a friend... some guy, dressed sharply like you... used to smoke the same as you."

"Oh, I don't always smoke these... I just prefer menthol."

"I know what you mean. It doesn't seem so damaging, somehow."

Vencat made a mental note to change his brand or try and give up. That sort of detail was important. He glanced around... Many of the girls were new. Philippe was still on roulette. Beth was on the other Black Jack table and.... this one.... Chrissy... well maybe, just maybe she'd have to be eliminated. He couldn't take any risks. No one must connect him to his old identity. He glanced towards the door; there was Stuart Allen just walking in with yet another beautiful woman on his arm. Vencat passed on his cards, stubbed out his cigarette and made his way to the lounge where he could have a bite to eat. He needed to think. Contact had to be made, but not yet... he wasn't ready.

*

They were outside again. Chanting their slogans, shouting obscenities. Three times this week, she had watched her mother struggle to wash the spray paint off the shop door. She put the pillow over her head to block out the jeering. It was no good. She could still hear them. Bastards! Bloody cowards. They always hid their faces. Wore ski masks to hide their identity. The police couldn't do anything without a description. Oh, she had an idea of who they were... but no proof.

Ghita had an idea. She got out of bed and without turning on the light she edged to the window. She tried to gently move the curtain a fraction and look out. There were eight of them. All in their hooligan's uniform. Doc Martin boots, tight blue jeans and bomber jackets or hoodies. Most of their faces were in shadow and a few sported black balaclavas, which hid their features. Their raucous voices were louder now. They had cans of beer or lager and were swilling it down and throwing the empty cans in the shop doorway.

"Go away, please... please leave us alone." Ghita prayed aloud.

Ghita was fifteen and the eldest of three children. Her parents had thought this was a new beginning for the family. They had worked hard to raise the money for the shop and had moved from the ghetto in Bradford to start life afresh. There were opportunities in Birmingham. It was the city of the future. All they wanted was to fit in. Ghita was doing well at school and things seemed to be on the up until the clan had targeted them; and all because her father had refused to turn a blind eye to the shoplifting by the local yobs, and because the Kumars were black. Racial hatred had been whipped up and directed at her family. There seemed to be no end to the violent abuse levelled against them.

Ghita strained to see the face of the lead man, 'Tough nut', as she'd nicknamed him. He stood directly under the street lamp and very slowly, almost as if he knew she was watching, he raised his head and appeared to stare at her through the window. Measuredly draining the last dregs of his beer from the can he flung it with such ferocity that she flinched. The curtain twitched. It was enough. He walked to the crumbling wall of the house next door, wrestled out a piece of brick and hurled it at her window. The glass splintered and smashed. Cutting shards landed at her feet and the smell of alcohol drifted through the window. The beast, for that's what he was, roared at her and deliberately removed his coward's mask and glared up at her; revealing his face for her to remember and be afraid. Then laughing with a demented glee he tossed a burning match into the wire wastebasket, which stood outside on the pavement and rolled it into the shop doorway. The smoke billowed up into her room while the beast laughed, and led his band of renegades away up the street. He paused and looked back at Ghita now fully framed in the window and delivered an obscene gesture before running off with the rest. Too late the police sirens bore down on the shop. Too late the police arrived to the vandalised newsagents. Too late! But this time Ghita knew him. And, more importantly, she would know him again.

*

Grace Clifton sat in her cell knitting. Her lips mouthed silent words as if counting the beads on a rosary with each stitch that she made. The endless squares which she knitted for blankets for church bazaars piled up beside her. She paused and furrowed her beetle brows that shaded those snake like hooded cobra eyes; eyes that gleamed with the light of the devil and belied the religious verses she spouted ad nauseum.

Jane Hoolihan stopped outside the cell and rapped on the door. "You all right Grace?"

"May the riches of Solomon reign on you and your family. Thank you for asking, I would like to see my son.... granddaughter, too, if that's possible."

"The request has gone in. No news yet I'm afraid."

"We are born to suffer ... The greater picture is yet to be... Am I to see the chaplain?"

"You have permission to attend morning Eucharist."

"Will you be there?"

"I'll be with you."

"You're a good girl... There's not many left in this world... You have seen what I know to be true."

"And the solicitor will be with you in the afternoon to write the codicil for your will."

"That's good. It's just a small addition."

"Okay, Grace... lights out soon."

"How long?"

"Ten more minutes."

Grace sighed heavily, her reedy tones continued to mutter her prayers and Jane Hoolihan moved forward on her rounds. Grace put down her knitting. She had been lucky. Not many had permission to use knitting needles. They were deemed to be offensive weapons. Grace had pleaded passionately for them. Remarkably, she had won a victory even if they were only soft plastic. They were what she needed. She had plans, plans that would upset the scheme of things... now, how could she make them work? She scrutinised her small cell. For the moment she was safe... no one to share it with, no one to give the game away. Her eyes swivelled over her hidden treasures; the stash of pins in blue tac hidden in the hollow leg of her bed, the dessert knife blade, honed on the granite floor after dark and taped between the wooden slats of the cot, the small tube of petrol fluid inside her shampoo bottle, the loose matches secreted in the boned part of her corset. Her time would come. She needed to get into the prison hospital. Grace was sure when the time was right that she would. But, she had reckoned without her granddaughter, Holly.

*

Rosie sat shivering miserably on her bed. The red digits on her radio alarm told her it was 2:20 a.m. The phone interrupted her thoughts and clamoured to be picked up. She stretched out her hand but couldn't bring herself to lift the receiver. The phone continued to ring, insisting on being answered. The noise seemed to be all enveloping and appeared to scream louder with each ring. Mustering all her courage she snatched up the phone to stop the impatient ring and then dropped the receiver back into the cradle. The room was silent for a few seconds. Rosie breathed more easily. She wiped her hand across her sweating brow and the phone began its persistent shrill call again. Rosie shrieked in anger and jumped from her bed. She yanked out the plug from the telephone extension, her room went quiet but she could still hear the agitated bell in the hall. Calmer now she forced herself to leave the temporary stillness of her bedroom and she walked briskly to the primary phone point. There, too, she pulled out the plug. The silence was deafening but comforting. The threat had been removed... for the present. She picked up her bag from the hall floor and took out her mobile. Rosie thought about ringing the police, but instead she retreated to her bedroom and slipped under the covers. She didn't sleep. She couldn't. Her heart was still racing. She vowed to follow police advice and change her number first thing in the morning and make sure that this time she was ex-directory.

Rosie's mind was racing. She couldn't think of any obvious enemies. Who would want to torment her in this way? Although she had recently broken up with Jake, her boyfriend of three years she was sure it was nothing to do with him. He would be horrified if he thought she even questioned his involvement.

Rosie tried once more to sleep. It was no good. She was too scared. With a groan she reluctantly tossed back the covers and padded to the kitchen. The street lighting reached into the room sufficiently for her to fill and boil the kettle and make a cup of tea.

Rosie was unaware that eyes were watching.

The ski masked observer had use of an infrared telescopic lens belonging to a night rifle. He watched Rosie sip her tea, shake her luxuriant locks and sit at the pine table. He watched her move to the cupboard and shake out a couple of paracetamol and drink them down. He watched her pace the floor... and watched... and watched. His breathing became more laboured as his excitement grew. He wanted Rosie and he wanted her NOW!

She rinsed her cup under the tap and padded back to her bedroom. Now that the phone bell had stopped harassing her, she felt more in control. She clambered into bed and at last, and exhausted she drifted off into a fitful sleep.

He watched for movement. He watched for lights. He tried her phone again. It rang... and rang... and rang.

"Bitch!"

She must have unplugged it! No matter. She would pay for that. And besides she'd have to plug it in again sometime. When she did, he would be ready. Right now he had another plan... another scheme to execute.

*

Vencat crushed the remaining cigarettes in their distinctive packaging and lost them in one of the freestanding ashtrays. He snapped his fingers at a waitress and ordered some Peter Stuyvesant. The pretty Chinese waitress returned, opened the packet and offered him one. He took it. Cigarette lighter at the ready, she lit the end. Vencat sucked a mouthful of smoke into his lungs and exhaled deeply. It tasted like cotton wool in comparison with his usual brand, but it would have to do for the moment. He took out his wallet and generously tipped the girl. She smiled sweetly and thanked him. He rose from his seat and watched the gaming tables from the doorway. There was Allen at the Roulette Wheel. Vencat was ready to test out his new appearance and sauntered to the table. Vencat coolly placed his bet. Five one hundred pound chips on black.

The silver ball was set spinning on the Roulette Wheel. The punters placed their bets. Stuart Allen placed his fifty-pound bet on even. Philippe took the note and shunted it through the slot into the table.

"No more bets."

The silver ball finished its dance of destiny and bounced assuredly into place.

"Vingt quatre noir. Twenty-four black."

Vencat's eyes gleamed. He was rewarded with the return of his bet and five hundred pounds more of chips. Stuart Allen acknowledged the Asian's luck with a playful salute as he too, had his bet returned plus another fifty pounds in counters. The two men eyed each other. There was no recognition in Allen's eyes. Vencat smiled. He had passed the first test. But more was to come.

Vencat took a handful of chips and placed them strategically on the baize straddling eight numbers. Allen did the same. The silver ball went bouncing as the wheel spun.

"No more bets," announced Philippe.

The ball sat in the curve of the wheel before tumbling into the winning number.

"Numero dix huit. Number eighteen"

Philippe slickly counted out the chips and slid them across to the two winners.

"Looks like we bring each other luck," smiled Allen.

"If it lasts," added Vencat.

Allen put out his hand and introduced himself, "Allen, Stuart Allen."

Vencat paused, then smiled. He removed the cigarette from his lips and took the proffered hand, remembering to change the way he practised this common courtesy. His grasp was firm and strong quite unlike his usual half hearted grip.

"Sharma. Bartlett Sharma."

Stuart Allen raised an eyebrow. He turned to the girl on his arm and gave her a handful of chips.

"Here go and have some fun. I'll meet you at the bar in one hour."

The leggy blonde brushed her glossed lips across his cheek and walked seductively across to a Black Jack table.

"I believe we have a mutual acquaintance," continued Allen. "Shall we adjourn to the bar? I'm sure our roll of luck will continue later."

Vencat nodded and smiled allowing Allen to lead the way. They pushed through the growing number of people and made their way from the gaming room to the bar and restaurant.

"I wasn't expecting you until the weekend," Stuart Allen's tones were soft and confidential.

"I got here earlier than expected. Thought I'd try out the local scene. The Rainbow comes well recommended."

"Our mutual friend, had some big wins here... loved the place."

"Seems he's not the only one to enjoy a big win," observed Vencat jerking his head at a beaming Chinese man.

"That's Kenneth Chung. He's a bit of a local celebrity. Fine musician. Won some top awards. What he can't play on the piano... also, has some interesting connections."

Vencat paid deeper attention to the young gambler. His fresh open face and ready smile, "Well, if he becomes useful let's hope he doesn't play the fiddle."

Allen laughed politely at the Asian's attempt at humour. Vencat frowned.

"I think we should get down to business don't you?"

Chrissy manoeuvred her way from her table into the bar. She noticed the two men with their heads close together, rapt in conversation.

She knew him... she was sure of it.

*

Ghita sat around the kitchen table with her family. She was worried about the strained expression on her mother's face, the dark shadows under her eyes and her continued weariness.

"What more can we do? I try to accommodate everyone and still my family and business are hounded." Her father's voice had a note of desperation in it that she had not heard before. "On the way to school, the children are picked on by white bullies. They must have something to do with this. They must be accountable."

"I know it's hard, Mr. Kumar," soothed the young WPC. "It often takes a while to be accepted into the area. If only we had an idea who was responsible, we may be able to do more."

"It's no good. They always wear masks or hoods. They are too cowardly to risk us seeing their faces."

Ghita said nothing. She just stared down at the table. The family had always helped themselves in the past ...if she said anything now, she was sure it would only make matters worse.

"Here's a number." The WPC handed Ghita's father a card. "This is a number of a special task force committed to eradicating this sort of prejudice. They have been really successful in the past. Call them. You've nothing to lose."

"I have tried every avenue. I wrote to our local MP about the harassment. Ghita even wrote to the Prime Minister himself."

"We had a lovely reply on House of Commons note paper," murmured Ghita's mother, Ranee.

"All talk!" exclaimed Ghita. "No one's really interested. No one cares."

There was a pause, "You tell us the police are doing all they can... but are they? Really?"

"You may feel that way. I'm sure you do. But, give this a try... It can't hurt, can it?" came the sensible tones of WPC Squires. "Well?"

Ghita's father sighed and took the offered card. "All right. But I don't hold out much hope."

"You may be surprised. Who knows?"

*

Rosie was aware of a strange sound. It infiltrated her restless dreams. She was walking through a long passageway, which twisted and turned. Sometimes the cavernous walls of stone narrowed so much she could only just squeeze through. Always she drove on, deeper into the heart of the labyrinth. The rocky corridor opened out into a huge cave with tunnels leading off in all directions. The floor of the cave appeared to grind, shift and turn as she stepped onto the moving floor. Unseen fingers plucked at her hair and face. The whispers started. Whispers and scrapes. No, not scrapes exactly, more like scratching, the scratching of a rodent's small sharp nails coupled with the whispering of siren voices, haunting, tempting, lying... Rosie awoke with a jolt and sat up in bed. It wasn't just in her dreams. The whispering was there still. In her room, a thousand voices calling her name, mockingly, threateningly, and whimpering.

"Rosie. Rosie... oh Rooosssiieee!"

Rosie flicked on her bedside lamp. Her eyes winced at the light. She wasn't imagining it. The whispering was still there, and the scratching. She put her foot out of bed onto the floor, and shook herself awake. The strange cacophony of sound like a radio station that hadn't been tuned in properly mingled with the whispers, bursts of tortured music and the scratching.

Rigid with fear she forced herself to move and switched on the main light. The warm flood of colour did little to calm her. She grabbed her wrap and opened the door. Rosie stepped out into the corridor of her apartment and edged towards the kitchen where the light spilled out from under the door in front of her.

Hardly daring to breathe she turned the handle on the door and pushed it open. There on the table was her cassette player. The decks were spinning, releasing the strange mixture of sounds. There was a mug, half full of steaming coffee, a cigarette lazily extinguished and still sending a spiral of smoke into the glow of the kitchen strip lights. Her eyes caught a movement. There on the tiled floor was a rat daintily eating the remnants of a biscuit and crumbs on one of her breakfast plates. Rosie stifled a scream and dashed back to the bedroom. She engaged the lock and leaned against the door panting heavily whilst the whispering tape continued playing, blending now into mocking, distorted laughter. She picked up her phone. Nothing. With trembling fingers she plugged it back in the socket. It rang immediately. Rosie stared at the phone, afraid to move, afraid to answer. It stopped. That gave Rosie the strength to move. Sobbing in fear she dialled for the police. As she gave her name and address she caught sight of her terrorised expression and something else. Dropping the receiver back into its cradle she cautiously stepped towards the mirror. It was unmistakable. There on her forehead was something red. Rosie took a closer look. It was the imprint of a red kiss.

*

Chief Inspector Allison grunted when his night's sleep was disturbed.

"Sorry to bother you. But you said to call you if we heard any more from Rosie Partridge."

Instantly awake he jumped out of bed. "Sorry, Mary," he apologised as she began to surface from her dreams. "Rosie Partridge, again... I have to go."

Mary nodded sleepily and tried to settle down once more

whilst her husband clumsily began to dress. The bedside light went out. The door clicked softly. Greg Allison was on his way.

*

Chrissy Stephens left the casino with two of her colleagues. They shared a joke as they walked across the car park together. Chrissy unlocked her Peugeot 206 and waved good-bye to her friends. She sat in the driver's seat and started the engine. She didn't see the driver of a dark Mercedes C220 flick his glowing cigarette butt from out of the window. Chrissy reversed out of her space and turned into Portland Road. She waited at the traffic lights before entering the sparse night traffic on the Hagley Road. A police car with its lights flashing raced up the opposite side of the avenue. Chrissy moved off comfortably down the tree lined street, past the Lychee Garden and Ivy Bush pub; On past the Plough and Harrow Hotel towards Five Ways, around the roundabout and off down Lee Bank. She didn't notice the dark Mercedes keeping a safe distance behind her. She didn't see him pull up and stop when she parked in the driveway of her house on the Bristol Road. She didn't see him make a mental note of her address. She didn't see him leave his vehicle. Nor did she see him walk up the path to check the names on the bells at the house where she lived. Chrissy was oblivious to it all.

*

Allison tried hard to comfort the terrified young woman who had been his daughter's friend. Mark Stringer had made a close examination of the flat along with two uniformed police who had been the first on the scene.

"We have to wait for Forensics but I think I've found where he got in."

Allison lumbered up from the settee and Rosie followed behind. Mark led them to the small bathroom. The frosted window was partially open and the wood had splintered where it had been forced up by a sharp instrument possibly a crowbar. Mark shone a flashlight out of the window to reveal a ladder propped carelessly against the wall.

"That's what he used to gain access," said Mark, "And

I'm not sure but I think that's a footprint in the flower bed below."

"Mmm," groaned Allison. "This isn't looking good. Have you anyone you could stay with for a few days?"

"I've got some leave owing me at work. I could go and visit my cousin in London. We've been meaning to catch up for some time."

"That still doesn't solve the problem about tonight... I don't think you should stay here," continued Allison. "Pack a bag while we wait for Forensics and come home with me. You can sleep in Cally's room. Do you have any spare keys?"

"Yes, I keep them by the biscuit barrel in the kitchen." Rosie led the way to the kitchen and hesitated before opening the door.

"It's okay," Mark reassured, "We've got rid of the rat. It was very tame and has gone off to the RSPCA."

They walked in the kitchen and Rosie snatched up the tin, "They've gone," she whispered, a fearful note entering her voice.

"Then the locksmiths must be called."

"But what about the front door? There are other people to consider..."

"I'm sure they'll understand. After all they don't want their safety compromised either."

Rosie nodded in agreement, "I suppose," she sighed.

A vehicle pulled up on the gravel driveway. Mark looked out of the window. "Forensics," he announced.

"Right, I'll let you deal with them, but first let them see this kiss or whatever it is and then I'll take Rosie back with me," asserted Allison.

Forensic got to work photographing and then transferring the imprint of the kiss. Finally the kiss was scraped from her forehead and then diluted and removed. Moments later Rosie and Allison left. Their departure did not go unnoticed.

*

"I won't!" screamed Holly. "I won't be forced to..."

"Holly? Holly?" Paul cradled her in his arms. "What's happened? What have you seen?"

"It's her.... she's playing some sort of game with me...

30

wants me to see her... if I don't she's going to... do something... something..." Holly screwed up her face trying to recapture the fleeting glimpses of what she felt was to come. "She has a plan... a plan to..."

"Yes?"

"She's going to try and get out and then..." Paul looked at her quizzically. "Then... she wants to settle with me... for informing the police about my visions and..." her voice trailed off. "Oh, no. What now, Paul? What now?"

Paul had no answer. He just held her all the more tightly. Holly convulsed in his arms. This would be yet another night when they would watch the hands of the clock move slowly around.

*

The special squad for race relations were a great bunch of men. Both Ghita and her brother were totally entertained by them and they had gained her mother and father's trust. The sad thing was that since their arrival each day at four. Nothing had happened. But that was about to change.

The family had retired for the night and Sergeant Jeffery and his men had settled down to another night of poker. All the equipment was in place as it had been for the past week. This was their last night of surveillance and if nothing transpired tonight then the plug would be pulled on the operation. There would be a lengthy procedure to get his team reinstated. It was tonight or nothing.

Ghita was writing in her diary. She found it therapeutic to retell the events of the day. The whole story was there with sketches to back it up, the entire rotten mess. Ghita stopped. She listened. In the distance she could hear them; hear their familiar chant, so well known now that it penetrated her brain like a repetitious jingle from an irritating advert. The sounds of boots on concrete stamped closer and cans rattled as they were hurled or kicked down the road.

Ghita peered out from her window. The gang was approaching with their taunting and Ku Klux Clan like behaviour. She slipped from her room.

"Sergeant Jeffery," she called softly. "Sergeant Jeffery... They're here."

Jeffery extinguished his cigarette and folded his cards. The rest of the squad got into position as the taunting barbs from the thugs below reached its peak.

"Dirty Coolies. Pakis out!" They screamed as they hurled cans and bottles at the shop.

On Jeffery's signal the windows opened and a flood of lights hit the street, blinding and arresting the gang. The lights swept around the pathetic group who stood uncertainly in the street below. Ghita shouted, "There! That's Tough Nut." She had singled out the muscular youth at the front in his balaclava and black bomber jacket. Jeffery swiftly gave the signal and the gang were hit on all sides by hoses and water cannons until they retreated into the night. Ghita laughed delightedly at their humiliation. They had gone.

"We cannot thank you enough," Jarnail gratefully affirmed as the squad packed up their equipment.

"Now, they know we're on to them, they should leave you in peace," smiled Jeffery, "But, if they do return..." he handed Jarnail a card, "Ring us and we'll be back." That night the family settled down to a peaceful night's sleep but somehow Ghita knew although they had been chased off... It wasn't over.

*

Chrissy sang along lustily with Whitney Houston, that she was "saving all my love for you" as she finished eating her buttered toast and downed the last of her morning cup of coffee.

She didn't hear the door rattle.

"Though I've tried to resist, being last on your list..." Chrissy sang her way out of the kitchen and into the bathroom.

She didn't see the door open and the protecting chain cut.

"No other man's gonna do-oo-oo", the silent figure stepped inside and the chain hung impotently in two. "So I'm saving all my love for you...."

Chrissy set the shower running while she scrubbed her teeth, "It's not very easy living all alone..."

She didn't see the figure of death assemble his pistol....

32

"My friends try to tell me find a man of your own..."

He clipped on his silencer...

"But each time I try, I just break down and cry..."

He pulled the mask completely over his face.

"I'd rather be home feeling blu-ue ...so I'm..."

He moved stealthily to the bathroom door and placed his hand on the knob. His head swivelled quickly to the right. A key was being inserted in the front door lock. He froze....

Momentarily panicked he stepped back from the bathroom and manoeuvred his way to the bedroom where he slipped into the closet.

"Chrissy! It's only me. I've got a surprise for you," shouted her boyfriend Mike.

Chrissy stuck her head around the bathroom door her mouth full of toothpaste. She grinned, her lips frothing with white foam.

"Help! Save me! Rabid woman!" yelled Mike in mock fear. He ran to the bathroom door pretending to try and lock her in whilst Chrissy gurgled and played up to him, continuing the game.

The masked assassin slipped from the closet and stepped into the hallway. Chrissy's unblinking eyes stretched wide with horror as she saw the metal barrel of the gun. She screamed as the intruder fired. Mike fell to the floor, the back of his head cruelly blitzed apart. Chrissy dived back inside the bathroom leaning her full weight against the door and shutting out the killer who fired as a young female golden retriever nosed her way through the front door. Snarling in fury the brave animal leapt at the murderer flooring him. Chrissy slid down the bathroom door to the floor. There were another three shots in quick succession. The valiant canine collapsed on top of the gunman her teeth grazing the hit man's neck. He shoved the creature's body off his chest and scrambled up uncertainly. His access to the bathroom was hindered by the weight of Chrissy, which had effectively closed the door. He fired once more through the thin plywood then hurriedly attempted to make his escape. He was now sweating profusely, and his breathing was erratic. He had to get out. He needed to get out fast and not be noticed. He tore the mask from his face and tried to calm his thumping heart. Hiding the pistol in his coat, he stepped into the morning and coolly crossed the busy road to his waiting rented Ford Focus and drove in the direction of Moseley.

The shower continued to run, Whitney Houston continued to sing and Chrissy groaned softly. The life's blood of the heroic retriever pulsed out over the hall floor.

*

Holly jumped. She inadvertently drew breath and a small sound escaped from her throat. Paul and Colin stopped their animated discussion on the qualities of red wine and stared at her.

Colin was the first to speak. "Holly? ... You okay?"

"I'm not sure... I've a series of vivid pictures in my head. There's a girl, she's hurt.... losing blood, dying..."

"Tony?"

"No. At least I don't think so... her boyfriend is dead... murdered."

"Where?"

"I'm not sure... the dog's hurt too."

"For God's sake, Holly ...where?"

"Birmingham..."

Colin groaned in exasperation, "Come on, Holly, Birmingham's a big place... where?"

Holly's head lolled back and her eyelids fluttered, "A big road... main road, tree lined."

"That could be anywhere ...think!"

"Don't shout," interceded Paul, "Let her concentrate..."

"It's okay, Paul... let me think."

"Edgbaston... Moseley.... not far from.... Bristol..."

"I thought you said Birmingham," interrupted Colin.

"No.... Pebblemill..."

"Bristol... Bristol Road? Holly, do you mean the Bristol Road?"

"Yes.... Hurry, she's dying."

"Where? Focus on the number..."

"On the left side, coming out of town.... an old Victorian property... argh... I'm shot.... I can't hold on... MIKE!"

The last word shrieked from her lungs then Holly

spluttered and coughed, "I don't want to die...."

Holly fell silent. Colin shook her, "Holly! Holly! ... The number, house colour anything..."

She revived for a moment, "Blue, it was going to be painted blue..."

"What colour is it now?"

"Black and white.... black and white...." Holly drifted into unconsciousness.

"Paul, get on the blower..."

Paul grabbed the portable phone and began to dial "What are we going to say?"

"Give it to me... you take care of Holly." Colin snatched the receiver and redialled.

"Allison? Chief Inspector Allison please... yes, it's urgent... come on.... come on... Chief! Got something for you, I just hope we're not too late."

*

The golden retriever whimpered on the floor and struggled to move, she valiantly dragged herself across the hall and pushed at the front door, which was slightly ajar, with her nose. The door opened wide and she manoeuvred herself onto the top step and howled a cry of melancholy sadness and pain before drifting into a place of darkness.

Sally Johns was struggling with her car door. The lock had frozen again. She heard the howl. The mournful cry made her jump. She dropped her keys into the gutter. She scrabbled under the car and secured them, but an uneasy feeling rippled through her spine and without really knowing why, she left her car and walked a few yards along the pavement. She stopped, gazed up the drive of Chrissy's house where she saw a dog lying on the top of a small flight of steps leading to the front door. The door was open and there was something else.... something red and dark was spreading from the animal's body.

Sally broke into a run. She reached the dog and smoothed the golden fur. The animal was shivering and whimpering softly but still managed to lick her hand. Acting braver than she felt she pushed gently on the door. Stifling a scream, she searched her bag for her mobile phone and rang the police.

3
Good Vibrations

"There has to be a connection," Brand slammed his hand down on the desk making the chief's in-tray quake. A piece of paper slipped off the growing pile and wafted to the floor. Allison grunted as he retrieved it from under his desk.

"Why do you say that?" queried the chief as his head reappeared above the desk once more.

"There has to be.... Chrissy was dealing Black Jack at the Rainbow last night. Stuart Allen was seen in there talking with an Asian, the same guy who was picked up at the airport by our driver friend turned informer. She must have overheard something or seen someone... It's too much of a coincidence."

"Do the Met know yet?"

"It's been reported, I'm meeting their man off the train at New Street. We can't let them blunder in and ruin our investigation so far."

"That'll be down to you... think you can do it?"

"I'll have to."

"What about the girl?"

"Chrissy? She's holding her own. We're hoping she'll be up to questioning by tomorrow."

"Boyfriend?"

"Didn't make it. Dead on arrival. She doesn't know yet...."

"And the pooch?"

"Looks like she'll survive. She's at the local vets. Sally Johns, the woman who called the emergency services is taking responsibility for her once the animal's been given the all clear until Chrissy is released from hospital."

"Lucky dog,"

"Lucky Chrissy! If it hadn't been for that little brave heart, she'd be dead!"

"What did you say? It was a rescue dog?" asked Greg Allison. Brand nodded. "Then she was doubly lucky. The dog hadn't had time to form attachments. So her boyfriend's surprise was her life saver."

"Certainly was; it just knew something was wrong and recognised the bad guy."

"I wish life was that simple."

"Well whoever it was would have been covered with the creature's blood. Someone must have seen or heard something, surely?"

"We'll keep asking. By the way, investigations in Columbia have turned up a massacre at a country ranch."

"Vencat?"

"Who else? A house obliterated by a bomb, Interpol think a remote control was used. Sources confirm a man of Vencat's description hiring the place. Five bodies so far."

"And Vencat?"

"No trace, at least the dental work doesn't fit. Further tests are being done."

"What does that say to you?"

"Could be that he pushed the button"

"So he's the one who got away. Very convenient."

"Especially if he'd changed his appearance."

"Think that's likely?

"Well, what would you do?"

"I suppose I'd change my face and remove all witnesses."

"That's exactly, what I think he's done."

"Plastic surgeon?"

"I expect that's one of the five. The Colombian police are checking on it."

Allison raised his eyebrows. There was a pause... "Right, keep me posted."

*

Grace Clifton had settled for the night. Jane Hoolihan checked the cell. Grace was sleeping soundly. "Harmless old biddy really," thought Jane. She couldn't get her head round all the atrocities this woman had done. Her son's girlfriend and all those prostitutes murdered. Jane shook her head and continued on her rounds.

As Wardress Hoolihan's footsteps faded, Grace peered out from under the covers. She crept stealthily out of bed and set to work. Gingerly opening her shampoo bottle she untied the cotton from around the neck of the bottle and gently pulled until her tube of petrol fluid emerged glistening with a covering of opalescent pearl shampoo. She wiped it carefully on her regulation towel and laid it down. Grace paused and listened, feeling secure in the silence and semi darkness she continued with her labour. Carefully extracting one of her pins from her secret stash in blue-tac hidden on the bedstead she heard a rustle and her head whipped round. She caught sight of her face, shadowed by the dark, in the mirror by the sink and drew a breath. Was that demonic looking face really hers? Was that wild-eyed shining, which glinted insanely, emanating from *her* eyes? She shook her greying, badly permed hair and the small curls moved with a life of their own like Medusa's snakes. For a moment she faltered, shocked at what she had seen and then as if with a new, steely resolve, her thin, rimless lips curled wickedly in anticipated triumph of what she was about to achieve. The honed blade was untaped and secreted inside the prepared panel in her corset; she removed the live matches and could hardly resist a hymn of joy. Words from the Scriptures rushed through her brain and she hurriedly murmured words of her own prayer that would lead to her liberation and Tony.

Now, came the difficult part, but the rewards, which would follow, determined her to continue and rise above the self-inflicted pain. Grace took the pin and raked it across her cheek. She did it systematically line by line, dragging across the thin flesh like the claws of a cat. Bright beadlets of blood popped through the scratches and ran in rivulets down her neck. Next she attacked her hands. She inserted the pin into the tube of petrol and allowed a fine spray of the fluid to anoint her forearm, the rest she put on the pillow with the withered jelly capsule. The pin was replaced with the stash and Grace placed two of the matches by the emptied tube and the remaining match she struck firmly on the floor. The flash of light and the smell of sulphur excited her.

She dropped the match onto the pillow and watched it burst into life. The pillow began to smoulder and her bed began to burn. Now she had to time things carefully. Smoke was beginning to drift across the cell and creep out under the door. The woman in the next cell started yelling, "Smoke! I can smell smoke.... Quick before we all burn to death."

The prisoner started shouting and banging hysterically, until the other inmates on the floor all joined her in shouting about burning. The piercing wail of smoke alarms reverberated through the corridor suffocating their cries. Grace had to listen hard. She waited until she heard footsteps hurrying towards her cell then baring her arm covered in petrol to the flame she flung herself onto the bed. Her nightclothes began to blaze. Grace screamed.

*

"I don't know whether going to Cornwall is such a good idea, after all," said Paul. "There's too much going on. Plus the fact the police want Holly to make a statement about that murder on the Bristol Road."

"I just feel a rest would do her good," answered Colin.

"I don't think she'd get too much of a rest with Dad. He can be a cantankerous old so and so."

"Then you haven't fixed it up yet?" queried Colin.

"No, Holly said to wait a few days and then if everything seemed quiet we'd go."

"I see."

At that moment Colin's mobile interrupted them, "Yes? ....When did this happen? ...I don't know. I'll get back to you." Colin's face was stern as he ended the call.

"What's wrong?"

"That was the prison.... Grace is in hospital... something to do with a fire, she's been quite badly burned."

"Burned? In prison? How?"

"That's under investigation .... but," Colin looked Paul squarely in the eyes, "That's not the worst of it... she wants to see Holly."

*

Things were proceeding according to plan. Vencat had survived recognition by Stuart Allen. The minor problem of Chrissy had been dealt with and now he was on his way to Devon. He was sure that with the recent crisis in the farming industry his farmer, Joel Macready would be more than happy to co-operate and may even want to extend his plans.

Vencat sat back in his new topaz blue, convertible BMW Z3. Divine driving? It was heaven on a day like today with a cloudless sky of Mediterranean blue and the wind in his hair with the top down. The M5 had been busy and fast but not over laden with lorries and when he hit the North Devon Link road he had pulled up at the first lay by and put the roof down. This was just the day to enjoy a car like this. Although it was only early spring it was one of those freak weather days, which resembled the summer, and that were happening more frequently at the wrong time of the year, as climate changes exacted their judgement on man.

He had checked the map and found the route to the farm just outside Newton Tracey, near Barnstaple, fairly straightforward. He felt comfortable on the smaller country lanes and backing up for larger vehicles presented no problem. In fact, today he was feeling so good not even the usual traffic delays at various road works had done anything to diminish his good humour.

Vencat turned up the long shingle drive leading to Harewood Farm and with a spray of gravel he turned his car to face the other way and parked.

He stepped out and replaced his sunglasses from off the top of his head and hammered on the large brass fox doorknocker. This was quite a beautiful property. Vencat decided that he would search for something similar for himself. A country residence would suit a man of his means, when the time was right, of course.

Bridget Macready answered his knock and ushered him into the farmhouse kitchen with its well-scrubbed pine table and offered him a seat. The old black and white collie looked up, curiously from his favourite spot in front of the Rayburn and then, disinterested rested his head back on his paws and nodded off to sleep.

"What can I get you? You'll have a cup of tea after your long drive. Or would you prefer coffee?"

Vencat flashed his brilliant smile, "Tea would be most refreshing. Thank you."

He studied Bridget as she moved around the kitchen. A

more homely woman you couldn't expect to see. She was round, and plump with apple pink cheeks. Her dark hair unfashionably pulled back that looked as if it hadn't seen a hairdresser in years. Her clothes were serviceable and plain, black slacks, which strained across her hips and a blue gingham cotton shirt.

Bridget set down the teapot with its steaming contents and placed a dish of home made fruit scones, blackcurrant jam and tub of clotted cream for the visitor to enjoy. Vencat assumed that Joel had married her for her cooking and not her looks and when he bit into the first scone he could see why.

"Joel shouldn't be too long. He's out in the field checking the cattle. Some of them have calved early, and there's still one or two, which might present a problem. When he arrives I'll leave you to it. I've got some orphan calves to feed." And she proceeded to make up some formula milk for the animals in question.

Conversation was stilted. Bridget didn't really know why this man was here; Joel was always tight lipped about his business. But, she knew it must be a profitable venture and the farm could certainly do with a profit after the recent lean years and foot and mouth crisis.

Bridget removed a plastic bucket from under the sink and placed her feeding bottles in warm water.

"Keeps the feed warm," she explained. "They don't like to take it cold."

Vencat noticed that her biceps were more suited to a man. Bridget Macready was obviously a hard worker.

The stable door to the kitchen from the garden opened and Joel Macready entered in his navy boiler suit, which had seen better days. He left a trail of straw and bits of hay as he walked. Joel lifted up the padded kitchen seat cushion and sat on the bare wood. He helped himself to a plate of scones and mug of tea.

"Could do with a few more, Maid," he grunted, "I'm as hungry as a rat."

"There's more in the larder. Help yourself," and she left with her bucket and bottles.

"So, what's there to talk about?" asked Joel. "I thought we'd settled on the details."

"And so we have, so we have. But I have another proposition to put to you."

The two men put their heads together and began to talk.

*

Grace Clifton, lay sedated in her hospital bed. Her arms heavily bandaged. She had made a fatal mistake with her nightclothes. The man made fabric had melted onto her skin and burnt her more severely than she had intended. Skin was taken from the inside of her thighs to graft and repair her damaged arms and back. She winced in pain as she tried to shift her position and feebly whined for the nurse.

"It's okay, Grace, I hear you... now, what can I be doing for you now?" said the attractive Southern Irish tones of Connie O'Grady.

"I'd like to sit up if I may." Grace murmured. She tried to be as polite as possible. She needed the nurse on her side. "I'm hoping my son is coming in today, to see me and maybe even my granddaughter."

"Won't that be nice for you... Hold on a minute and I'll give Clive a call, I need a bit of help to move you. We don't want to be disturbing the dressings, now do we?"

Connie moved to the edge of the ward and shouted to the nurses' station, "Clive! Can you be getting yourself down here, I'm in bay two?"

Moments later, a muscular blonde haired male nurse of about thirty came into view.

"Ah, there you are. Give me a hand with getting Grace up, if you please."

Together they carefully lifted Grace into a sitting position, propped up on a bank of five pillows on the steel racked bed head."

"There now! Is that better for you?" Grace nodded and Clive moved away. "Is that it? Or is there anything else you'll be wanting me for?" asked Connie.

"A sip of water would be nice," came the nasal twangs of Grace's voice.

Connie filled a cup with iced water, put in a straw and

placed it on the mobile bed table and pushed it in place for Grace to drink.

"There you are, all done."

"Thank you," muttered the reedy tones.

"Give me a shout when you want and I'll help get you ready for your son's visit... Tony, isn't it?"

"Ar, I will. You'd like our Tony and he'd like you... I'm sure of it."

"Ah, you old flatterer, you're only saying that because it's true," Connie mused and the old cliché sounded sincere in her soft Irish brogue.

Grace watched the nurse as she walked away. "A nice child", she thought, someone like that would suit Tony that is if she, Grace, could bear to share him with anyone else.

Grace attempted to focus her mind but found the task impossible. She was so uncomfortable. The pain kept getting in the way. But, her time would come. That much she knew and then... then, who knows what havoc she might wreak?

*

"I like it.... I like it Mr. Sharma. You tell your Mr. Vencat that I'm in. Times have been hard for me what with Foot and Mouth and all. It could work well for all of us. I been thinking I may have one or two other interested parties. What do you think?"

"Go steady, Joel. This is an experiment this year. Let's see how it works out in practice before enrolling anyone else. The fewer people are in the know, the better... loose tongues and all that?" he gushed and smiled knowingly.

"As you wish, Mr. Sharma, as you wish."

"Later on who knows? So, when do you plant?"

"All ready done and in the ground... the first harvest will be this summer. I've been ordered by the police to plant the hemp away from fields adjoining roads and walkways. The forty-foot square in the centre will hold the real cannabis and no one will be any the wiser. The plants are almost identical. Needs an expert to tell them apart. It should be a doddle."

"And you have somewhere else conducive to growing more?"

"Just like you suggested I've got some redundant farm

buildings, ideal really, tucked out of the way. I'll set up some cold frames, get the places heated and turn on the lights and away we go... I'll even have a bash at the poppies... as an experiment and see how they fare. Although, I don't see how we could get the quantity needed or even if they're right for our climate."

"Don't worry, it is as you say merely an experiment. If it works, it works. If not then we've lost nothing. I'll explain to Mr. Vencat. He will, I'm sure, be delighted. Here is your first payment, on account." He handed Joel a wad of notes, "Ten thousand there, for the risk. A further five when everything else has been planted and inspected, say about three weeks?"

Joel touched his cap in a gesture of acceptance.

"The balance will be paid on receipt of the goods. It's quite ironic really, you being paid by the government to grow the stuff... the harmless kind of course."

"Yes, I suppose it is... subsidy for old rope..."

Both men laughed, and Vencat took his leave.

*

Brand who had followed the Asian watched the BMW roar away and checked the time. He shook his head, "What could this guy possibly want with a farmer in North Devon?"

He radioed his partner, Woodward, to take up the tail. He was going to stick around and find out a bit more about the owner of Harewood Farm. A good place to start would be the local pub, The Hunters' Inn. There he hoped to get a bed for the night and some valuable information.

*

Allison's wife, Mary and Rosie were chatting over a pot of tea.

"Do you really think you ought to return to work, Rosie? Especially after those threats?"

"I'll be fine. I won't be got at there... I'm not returning home, not yet anyway. I've some things to sort out, first: a couple of features, which need finishing and I've got some leave owing me so I'll head for London. No one will find me there."

"Mm, I think Greg would prefer it if you stayed here and

travelled to London without seeing anyone at all. It would be safer."

"I don't think it could possibly be anyone to do with work... My God, paranoia really would set in. And I do want to keep my job. I need to keep my boss sweet."

"Okay, but please ring Greg first and tell him what you're going to do... I don't want it on my head," said Mary.

"Now, who's paranoid?" laughed Rosie. "You worry too much. I'll be fine," she pressed, "but if it will make you feel any happier I'll call, Popsie."

"The number's on the pad by the phone. It's a direct line... do it now," Mary insisted.

*

"Your mother is in considerable pain, she is. The burns suffered on her body means her movement is severely restricted and she can't adjust her position in bed without help. Naturally, she gets quite tired but she is looking forward to seeing you. So she is."

"How long may I stay?"

"I'll let you have half an hour, then I'll pop in and review the situation."

"You say she's got to have further operations."

"She needs another skin graft. The one on her left arm doesn't seem to have taken but she needs to be stronger in herself first before we attempt that." Connie O'Grady smiled sympathetically at Tony, "I'll leave you to it. She's in there," and she pointed to a side room off the nurses' station. Tony noticed the uniformed copper sitting outside reading a paper who had barely glanced at him as he approached the door.

Tony composed himself before sweeping into the room with his bouquet of flowers. He fixed a broad smile on his face and greeted his mother.

"Hello, Mum. How are you doing?"

"Oh, Tony. It's lovely to see you. I wondered if you'd come."

"I couldn't ignore the fact you were in hospital, now could I?" He pulled a chair up to the side of the bed and sat awkwardly. "These are for you."

"They're grand. I'll get Connie to put them in water."

"Connie?"

"My nurse, she's a smasher, Tony. You'd like her. Ring the bell for me."

Tony did as he was asked; he was feeling uncomfortable and hot. Hospitals always had the heating turned up too high. He didn't think it was healthy. There was an embarrassed pause whilst Tony tried desperately to think of something to say. He was saved by the timely arrival of Connie O'Grady.

"Ah! So, you'll be wanting these to be put in water. Will you not? They're beautiful. I only wish I had someone to bring me flowers like this."

Tony wanted to scream that he hadn't wanted to bring flowers. His mother didn't deserve them. He was only doing it out of duty and guilt. Guilt, which haunted him night, and day when he was made to confront his demons and his own fears.

Voices were screaming inside his head that it would be better if his mother had died then he would be truly free. But he said nothing. He didn't hear the rest of what Connie O'Grady had to say. He meekly let her take the flowers from his grasp and watched her as she marched briskly away.

The reedy tones of his mother impinged on his thoughts and he realised she was talking to him.

"I knew you'd like her. You'd get on really well you two. I can see you would."

"Mother, why did you do this? It can't have been an accident." Tony found himself asking.

"I did it for you, Son. You wouldn't see me. I had to make you come. I had to."

"Why Amy, Mum? Why kill her? She was good for me. Kept me out of trouble."

"She reported you. She was evil. She stole away your liberty."

"No, she was standing by me. She wanted to help me. She was the only one who truly understood me."

"Now, that's a slap in the face after all that I've done..."

"After all you've done? Mother, what have you ever done for me? You've always had your own interests at heart."

"And was I looking after my own interests when I

46

engineered your release? You'd have been locked away for good in a mental institution or prison hospital... a serial killer... you'd have never got out. You're free, thanks to me."

"But at what price, Mum? What price?"

"Thou shall not bring the hire of a whore, or the price of a dog, into the house of the Lord thy God for any vow: for even both these are abominations unto the Lord thy God.... Deuteronomy 23 verse 18."

"What are you saying? Amy wasn't a whore. Neither was she a dog. You're not making any sense."

Grace Clifton's serpent's eyes began to glow with the fiery light of righteous fervour and she rambled on incoherently quoting verse upon verse about price. All of which added to Tony's deep confusion until he roared,

"Enough!" Then his voice diminished to the quiet deadly calm, which Grace knew was more threatening than any shriek of anger. Her thin lips fell silent, spittle dribbled down her chin. Her cobra hooded eyes stretched in fear. She knew she had gone too far.

"This is it, Mum. Finally, at last. You can end your days here because I will not see you again."

The copper posted at the door stuck his head in, "Everything all right in here?" he asked.

"We're fine, aren't we mother? Just dandy," responded Tony.

"Yes, no problem, Officer. No problem. I think I'd like to rest now, if you don't mind, Tony." She paused momentarily, "Will you be coming again, Tony. I'd like to see you again."

The policeman retreated back outside the room as Tony replaced the chair upon which he had been sitting.

"I don't think so."

"Not even to see Gillian?" A note of cunning had crept into Grace's nasal whine.

Tony stopped abruptly at the door, "Gillian?"

"Well, she's called something else now. I'm not sure what... I've asked to see her," she said plaintively.

"Leave Gillian, Mother. She has another life, a good life. Don't corrupt another innocent soul."

"Corrupt? I'll show you corrupt," hissed Grace. "She's

different your Gillian. She has the gift. But you go. Go out of both of our lives"

Tony was now deeply confused and he started to whimper like a small child. With a small yelp of anguish he straightened up and brushed the lock of blue-black hair, which had fallen, across his forehead. He stilled further cries and left the room, his head held high just as Connie returned with the flowers in a vase.

"There now, don't they look pretty? Oh, are you all done then?" She glanced at Tony his handsome face furrowed in a frown and a vein pulsing dangerously at his temple. "See you again then, sometime," said Connie cheerily.

"Maybe. Good-bye, Mother." And with that he defiantly raised his head and left the room.

"Don't worry," whined Grace Clifton, "He'll be back. He's just upset to see his old mum like this," and she curled her mean lips into a satisfied reptilian grin.

*

Ghita wrote in her diary. The waiting was almost unbearable. Her family seemed convinced that the persecution of them at the family shop was over.

Her little brother was even starting to attend the afternoon school clubs he had enjoyed prior to the attacks. The family appeared to be happy.

"Ignorance is bliss," thought Ghita. She knew the yobs, for that's what they were, would start again. That their intimidation of the family was far from over. But when they came again she would be prepared, someone had to make a stand against these racist hooligans.

She closed her diary, and locked it, hiding it away in her secret place, away from prying eyes and returned to her homework. There was a knock at the door.

"Come in."

Her little brother, Ajay poked his head round the door. He smiled his most appealing toothy smile at her. Ghita studied his face. He was far too pretty to be a boy. He had long, dark, curling lashes, which would be the envy of any girl. His dark, thick, shining hair was wasted on a boy. Ajay took his sister's silence and scrutiny of his face as encouragement.

She usually asked him not to bother her when she was doing her homework. He bravely, stepped in to Ghita's room and closed the door behind him.

"Can I talk to you?"

"Course. What's the problem?"

"I want to stay after school for the stamp club."

"And?"

"That's the one I had problems with. There are a couple of year six boys who go."

"So?"

"They're the ones who used to pick on me."

"Tell your teacher."

"She knows. But it's not that. They are always nice as pie when she's around; in fact they're too nice. They've even asked me if I was coming back to the club."

"And what did you say?"

"I said I wasn't sure. They said I should come and that things would be different."

"Do you think they're telling the truth?"

"I don't know... I wondered if you'd come and meet me afterwards. They won't bother me if you're there. They never do when I'm with a grown up. Mother said to ask you."

"How have the other clubs been?"

"They've been fine. But, they've only been for my year. I don't have problems with my own class. I've got lots of friends there."

"So, this is the only one for the whole school?"

Ajay nodded vigorously, "Please, Ghita! It would mean so much to me."

"What night is it on?"

"Every Wednesday three thirty until five."

Ghita thought for a moment and then gave her pronouncement, "It doesn't clash with any of my activities... so, ...Okay I'll do it."

"Thanks Ghita, you're the best," and her little brother flung himself at her and hugged her hard.

Ghita laughed, "All right. I'll do it for a few weeks and we'll see how it goes. Maybe things are changing after all."

Ajay beamed and skipped out of her room, calling to his

mother that Ghita would meet him and so could he go after all?

"Little rascal," she thought. She'd fallen for that one all right. Never mind. She didn't mind helping him out. As long as her other brother didn't want baby-sitting too. But Gurdip was not as outgoing as Ajay and preferred to race home and play on his computer.

Ghita went to the window to close the curtains. It was dark. She froze as she saw someone lolling against the lamppost with his back to her. It looked like 'Tough Nut'.

He must have felt her eyes on him and he slowly turned, exhaling a stream of smoke from his lips before grinding out the cigarette stub under his boot. He looked up at the window and smirked challengingly at her. He was alone.

"Yes, there's safety in numbers, isn't there, you bastard?" muttered Ghita.

He straightened himself up and waved. Ghita drew the curtains blocking out that smug, mocking face and his self-satisfied grin.

She was shaking.

*

Dempseys store was buzzing. Tony Clifton was returning to work. Taking up his old position in Sales. Most of the staff hadn't believed that the charming Tony Clifton could possibly have had anything to do with the awful murders that had terrified the city of Birmingham. They were more than willing to place the blame on his nutty mother.

Susan Hardy, the friend of the girl who had died, Janet Mason, was not so certain, but she resolved to be polite if their paths crossed. She continued to type vigorously as Charles Payne interrupted her thoughts. "Er Susan, ... I've just had a call from upstairs. It appears that Mr. Clifton's old secretary has reservations about working with him. She has put in for a transfer and is moving to our Wolverhampton branch. They would like you to take up her position until a replacement is found."

"What about you?"

"I'll make do with a temp. We haven't anything urgent that needs addressing. Anyone with good skills can fill in for a short time. Sales need someone who understands the business and has been with the firm for some time. You fit the bill unless...."

"How long for? I like my job here."

"I would say a month tops. Do we have a deal?"

Susan Hardy sighed resignedly, "No longer than a month you say?"

"You have my word."

"Okay. But you owe me... I'll expect you to do the cake run on Friday, until I'm back in situ."

"You drive a hard bargain. It's a deal then?"

Susan smiled and assented, "When do I start?"

"Now, this morning. Mr. Clifton is in and being appraised of business developments. Use this time to prime the new temp who should be here by now," and he glanced disapprovingly at his watch. The door swung open and in breezed a young girl of about eighteen with brightly streaked red hair and nails to match. Her skirt was short as was her top revealing a pierced belly button and jewel. She was chewing gum and blowing bubbles as she entered. She waltzed up to Susan.

"Hi, I'm Melody. Melody Harper, the new temp. I've got a training session with you?"

Charles Payne frowned disparagingly and curtly added, "You'll be working for me, Melody. Susan will show you the ropes." He paused, " I will look forward to seeing you, Miss Hardy, back at your desk in one month," and with a final critical look at the new girl and her flowing Isadora scarf, he returned to the safety of his office, out of earshot of the pops and bangs as the pink bubble gum burst its sticky mess over her over painted face and lips.

"A word of advice," offered Susan, "Lose the gum. Mr. Payne doesn't like it and it doesn't look too good chewing in front of clients."

Melody immediately spat out the offending pink ball into the bin, "Sorry, I didn't think. I always chew when I'm nervous."

"Then it's a habit you'll need to get out of... And there's no time like the present." she added chirpily. "Don't worry,

Mr. Payne is a sweetie when you get to know him. He's a stickler for time keeping, but not a bad boss. Now, let's see, where shall we start? I think I'll show you the files first. I have a fairly unique way of filing... makes me indispensable," she smiled and Susan began to explain the running of the office and the idiosyncrasies of the switchboard, which was prone to play up from time to time.

The telephone system in Dempseys was notorious throughout the store for its eccentricities. It seemed to have a mind of its own at certain times and always when they seemed to be at their busiest. Susan was just preparing a trouble-shooting list for Melody when the door opened and Tony Clifton came in. He spoke impeccably, as always, "Ah, Miss Hardy. I understand that you are working with me temporarily, until a effective substitute has been found." He shook her hand warmly, "Shall we say half an hour? ... Will that give you enough time to appraise Miss...?"

"Melody, Melody Harper," gushed the teenager as her eyes lit on the handsome Tony Clifton.

"Miss Harper," he affirmed. He hesitated a fraction as his eyes caught the drape of the silk scarf at her neck. "Half an hour then?"

"That's fine," agreed Susan. She was surprised to see a flush of colour spread up from his neck. Tony Clifton left quietly and Susan began to doubt whether the blush she assumed she had seen was imagined or not.

"Cor, he's a cracker, he is. He could put his shoes underneath my bed any time."

Susan smiled at the comment and wondered whether a word of warning was in order. But, as she told herself, Melody would be bound to hear the gossip in her own time and she was sure Melody could make up her own mind. And so, she said nothing.

That was a mistake.

4
Would I lie to you?

"Take as long as you need, Rosie. I'll get Audrey to cover your section. And take care."

"Thanks, Geoff. I'm hoping I'll only be a week, just until the locks have been changed. I need to get out of the way for a while. You understand?"

"Don't worry. We'll cope. I'll brief Audrey. Anything else I should know?"

"I've been following up on the race relations story and have an interview with the youth social worker Thursday at two. I hope to be back but if I'm not can you reschedule for me?"

"Not a problem. Look after yourself now, won't you?"

"I intend to, Geoff, don't worry."

The editor of the Birmingham Mail looked concerned as he watched Rosie cross the office to her desk. She placed her in-tray on the adjoining desk and smiled at her colleague, Audrey.

"I won't overload you, most of it's cleared. There are just a couple of enquiries that need following up. Can you manage?"

"I'll be fine," smiled Audrey. "Just make sure everything is secure for you."

"Word travels fast!"

"You know journalists, can't keep their snouts out. News travels faster in this place than Linford Christie. Just take care, do you hear?"

"Will do. I'll take a couple of files with me. I've still got some research to do. Might as well do it while I've got the time. I can't sit here and twiddle my thumbs."

"I know what you mean," agreed Audrey and then returned to her PC.

Rosie opened her desk drawer and removed two files. She flicked a strand of her shining chestnut hair back from her face and made her way to the exit where she bumped shoulders with Lex Montague who was chatting with Brian Bates, one of the photographers.

"Hey, Rosie, where've you been? We've missed you."

"Long story."

"I've got time, fancy a drink?"

"Can't. I've got a train to catch. I'll tell you when I get back."

"Going anywhere nice?"

"Only London. Catching up with my cousin."

"That would be... Linda or is it Denise?"

"You've got a good memory,"

"Never forget a funny story and you have plenty of them about you and is it Linda? Like the time your aunt passed her a china cup and saucer of tea when she was on the motorway driving to see you in Brum."

Rosie chuckled, "I'd almost forgotten ... yes that's right, poor Linda had to do a strange balancing act, nearly crashed the car."

"Have a good time and we'll have that drink when you get back."

"Sure."

"Maybe you'll get to see a show," interjected Brian. 'Blood Brothers' is good if you can get tickets."

"Thanks, I'll remember that. Bye now," and she made her way to the corridor and the lobby, muttering good-byes to all who crossed her path.

*

Ajay giggled happily, everyone was being so friendly, even the two older lads, who used to pick on him. He felt if things continued to progress like this he may not even need Ghita to collect him each week. Then he really would seem grown up. After all he didn't want to be teased for being a baby. He sat down on the steps at the school entrance to wait for his sister.

"Fancy coming to the reservoir after club?" asked Wayne.

"I have to wait for my sister."

"Oh, go on. It'll be fun we're going hunting for frogs and lizards," added Kevin.

"I'd better not," murmured Ajay uncertainly.

"You won't get into trouble will you?" Wayne questioned.

"No. No nothing like that, I just need to ask first."

"Maybe next week then?" prompted Kevin.

"Possibly."

"Ajay!" called Ghita as she entered the playground. Ajay grinned and scrambled up.

"See ya!" he cried and ran to meet his sister.

"Everything all right?" asked Ghita as Ajay bounced up to her.

"Couldn't be better," gushed Ajay and he beamed at Ghita. "I've had a terrific day. Everyone's been smashing."

"Great! Who were they? They look a little old for you"

"They are the two who were so horrid before, but they both said sorry and that they were only mucking around. They even asked me to go out after club."

"I don't know about that. You'll have to ask mum."

"That's okay. I said I couldn't go this week. Maybe another time."

Ghita turned back to look at the two lads who were now deep in discussion. Kevin must have felt her eyes on him because he looked up and met her gaze. He smiled and gave a friendly wave, but his eyes remained cold. Ghita walked on watching Ajay run gleefully along the pavement dragging his ruler across the metal railings on the bridge that spanned one of the many canals that were in the area.

*

Tony Clifton closed his office door and turned to Susan Hardy.

"You did well today, Susan, very well. Do you have to dash straight home?"

"Why?"

"I just thought after all your efforts you deserved a drink. There's a neat wine bar in Temple Row. I like to unwind there after work. Wondered if you'd care to join me."

"Thank you, Sir, but I'd best be off home. My mother is unwell and it's my turn to cook dinner tonight."

At the mention of the word mother, Tony flushed guiltily as he remembered her plea for him to visit. But he put that thought to the back of his mind and smiled broadly, "Another time perhaps?"

Susan Hardy nodded and moved out of the office almost bumping into Melody Harper.

"Hi! How did you get on today?" asked Susan.

"All right. Although, I did get a little flummoxed with your filing system, but I'm getting the hang of it now."

"Good, any problems I'm on extension 139."

"Thanks."

"See you tomorrow," called Susan as she stepped out of Dempseys' side door.

Melody's scarf was caught in the gust of wind that blew through the door and Tony fell into step beside the young temp.

*

At the hospital, Detective Mark Stringer asked the question again, "I know this is difficult for you, but can you think of anyone, anyone at all who may have wanted to harm you or Mike?"

Chrissy turned her haunted eyes on the young detective. She blinked firmly as she struggled to shake her head. She had just regained consciousness and every movement was excruciating. She tried to moisten her dried cracked lips.

"No, I've never hurt anyone in my life. How's Mike?"

Mark looked uncomfortable as he tried to find the right words to say, "I'm sorry, Chrissy."

"He didn't make it?"

Mark's eyes gave Chrissy her answer and her expression crumpled into one of despair.

"Why?" was all she could muster before turning her head into the pillow.

Mark continued, "We want to get whoever did this to you and Mike. If you think of anything, anything at all, you must contact us." He took a card from his wallet and placed it on her locker. He turned to leave and then paused, "At the Rainbow Casino, I have a feeling that you saw or heard something you shouldn't. Can you remember?"

Chrissy winced as she shook her head once more, "I can't remember..." her voice trailed off.

Mark removed a flyer of Vencat from his pocket and showed her. "Do you know this man?"

Chrissy squinted at the photograph before letting her head fall back on the pillow. She nodded. "A big player and a big tipper. Used to come in a lot. Haven't seen him in a long while."

"Oh, well it was just a thought. Hang on in there."

*

Holly was pacing the room. She stopped for a moment and stared at the suitcases ready for their journey to Cornwall.

Paul walked in and paused, "Not having second thoughts are you?"

"I don't know. I'm not sure if it's the right thing to do."

"Colin feels you need a break. You need time to think."

"That's just it. I keep going over and over everything in my mind. It's relentless. I don't know if I should just face her out. But, then again...."

"You're scared?"

"Terrified more like. Oh, Paul, is this wise?"

"What do you mean?"

"Well, what if she does something else?"

"Holly, she can't. She's in hospital and when she has recovered sufficiently she'll be back in prison. Nothing for you to worry about."

"It's all right for you to say that, it isn't you she wants to see."

"If you decide to see her and I'm not sure you should, I shall be with you every step of the way. Now, do I put these in the car or not?"

Holly pursed her lips in that prim way that he so adored and nodded.

"Great. Is that everything? What about coats?"

"Oh yes!" exclaimed Holly and dashed to the hall closet to retrieve a couple of waterproofs.

"Right! Then let's go."

As Paul pulled the door closed behind them, he didn't notice the sudden drop in temperature, nor the draught, which appeared from nowhere and seemed to whisper and sigh through the house. If he had, he would have known there was mischief afoot.

*

Vencat swept his hands across the table and scooped up his winning chips. He pushed a small pile to the red headed escort he'd booked for the evening from Smart Girls.

"Here, have some fun. I'll meet you in the bar at..." he glanced at his watch, "say three quarters of an hour?"

The full-lipped beauty simpered her delight and suggestively wiggled her way across to the cashier's desk and fruit machines. She wasn't going to blow the lot on the tables. He had passed her well over a thousand pounds she could do a lot with that, not least of all to get a portfolio together for some modelling jobs. She'd often been told she had the looks to succeed. It would certainly beat this escort work.

Vencat turned to Stuart Allen at his side, "I'm ready to talk now."

"And I'm ready to listen although it does seem a pity to break the winning streak."

"I'm sure Philippe will be thankful that we'll give the bank a chance to recover!" He tossed a hundred pound chip along to the croupier.

The two men retired to the bar and chose a secluded table away from the rest of the clientele. They ordered their drinks, falling quiet when the pretty waitress delivered them to their table. Stuart tipped her and caught her by the wrist.

"By the way, what's happened to Chrissy? I haven't seen her in a while."

"Haven't you heard?" replied Colette. "She was attacked and left for dead."

"What? No, how shocking. "

Vencat leaned forward, interested in the interchange, his eyes gleaming with apparent concern.

"Chrissy? Does she work here?"

"Dealt Black Jack."

"What happened?

"Don't know."

"Will she be all right?"

"It's been touch and go. She's woken out of her coma but doesn't remember anything."

"Here, get her some flowers. Tell her get well soon. Which hospital is she at?" Vencat gave her a fifty-pound note.

"Dudley Road, in Intensive Care. Thank you." She placed the note under her tip tray. "Who shall I say they're from?"

"Just a couple of punters." Vencat smiled dismissively and Colette went back to her work leaving the two men to continue their discussion unaware they were being watched.

Woodward swallowed the last of his drink and called Colette over. "Same again please, Colette," he gestured to Allen and Vencat. "Big tippers, yes?"

"What? Oh yes, but this fifty is for Chrissy. They want me to get some flowers for her."

"That's kind. Wish I could do the same, but I don't seem to have the luck."

"You'd be better off going home to your wife and saving your money."

"You're probably right but I don't think the management would agree with you."

"They'd have my job if they heard me. You won't say anything will you?"

"Your compassionate views and counselling will go no further."

Colette passed him his drink and moved off from around the bar. Woodward watched the men discretely for a moment before trying to move closer. It was unfortunate. He couldn't catch anything that was being discussed. Allen raised his hand to Kenneth Chung who had appeared in the bar. Allen signalled him across and the conversation became more intense between the three men. Woodward couldn't risk making his interest obvious and so he tossed a fiver on the table for Colette and left the bar and the casino.

Once in the car park he got on the phone.

Allison answered gruffly, "What have you got?"

"Allen is up to something. He's meeting with Sharma. I don't know if he's a relative of Vencat, but there's a certain similarity. Kenneth Chung is with them now."

"The musician?"

"With alleged Triad connections. But, we've no proof. Why would he be mixing with Allen?"

"He does have a certain charm," mused Allison.

"Also, they gave one of the waitresses fifty quid for flowers. For Chrissy."

"Why would they do that?"

"Exactly. Guilty conscience perhaps?"

"Where are you now?"

"In the car park. Thought I'd wait a while. See what goes down."

"Need any back up?"

"I've called Brand. He can take over inside. Hold on! Sharma's coming out with his lady friend. I'll call you back." Woodward hung up and watched.

Vencat unlocked the blue topaz BMW Z3 and opened the passenger door for his companion. They were smiling and laughing. Woodward started his modest red P reg Fiesta. He watched them take the Portland Road exit and travel to the lights at Hagley Road. Woodward followed.

*

Rosie waved good-bye to Mary Allison on the platform and settled herself down on her reserved seat. She took out her book a Dean Koontz novel and settled herself down to read. She was a real fan. How he managed to think up such impossible plots was beyond her but the real skill he had was in making the reader believe them, absolutely. He made the bizarre perfectly plausible. Rosie had lost herself in the story and jumped when one of the stewards tapped her on the shoulder.

"Miss Partridge?"

"Yes?"

"I was asked to give you this."

He handed her an envelope. She examined the writing with trepidation. The steward began to walk away.

"Excuse me."

The Steward stopped.

"May I ask who gave you this?"

"I'm sorry, the guard on the platform indicated you when

you were saying good-bye to your friend and asked me to deliver it. Is there something wrong?"

"No, no. Not at all. Thank you." Rosie turned the envelope over. There was a kiss marked on the back. With shaking hands she opened it and read,

'You won't escape me. I'll be waiting for you.'

Rosie looked around the carriage nervously. Everyone travelling was wrapped up in their own affairs, in their own worlds. She took out her mobile and dialled Greg Allison's number.

*

Tony smiled at the young temp as she finished her wine. "Would you like another?"

"No. I'd better not. I'm supposed to be going out tonight. I need to have something in reserve."

"Going anywhere nice?"

"Doing the rounds. You know, starting off at Chaplins and Kelly's Wine Bar and then in and out of the bars on Broad Street."

Tony's mouth went dry at the mention of those places. Memories of Annette muscled their way into his mind.

Melody smiled brightly, "May see you tomorrow then?"

Tony responded, "If not before." He took another sip of his wine. His eyes narrowed as he watched her leave the bar. For a moment he abandoned himself to his thoughts and his eyes grew darker, some would say they turned to black. He was snapped back to the present with the annoying Toreador ditty, vibrating out from his mobile phone.

"Yes?"

"Tony! Glad you're out mate. Bit of a rum do for you. You planning on singing again?"

"If I can get the work. Beats staying in with my thoughts after mother...."

"Quite! Quite. Peter Sherratt, manager of Chaplins, has had someone let him down. Can you do a couple of spots tonight? Rehearse about eight thirty for nine, when the club opens? Steve Jenkins is still resident pianist, he knows your stuff."

Tony glanced at his watch. He just had enough time to get

home and change, sort out his dots. "Sure." He smiled; he may be seeing Melody sooner than tomorrow after all.

"Great. I'll put you back on my books then?" said Billy Clarke who ran a local entertainment agency.

"Why not? It's time things got back to normal." Tony left the rest of his drink, put on his blue Crombie and disappeared into the street.

Pooley finished his orange juice and followed at a discrete distance.

*

Vencat's car turned into one of the big houses on the Pershore road. Woodward cruised past and noted the number. He caught sight of the couple getting out of the car. Woodward continued along the road and turned into Speedwell Road, where he could park the car safely out of sight. He stopped at the barriers which adjoined Alexandra Road, put there to stop kerb crawlers from the old days when Varna Road had been the most notorious red light district in Birmingham, now innocuously renamed Belgravia Close. Woodward strolled past the park and positioned himself opposite the house. He saw the lights go on in an upstairs room and the curtains were pulled shut. He was going to have a bit of a wait that much was clear.

He walked up to the crossing and joined the queue in the fish and chip shop. He'd forgotten how hungry he was. There was a pub one door down, although it looked a bit rough, it could no doubt offer him a friendly pint. After all, it may be a long night.

If Woodward had realised that Sharma and Vencat were one and the same, he may have been more concerned for the red headed escort.

*

Rosie alighted from the train at Euston. The railway police were there to meet her and placed the envelope with its threatening note into an evidence bag. Rosie was uncertain how much use it would be after being handled by a guard, the steward and herself. She answered a few questions and was escorted to the taxi rank where she was lucky enough to be third in line.

Rosie got in the black cab before giving out her cousin's address. She didn't know who might be listening.

Her mobile started to bleep. It was a text message. She opened it. 'hpe u hd a gd jrny. Thnkng of u. Nt lng nw." Rosie almost dropped her phone. She started to cry.

*

Holly was finishing unpacking their bag in the spare room while Paul was catching up with his dad downstairs. There was a promise of a cup of tea when she had finished and a visit to the local pub later, which specialised in the most fantastic seafood.

Holly caught sight of her face in the dressing table mirror. Her eyes looked frightened. They reminded her of a young roe deer, which had been caught in the headlights of a tractor, at night, in the mowing grass. She stopped. Is this what she had come to? Chased out of her home for fear. Fear of a grandmother she had never known and fear of a gift stronger than hers? Was it stronger than hers? That she didn't know. In a battle of wills, who would be the victor? Little did Holly know that her thoughts of her grandmother were helping to create a stronger link between her and Grace Clifton.

She heard music begin to play downstairs, Gustav Holst's Mars, the Bringer of War from the Planet Suite. It provided a suitable backdrop for what happened next.

Holly hung up the last item of clothing in the wardrobe and thought about changing her clothes before they went out. There was an almost indiscernible drop in the temperature in the room as she began to undress. She threw aside her jeans and selected a pair of black slacks. The air grew colder. Holly shivered slightly, before pulling on a fluffy, kitten tongue pink sweater with matching belt. The room was becoming colder by the second and Holly checked the windows. There was no draught. She turned her attention to the radiator in the room and turned it up a couple of notches. She grabbed her handbag and removed a small brush and began grooming her hair that was untidy from the journey. Holly paced to the mirror and paused mid stroke as she watched the mirror cloud up as if Jack Frost himself had breathed his very essence onto the glass. Holly took a step backwards and sat on the bed. She stared with a mixture of fascination and horror as an unseen hand began to write on the mirror. The ghostly hand inscribed her name 'Holly' followed by an exclamation mark.

Holly tossed down her brush and rubbed the spirit words off the mirror. She gave a small cry as her reflection disappeared under another blast of an opaque silver mist and a circle was drawn with an unhappy face. Holly determined she would deal with this herself and alarm no one. She wiped the offending marks off the mirror, picked up her bag, forced a smile on her face and went downstairs to join Paul and his Dad. She would not be hounded or rattled by this woman. Not now. Not ever.

*

Chaplins was fairly quiet. Steve shook Tony's hand warmly.

"Good to see you." He paused before adding, "We were all sorry to hear about Amy.... but we knew you had nothing to do with any of it. It must have been hard."

Tony acknowledged the kindness offered and began the rehearsal. It was as if he had never been away. Everything just slotted right back into place. The girls were friendly, the band, and the manager, Pete.

Tony and Steve adjourned to the bar for a drink and the doors were opened. Tony scanned the customers for a glimpse of Melody but she wasn't there. Not yet, anyway. Steve nudged Tony and they returned to the small stage and began the first set.

'Laughter in the rain' segued into 'Proud Mary' the lights softened and Steve struck the opening chords of 'Home Thoughts from Abroad'. Tony's poignant tones filled the club and people stopped talking in order to listen. His eyes searched the club and he saw Melody and a friend watching from the bar. She caught his glance and smiling with both surprise and pleasure gave him a tentative wave. He raised his hand in recognition and nodded to her as he continued the song. He didn't notice young WPC Beck, sitting in the corner with a glass of wine. She studied his handsome face, the line of his jaw, his soul-searching eyes, his perfectly groomed blue-black hair, and his muscular body. She had to admit he was more than attractive. And he had this air about him, more than charm, more than charisma, one of power. There was something compelling and strangely disturbing about him but nevertheless very exciting about this talented singer. It was hard to believe he was involved in any murderous activities.

*

Linda hugged her cousin, "We're going to have so much fun. It'll be terrific having you here... what's the matter?" She broke off sensing the tension in Rosie's manner, so Rosie explained.

"Well no nut case is going to ruin your break. Give me your phone."

"What? Why?"

"Just do it."

Rosie handed Linda her phone obediently. Linda switched it off and shoved it in her sideboard drawer.

"There! Forget about it. You don't need it here anyway. If you have to make a call you can use the house phone, just remember to mask the number. I'm not ex directory. Tomorrow I've got the day off. We'll trot along to the BT shop and get you a new sim card. That'll give you a new number. It's only about twelve quid. I'm sure you can manage that?"

Rosie nodded, already she felt so much better. Linda had a way of dealing with things, which inspired confidence. Everything she said made perfect sense.

"I'm going to pour you a glass of wine. Ring Popsie and tell him the latest. Come on. Smile! We're going to have mega fun. You'll see."

*

Back in Birmingham, Rosie's mobile number was dialled again. He reached the BT voicemail 901 service. "Bitch!" she must have switched it off. No matter, let her have her day of respite. There was always tomorrow and if it was still switched off, he would have to ring her cousin's phone. What was her name again? Linda, that's right, Linda ... Gilchrist. And if his memory served him correctly she lived in Swiss

Cottage. It shouldn't be too difficult to find her number. Let Rosie wait. It would be all the more shocking and all the more satisfying when he did make contact. She would learn the hard way that he always got what he wanted.

*

Woodward had enjoyed his cod, chips and tub of mushy peas. He did feel however that wrapping the items in clean plain paper didn't do as much for the flavour as in the old days when the nation's favourite was parcelled up in newspaper. He'd strolled back to the house. The car was still there and a more subdued lighting shone through the curtains of the upstairs window. He had heard strains of something playing in the background, which sounded like the tin pot sounds of nondescript music that usually ran behind a porn movie. Woodward had checked his watch. He was probably good for another half an hour, maybe even all night so he decided to grab that pint he'd promised himself and then, check back with Brand.

Woodward sat as unobtrusively as possible at a corner table near the Gents. He took a passing interest in the game of Pool being played as he supped his pint. He took out his mobile and dialled.

The jangling of the phone on his outside line made Allison jump and he bit the inside of his cheek as he was enjoying the melting creaminess of his adored Mars Bar.

"Allison," he answered gruffly as he winced in pain.

"You're working late, Sir."

Allison grunted. Mary had already had a go at him about that. But he needed to wait to see what the forensic report had picked up on Rosie's envelope.

"Woodward here. Any news on Brand?"

"Brand seems to be on a round of club nightlife following Allen around and his various females. Kenneth Chung was picked up by his father. He's performing in some classical concert or other at Studleigh castle. But, he scribbled something on a piece of paper and left it with Allen. Brand's got someone attempting to check Allen's coat pockets in the cloakroom."

"Where are they now?"

"Some gentlemen's lap dancing club I believe. I think Brand is enjoying himself."

"I wouldn't be surprised."

"And you?"

"Just about to check on Sharma's house. I'll be in touch." Woodward ended the call when he spotted a thin weasily looking man with lank sandy hair. The face registered immediately with Woodward. Here was the truck driver who had transported the cocaine hidden in the frozen beef carcasses from Bristol to Rhyl on that big bust. This was the same guy who acted as Sharma's driver from the airport, who, it was said, had turned informer. Brand had persuaded him it was in his best interests to report on anything at all dodgy. The guy was playing a dangerous game.

Woodward, to all intents and purpose appeared absorbed in the crossword, which had been left on the table but he took note and watched the man who had once been one of Vencat's verminous crew.

The pager rang on the man's belt. He checked it and went to the public phone near the lounge bar. Woodward edged as near as he dared whilst feigning interest in a darts match between two local teams but the noise was too great and the man was speaking too quietly to be of any use.

The man replaced the receiver and headed for the exit. Woodward drained his glass and followed him out quietly. He observed from the shadows of the pub and saw the weasel unlock a dark Mercedes C220 and climb into the driver's seat. He lit a cigarette and Woodward noted the number. The man appeared to be waiting for something and Woodward thought he might just have time to get to his car and be ready to pursue the driver wherever he was off. He jogged across the crossing, along the road by the park until he reached his Fiesta. He scrambled in and started the engine and made his way to the corner of Speedwell Road where he could watch the pub car park without detection. While he waited he put a call through to trace the owner of the dark grey Mercedes. Moments later the C220 swung out into the line of traffic on the Pershore Road and headed towards the city.

Woodward pulled in two cars behind. The vehicle indicated left and Woodward could see it was turning into the driveway of the house where he had followed Sharma. Woodward proceeded past the house and up to the lights where he signalled right. He ducked out of the main stream of traffic and managed to turn around and return the way he had come. He slowed as he passed the drive and was able to see the weasel helping the leggy redhead into his car. There was no sign of Sharma. The redhead however, was not looking good. She was being supported, no, almost carried into the car. She was also holding something to her face. Woodward couldn't quite see. He turned back into Speedwell Road and waited to see which way he needed to turn into Pershore Road. The Mercedes purred to the edge of the drive. It was signalling right. There was a pause in the traffic and the weasel drove out and swept down the street passing Woodward waiting on the corner. He managed to slip in two cars behind his quarry. They pushed on and turned right in the direction of Moseley, along a leafy lined avenue and into the heart of student bed-sit land. Woodward watched the vehicle slow and stop at the driveway of a typical three storey Victorian House. Woodward waited at the kerb a few doors down. The driver left his engine running as he struggled to help the girl out of the car and up the drive. She stumbled and sat her down with a bump on the steps leading to the front door. The wall at the side was studded with bells. He pressed one and hurried away, got into his car and was gone. Woodward cruised up to the same driveway and stopped the car. He could clearly see the woman sitting on the steps. She was slumped over; her head in her lap and her legs lying crooked like a broken doll. He turned off his engine and ran up to her. Just as he arrived the front door opened and a young blonde came out. She stooped down and looked at the redhead.

"Rhonda? Rhonda? Are you all right?" She glared at Woodward as he bent down on the step and laid into him, "You bastard, what have you done to her? You need your bollocks nailed to a tree!"

Woodward grimaced when he saw the towel soaked in blood fall away from her tear stained face. What had been done to the beauty? Her bottom lip was swollen and split, her cheeks puffy and bramble bruised. Her right eye was almost closed with livid, distended lids, her nose bleeding and broken. He put his hand in his jacket pocket and flipped out his warrant card. He spoke to the blonde, "I didn't do this to her, but I want to know who did. Let's get her inside."

Woodward lifted Rhonda up into his arms and followed the blonde indoors. She led the way to a first floor flat; Woodward laid Rhonda down on the settee.

"I'll get some hot water, clean her up."

"No!" ordered Woodward. "If we're going to get this guy, we need the evidence. Just hang on. Get her a drink, a brandy or something."

"Brandy! Where do you think you are? The Ritz?"

"What have you got?"

"Hot sweet tea. That's supposed to be good for trauma."

"Fine, go and make it."

The blonde rushed into the kitchen, he heard the kettle being filled.

"Make us all one while you're at it," he called out before turning his attention back to Rhonda.

"Rhonda! Can you hear me? Listen Rhonda, who did this to you?"

Rhonda's once beautiful blue eyes filled with tears, which spilled over her lids and cascaded down her cheeks taking with them her blackberry juice mascara. She winced, as she wiped her hand across her cheeks. Woodward was sure her cheekbone was crushed.

She recoiled back in her seat her voice little more than a whisper, "Who are you? What do you want?"

"A friend. Believe me, I mean you no harm. I just want the person who did this to you."

She shook her head and her glossy tresses curtained her face, her voice cracked with emotion "I can't, he'll kill me."

"And if we let him go he could do it to someone else and possibly kill them."

"I've been paid to keep my mouth shut." She faltered and

then thrust her bag at him. He opened it; it was stuffed with fifty-pound notes. "Where's Coral?" she asked faintly.

"Making some tea."

"I'd prefer a drink," she croaked, "My throat's so sore."

"There isn't any."

"In my room under the wash basin. Some Scotch."

Woodward shouted, "Coral!"

"I heard. I'll get it. She can have it in her tea."

Rhonda's head lolled forward onto her chest. She was in no position to argue.

"You need a doctor." Woodward took out his mobile and strode to the window to get better reception and dialled the station, while Coral helped Rhonda to sip some tea.

"We need a doctor pronto and Forensics. If I'm not mistaken, our Mr. Sharma and Vencat are the same person... well, Vencat's predilection for sadism is well known. I've seen his handiwork before. This could be just what we need... What? Yes, pick him up too. The driver of the dark grey Mercedes license number T618 RRB... Who? That's right, Graham Gibson, of course, now I remember." He gave the girls' address and sat back down to wait.

Coral sat with Rhonda on the settee and she started to talk in fact it flowed from her.

"I warned her after the last time. I told her not to go but she was more interested in the tip. Wants to be a model, reckons it would pay for a portfolio get her registered with a top modelling school. It took her ages to heal last time. This time it's worse. Let me loose with him and I'd give him something to think about."

"What's the guy's name?"

"Some smart ass called Sharma, she met him in a night club. Perfect gentleman to begin with, then after the third date he started beating up on her. Shackled her inside a closet, like a torture chamber she said. Bastard I'd like to shackle him, cover his dick in chilli powder. And stick a radish up his fundament. That'd make him hop."

Woodward had to suppress a smile at Coral's imaginative punishments for Mr. Sharma. He had to admit he wouldn't mind seeing a few of them being carried out.

There was a grating rumble on the gravel outside. Woodward peered through the window, the doctor had arrived, and so had Forensics. Now he was on the way to finding out if his hunch was correct.

*

Tony finished the set and strolled across the dance floor towards the bar where he'd seen Melody with a friend.

"Hello, there. Can I buy you a drink, Melody isn't it?"

"Right! Melody Harper. I'll have a vodka ice," murmured Melody.

"And your friend?"

"The same," responded Melody's mate, "The name's Tina."

Tony ordered their drinks and himself a lager. "Did you say Harper? No relation to George Harper?"

"Who?"

"Old guy, good at chess. He was good to me."

She pulled a face, "No one of that name in the family, not as far as I can remember... You sing well," she added after a pause.

"Thanks. You sticking around? There's more to come."

"Nah! We've got places to go and people to see. What time do you finish?

"I'll be through about one."

"In that case we may pop back, right, Tina?"

"Whatever," exclaimed Tina, obviously bored. "Come on, Mel, drink up. It's time to move on."

Melody smiled apologetically, "May catch you later then?"

"You may," and he sipped his lager slowly allowing his eyes to wander over her smooth swan like neck, which displayed a butterfly choker. It reminded him of Amy and his eyes turned misty. He turned away abruptly and walked back to the dance area and sat at one of the tables. He didn't feel like talking now and he didn't want company. He stared morosely ahead, but could feel eyes upon him, staring. He spun his head around and peered into the corner where he could just make out a figure sitting at the table. The woman raised her glass and smiled. She looked familiar, who was she? Faces of other women kaleidoscoped around his head, images of Amy, Annette, Janet Mason, Natalie Blakeney Sandra Thornton and his mother whirlpooled in his brain. He forced his eyes shut but he could still see them, their laughing faces and his mother with her red damson coloured cheeks and raspberry smeared lips, his mother reciting the Bible and urging him to be cleansed; and her fat pudgy hands exploring his body and her relentless chanting of the psalms. Tony slammed his hand on the table. She had to stop, get out of his head before he lost it again. The noise of the bar and the disco music came to a crescendo in an ugly climax and then diminished into the ordinary nightclub sounds once more. He opened his eyes. The woman was still staring. She rose and approached his table.

"Tony, isn't it? Mind if I join you a wee while? Came the lilting Dublin tones of WPC Beck.

"How...?"

"We met the other week at your house."

"I'm sorry?" Tony was at a loss.

"The disturbance... your electricity was off."

"Of course, the WPC," he licked his lips.

"I'd prefer it if you called me Kirsty."

"Kirsty it is," he said and he smiled, his head was beginning to clear. That was a good sign. He hadn't felt this calm since Amy. He was definitely feeling better.

"Let me buy you a drink," he insisted and Kirsty nodded.

"Dry white wine spritzer, please."

Tony pushed the chair away from the table. That's what Amy used to drink. This was definitely a good sign. Definitely.

5
Broken Wings

The hand tapped on the computer keys and entered a favourite site 192 directory enquiries. The accessed menu selected a name, Linda Gilchrist and a place, Swiss Cottage London. He was right. It was easy. There was one match and clearly on screen for anyone to read were her full address, phone number and conveniently there was a map showing how to get to her house. Excellent! Now, he could phone her, send her flowers, even visit if he wanted to, as long as he could get the day off work. It was all worth considering and planning. He set to work.

*

Coral travelled with Rhonda in the ambulance. Woodward followed in his car. Coral would need a lift home if they decided to keep her friend over night. The doctor was insistent she went to Casualty straight away. Her face was a mess. Rhonda's nose needed to be set and her cheeks repaired; the sooner the better. So, thanks to Coral's nagging, Rhonda had seen sense, if she had any intention of following her dream of a modelling career then she was going to have to break her silence. When she did, Woodward would be there.

Swabs from her vagina had already been sent to the lab, a mould of the teeth marks on her breasts plus prints taken off the bundle of notes. This should prove conclusively whether Sharma was Vencat or just another pervert with a predilection for hurting beautiful women.

*

Grace Clifton whined for the nurse, "Connie! Connie are you there?"

"Now, what's all this fussing and yelling? Surely, you can see I have my hands full with the new admission."

"Sorry, Connie. I seem to have slipped down the bed. I'm getting a crick in my neck trying to get up."

"We'll soon have you up and surveying the world again.

73

Clive!" She called for the male nurse to help her lift Grace into a more comfortable position. "There now, is that better?"

"Much better, thank you. Can you pass me my Bible? I'd like to read the Lord's words they give me comfort, so they do."

Connie reached down and picked it up, "Although, I wouldn't have thought you needed it. Why you can recite practically the whole thing word for word."

"The memory's not as good as it used to be. I sometimes get the words wrong, but not the sentiments," she added quickly.

"Will that be all, now?"

"I just wondered if there'd been any word on my granddaughter or my son."

"I promise you, if there is, you'll be the first to know."

Nurse Connie O'Grady left Grace's bedside with Clive. Grace looked around craftily. She had been taking great note of late, of the busiest and most relaxed times on the ward. Visiting times in the evening may look busy with people coming and going, but the nurses were more relaxed. They didn't have time to keep watch especially if they had an admission to deal with. The copper on duty usually helped himself to a cup of tea while waiting for his relief. Yes, the evening was a good time. At night there wasn't enough activity except for emergencies and she couldn't rely on that. Similarly, people were too alert in the morning with doctors on their rounds. No, evening would be best.

Grace was keen on prolonging her stay, pretending she wasn't healing as well as she should be. That had caused a few problems at first but now the staff seemed resigned to her staying there till the end of the week. She would soon have to make her move. Her scheming and future plans were almost sorted out, almost, but not quite. A little more thought needed to go into her disguise. The key to the linen closet containing doctors' white coats, amongst other things, was housed on a hook on a keyboard at the nurses' station. She needed to get at that without being seen. The rest would be easy. She knew where there were spare trolleys, where she could load the linen. There was an old lady in a bay near the swing doors of the same height and build as herself, so the old lady's clothes would fit. With a bit of luck she may even manage to get the old dear into her bay. Grace opened her Bible at random and pointed with her finger, which fell between two verses 21 and 22 of Genesis 39. She read,

"But the Lord was with Joseph, and shewed him mercy, and gave him favour in the sight of the keeper of the prison.

And the keeper of the prison committed to Joseph's hand all the prisoners that were in the prison, and whatsoever they did there, he was the doer of it."

Her eyes glistened with the fervour of righteousness. This was an omen, an omen that she was on the path to victory. Grace burst into song, praising her soul the King of Heaven.

*

Kirsty Beck had a delightful way of putting her head on one side as she listened to him. She was a pretty little thing and her voice. Her voice with that soothing, charming Irish accent added to her appeal. In Tony's eyes she was already becoming the ideal substitute for Amy. Amy who he had loved so dearly and whose life had been so cruelly stolen away by his mother, for which, he would never forgive her.

"I must say how surprised I was to see you here. That you'd resumed your singing career." If Kirsty Beck was unnerved by Tony she certainly didn't show it. In fact, she even appeared to be warming to him.

"It's in the blood. I can lose myself in the music. It chases away all the bad memories." Tony found himself talking to her as if he had known her forever. The timbre of his voice was resonant, melodic. He was so easy to listen to; it was part of his charisma.

As Kirsty listened and chatted she could scarcely believe him guilty of the murders, which had struck fear in the heart of Birmingham. It seemed much more probable that his religious freak of a mother was solely responsible. And, of course, he had been released; the evidence had been shaky and circumstantial except for Sandra Thornton who claimed to have been attacked by Tony and threatened by his mother. Kirsty made up her mind to fully examine the files and case notes and draw her own conclusions. For the moment she was enjoying his company. She didn't notice a young woman watching her carefully from the bar.

Tony went to order some more drinks before beginning the second set and Kirsty excused herself to visit the Ladies Restroom. The young woman who had been watching pushed her way through the throng of clubbers that was beginning to grow and followed Kirsty into the loo.

Sheena replenished her lip-gloss and teased her hair around her face as she waited for Kirsty to emerge. The toilet flushed and Kirsty went to the hand basin to wash her hands.

"Excuse me,"

Kirsty glanced up surprised. "Yes?"

"I have to tell you... warn you," continued Sheena.

Kirsty dried her hands and looked expectantly. "What is it?"

"That man you're with. Do you know him?"

"I do. Why?"

"He's not what he seems."

"And how do you make that out?"

"Please for your own sake, leave the club now, and don't come back."

"But why?"

"He's dangerous. Trust me, I know."

"How? How do you know?" Kirsty was beginning to feel alarmed.

"My best friend... she was his girlfriend. She's dead now."

"Amy?"

"You know about her?"

"It's my business to know. I'm a police woman."

Sheena began to fluster, "Oh, I'm sorry. I just thought..."

"It's okay. I'm not getting into anything I can't handle. For what it's worth, the story about a miscarriage of justice could be right."

"No!" Sheena was adamant. "Listen," and she took a scrap of paper out of her bag and scribbled a number on it. "If you want to talk, call me. I can tell you things about this man that no one would believe."

"And how do you know they're true?"

"Because Amy told me and she loved him. Please be careful."

The door to the ladies burst open to admit three giggling young women. Sheena retreated to the door, "Remember what I said," and she disappeared into the crowded club.

Kirsty stuffed the note into her bag and returned to her table. There was a drink waiting for her. Tony had begun the second set. He gave her a wink as he launched into the chorus of an old James Taylor number. Kirsty smiled back and Sheena watched from the bar, clearly very concerned.

*

Linda and Rosie were happily reminiscing, "And do you remember us going up and down in the lift at the flats opposite?"

"And it got stuck and we were afraid to ring the alarm."

"Because the caretaker had already told us off and threatened to tell your mother."

"We were there for hours!"

"Missed our lunch."

"We were stuck there until Mrs. Scooter got us out."

"Her name wasn't Mrs. Scooter."

"That's what you called her."

"That was her dog, her dog was called Scooter. Her name was Salmon."

"Mm! Sounds fishy to me."

"Oh, Linda!" groaned Rosie as she took another sip of wine.

The telephone rang. "Hello," said Linda still laughing. She put her hand over the mouthpiece and offered the phone to Rosie, "It's for you."

The laughter fell away from Rosie's eyes, "But no one knows I'm here..."

"Except the police!"

"Of course." Rosie took the phone and spoke tentatively, "Hello?"

"Are you missing me?"

Rosie stiffened and her eyes widened in fear. The voice went on, "Cat got your tongue? Come on... Surely by now you realise I know your every move. Have fun with your cousin, it won't last long." Rosie dropped the phone and began to sob. Linda grabbed it and demanded, "Who is it? Who is this?" But the receiver went click, punctuated by the dialling tone. Linda immediately punched in 1471. "... The caller withheld their number."

"Call the police, now," insisted Linda. With shaking hands Rosie began to dial.

Allison was just tearing the wrapper off one of his Mars Bars when his direct line rang.

"Popsie?"

"Rosie? What's wrong?"

Rosie's anguished voice began to recount what had happened. Eventually her voice cracked as she tried not to weep. Linda grabbed the phone from her,

"The pervert has tracked her down, somehow. What shall we do?"

"Sit tight and I'll get someone from the Met to see you. They owe me a few favours. Who knew she was coming?"

"I don't know. I'll ask."

Rosie stretched out her hand, "It's okay. I'm all right, really. I'll speak to him."

Greg repeated his question.

"Lots of people at work, folk at the flats, a couple of family members and the police."

"I thought we said no one was to know."

"We did but word seems to have got around somehow."

"Try not to worry, I'll ask a few questions myself if need be. The locksmith is fixed for tomorrow and BT is changing your number. I'll get someone to check your cousin's line. Oh and leave your mobile off."

"We've already thought of that. I'm getting a new sim card and I shall be very careful about giving that number out."

"Okay. Just try and keep calm. You're safer there than in Brum at the moment."

"How do you know?"

"Trust me. I'll have someone with you within the hour." Greg ended the call, his Mars Bar forgotten he rang home. "Mary? I'll be later than I thought. Don't wait up."

Woodward and Brand faced Graham Gibson across a desk. The sandy haired weasel looked uncomfortable.

"I told you. I didn't do nothing. For Christ's sake I been trying to help you lot out."

"Tell us again, from the beginning."

"Oh, Lord love us!" he exclaimed and launched into his third explanation of the night.

"I picked up Mr. Sharma from the airport and I ferried him around until he got his own motor. But you know all this, bloody hell you was following me!"

"Right. What else did he have you do?"

"I ran a few errands for him. Chauffeured him when he went out on the town. That's all. Until tonight, and I didn't like that. What he'd done to that girl. Weren't nothing to do with me."

"We've established that. But, these errands, you've not said what any of them are."

"All sorts, pretty boring really. Taking his stuff to the cleaners, picking up champagne, cigarettes and so on. Tracking down some female's address."

"Hold on. You've not mentioned that before. What female?"

"Some bit who works at the casino."

Brand raised his eyebrows and looked across at Woodward, "Go on."

He got me to follow one of the dealers. Black Jack, you know. Wanted to find out where she lived, to send her some flowers by way of thanks. He won big on her table, see? Don't know why he couldn't just ask her or send it to the casino. He made enough fuss about keeping it a surprise."

"Where did she live?"

"I followed her to some place on the Bristol Road, black and white house. Three flats there and I had to check the bells."

"So, who was she?" interjected Woodward.

"Some bird called Chrissy, Chrissy Stephens."

Woodward leapt up, "You stay right there, Sunshine. I'm not finished with you yet." Woodward left the interview room and a uniformed copper entered and stood by the door.

"Come on Mr. Brand. This ain't hardly fair. I've done what I'm supposed to do. If he finds out I'm talking to you. I'm done for."

"Then you may be safer here than on the streets. Just once more tell me about the girl, Rhonda."

"I've told you, I've driven them out a couple of times. One time he hurt her quite badly, gave her a black eye and such. I had to take her home. I didn't like what he'd done then."

"And tonight?"

"I got a call to collect her from Mr. Sharma's and take her home as quick as possible. I had to help carry her out she was in a hell of a mess. I made up my mind then that it would be the last of it. I don't like blokes who beat up on women. Vencat was the same, used to enjoy hurting them."

"I'll get a statement together for you to sign, then I think we may need to put you into protective custody."

"Come on, Mr. Brand. Do I really need that?"

"Yes, Gibbo I think you do. I'm impounding your car, for Forensics."

Graham Gibson rolled his eyes in a gesture of despair, "At least can I have a coffee?"

Brand nodded at the copper. "See to it. And keep him out of sight, at least for the time being."

Brand went off to find Woodward. Things were hotting up now and he'd soon have something to tell the officer from the Met working on the Friel killing. It looked like a number of crimes were to be wrapped up if Woodward's hunch was correct.

*

The final set was in session. Couples danced slowly and closely to the last number of the night. The glitter ball's silver lights spiralled around the club in time with Tony's exceptional voice, which claimed that a house was not a home unless she was there still in love with him. Kirsty tried to swallow the lump of emotion, which had risen. She wasn't used to this. He was getting to her. How could someone over flowing with such emotion possibly be a serial killer? Forget

Robbie Williams and Jack Jones. He had the voice and looks of an angel. Kirsty felt drawn to him, comfortable with him and wanted to see him again.

Tony's nostrils flared with the depth of feeling in his song. His hands cupped the microphone in the gesture of a prayer and he lowered his head as if overcome with the power of the song.

People clapped and applauded. Kirsty stood up and beamed. She too clapped and a tear escaped and ran down her cheek. She quickly brushed it away.

"Great set!" congratulated Steve as he collected his sheet music. "Are you on tomorrow? I've got a new song I'd like you to try."

"If Pete wants me, I'll be here." Tony sounded supremely confident and exactly like his old self. That had to be thanks to Kirsty. He scanned the club. There she was collecting her coat. He excused himself from Steve and hurried over.

"Kirsty!" He stopped, suddenly feeling shy. What if she didn't want to see him again? What if he had imagined her interest? Kirsty turned her head and smiled. Tony pressed on and spoke to her. "I was wondering that if you liked the show … do you want to come again?"

"I've a day off tomorrow; that is if you're performing again?"

"Can you hang on a minute?" Tony ran across to the manager, "Pete? Do you need me tomorrow?"

Pete nodded. "I'll sort the contract, let's have you back on a regular basis. Same as before. Our regular singer, Lionel is laid up with the flu or some such thing. I'd like you to cover his spots until he's better. If that's okay?"

"Fine! Fine. Tomorrow it is," he turned back to Kirsty who had heard the interchange. She extended her hand to him, which he took, "Until tomorrow?"

"Tomorrow," she responded and joined the drifting crowds on their way in search of another venue open until the early hours.

Tony praised God in his heart, the God he'd turned his back on. He was being given another chance. This time his mother wouldn't mess things up. He'd make sure of that.

Allison and Stringer made their way to the night desk of the Birmingham Mail. They showed their cards and were ushered through to the Chief Editor's Office. Geoff Franks looked up curiously at the two men approaching him.

"Mr. Franks?" questioned Mark Stringer, "Police, we need to ask a few questions."

"Be my guest," and he offered them a seat. "Is this to do with Rosie?"

"I'm afraid so," continued Mark, "As you know Rosie has gone away for a few days,"

"Yes, to her cousin in London."

"I understand she was in the office earlier."

"Very conscientious is Rosie, she wanted to leave things tidy."

"Who else knew she was going to London?"

"Most of her colleagues in this office and a few from downstairs."

"We'd like a list of names and where they can be contacted."

"Mm. Not sure I can remember everyone. I expect Audrey can help."

"Audrey?"

"Audrey Hooper, next desk to Rosie. She's finishing off a couple of Rosie's assignments."

"What was she working on?"

"Something on the racial tension that's been brewing... and the fund raising project for the new children's hospice amongst other things."

"Ask her to come in," instructed Allison.

Audrey Hooper entered, a petite girl with pearl blonde hair and owl glasses, which seemed too big for her frame and face.

"Audrey, can you remember who was in the office when Rosie dropped by?"

"Who wants to know?" she asked suspiciously.

Allison introduced Mark and himself and continued, "We need a list of everyone who may have known her plans."

Audrey chewed on the end of the pencil she had been

twiddling, "Let's see... Geoff here and of course me, Brian Bates, Carol Farthing, John Dorsey, Katrina Purvis, um..." She paused and Geoff carried on with a list of more names.

"Oh and Lex Montague," added Audrey as she saw the photographer walk into the office.

"I'll get Personnel to give you their addresses and contact numbers and you better have a word with Parker from downstairs, he'll tell you who was in from his department."

"Can you think of anyone who may hold a grudge against Rosie?" asked Allison.

Audrey shook her head, "She was pretty much well liked as far as I know."

"Good at her job too," added Geoff.

"Any boyfriends, ex boyfriends?" queried Stringer.

"Not really. She went out with Brian for a while."

"Brian Bates?" questioned Stringer consulting his notes.

"Mm. But they remained friends. She was quite pally with all the photographers."

"I'll need a list, whether they were in today or not," grunted Allison.

"That's easy," said Geoff and went to his filing cabinet and took out a folder, "Competition entries for the Mail Shot of the year, take it. It's a duplicate."

Stringer thanked the editor and the two coppers left.

"Fancy a night cap?" asked Stringer.

Allison looked at his watch, "Why not? I told Mary not to wait up. It'll give us a chance to look through these.'

"Peppermint Park? That stays open till four."

"Peppermint Park," Allison affirmed.

*

Grace Clifton crept stealthily from her bed. She screwed up her face as she moved. She was still in discomfort from her injuries. Grace peered outside her bay. The duty policeman was asleep, no worries there. It all seemed quiet. She made her way to the swing doors and the old lady's bed. There she bent down by the locker and tentatively opened the door. There was a bag inside, open. Grace could see the woman's clothes, shoes and a purse with money and credit cards. She stopped as the old dear turned in her sleep dropping her hand down the side of the bed almost touching Grace's shoulder. Grace held her breath and waited. The woman turned again. Grace moved. A sleepy voice opposite stopped her in her tracks.

"Hey what do you think you're doing?"

Grace turned. An elderly woman was talking in her sleep. But Grace couldn't take the chance. She padded over to the patient taking the bag with her. Her eyes darted around. She licked her lips and made sure her deed was not witnessed by anyone. Taking one of the pillows from the chair by the bed she placed it over the unsuspecting woman's face. The body convulsed and twitched. Grace held her position until all life had drained away and she was still. She replaced the pillow and made her way back to her bed. She shoved the bag in her own locker and sat on the bed sweating with her exertions.

"And what are you doing up and about?" asked the night sister as she looked in.

"I was just going to the toilet," Grace whined in her reedy tones.

"Then you should have buzzed..."

"Most folks are asleep and I wanted to see if I could go on my own. It's not very dignified having to use a commode. Everyone can hear you go."

The sister sympathised and helped Grace up. "All right, come along with me and I'll help you. My, my, you're soaking wet."

"Night sweats. I get them sometimes," lied Grace.

"We ought to change you,"

"I'll be all right till morning. I'll have a bit of a swill in the basin."

"If you're sure?" replied the sister glad of the excuse not to wash and change her.

They came out from the bay. The policeman now alert from the commotion stood.

"No worries officer, just a loo trip," came Grace's nasal twang as she shuffled past. The constable stretched and sat himself down again.

"I'll be along with a cuppa in a minute," offered the sister to the policeman, as she helped Grace into the lavatory and closed the door. "Tea or coffee?'

"Coffee I think, I need the caffeine," joked the copper.

Grace leaned against the door and gave grateful thanks to the Lord. Right was on her side. Tomorrow evening couldn't come quickly enough, tomorrow evening and freedom.

6
Feelings

Dempseys was buzzing with the news. The police had arrested Tony Clifton. It was something about the disappearance of a girl.

Melody Harper had not turned up for work that morning. When Charles Payne had telephoned, her distraught mother said that Melody's bed had not been slept in. Melody had not returned home. Mrs. Harper had immediately called the police and reported her missing.

Susan Hardy was already admonishing herself for not having said anything to the young temp. If Melody *was* found dead, she would never forgive herself.

*

Tony Clifton was in an interrogation room being questioned. He had no idea why he was there. His head was beginning to pound; fireworks were going off behind his eyes. The room was whirling like a carousel. He threw back his chair and slammed his knuckles into the wall with a bellow of rage. Sergeant Pooley was up and on his feet, and with the help of PC David Taylor they managed to restrain Tony who seemed to have an abnormal surge of strength. Young PC Taylor returned Tony to the cells whilst Pooley grabbed the phone and demanded a doctor to examine Tony Clifton.

It was to this chaos that DCI Greg Allison arrived back at work. His temper was none too sweet from the after effects of the previous evening's impromptu night cap with Mark at Peppermint Park where one drink had turned to four and he'd taxied home in the early hours and as a result had slept none too well. His lack of rest showed in his grizzled appearance.

"Jumped the gun didn't you? Where's the surveillance report? Who ordered him brought in?"

Pooley looked uncomfortable under Allison's accusing gaze.

"Who was on watch last night?"

"Beck, Sir from nine p.m. until one a.m."

"Where's her report?"

"Not filed yet, Sir it's her day off."

"And afterwards? Who staked out the house?"

"Juniors in CID had the graveyard shift."

"What do they say?"

"The notes are incomplete." Pooley didn't know how to convey the next piece of information. He knew he was going to be blasted by Allison, so he just came right out and said it, "They fell asleep on shift, Sir. Woke with the dawn chorus and people going to work."

Allison was practically apoplectic, "What?" he roared. "I want their names and in my office now."

"They've gone off duty."

"I don't care where they've gone. Get them back." He jerked his head to the door dismissing the sergeant. He thumped his desk in anger sending his in-tray sliding.

"Is everything all right?" asked Maddie nervously as she poked her head round the door. She wasn't used to seeing her boss like this. He always looked as if he could blow a gasket but he rarely did. His gruff demeanour was strong enough to have his team jumping to attention.

"I'm surrounded by idiots. Do I have to do everything myself?"

"Can I do anything, Sir?" asked a bemused Maddie.

"You can get me a cup of tea and ring Mark. Tell him to get his arse in here."

"Yes, Sir." Maddie closed the door quietly and went to warn Mark Stringer.

Allison scooped up the papers, which had tumbled from his tray and thrust them back with a resounding slap. He wrenched open his drawer and grabbed a Mars Bar. He needed one right now. He didn't care if it was early. Still smouldering he lumbered to the window and stared out at the view of the General Hospital. The comings and goings of the medical building always seemed to have a calming effect. That and his Mars Bar, he thought, as he ripped off the paper.

He'd just demolished the last mouthful when there was a

tap at the door and Maddie entered with his tea, followed by Mark.

"Get him a cup too, Maddie." Allison growled, "And Maddie?"

"Sir?"

"I didn't mean to sound off at you."

"No, Sir."

That was the nearest to an apology he was going to give. But Maddie didn't mind. She liked her boss and forgave him the occasional outburst.

"Mark? How's the head?"

"Fine. I was on the Kaliber. Remember? Driving," he added lamely.

"That low alcoholic rubbish, don't know how you can drink it."

"Yes, Sir. So you said."

"Mm, well... we didn't do much analysing last night. If Rosie is to remain safe, we'd better get onto it now. Have you organised anyone to question those on the lists?"

"All in hand, Sir as we speak."

Greg grunted and spread the contents of the photographer's competition file on the desk. He gave a low whistle... "Would you look at that?"

There on a black and white glossy print was a picture of Tony Clifton upon his release facing a horde of reporters vying for position and at the front of the line with the tails of her Isadora scarf flying in the breeze was Rosie Partridge. The look on Clifton's face was intense and Allison could swear he could see the beginning of a smile. Clifton's eyes were fixed on the scarf.

"I wonder..." was all he could muster for the moment and the two men looked at each other.

Just then Maddie entered with Mark's tea and broke the silence, which had fallen between them, a silence that was filled as both men's brains were sent whirling.

Allison was the first to move and he searched through the rest of the pictures, "That's interesting..." There was another picture, this time of Darleston's newsagents. A stream of water from a fireman's hose was extinguishing a wire basket aflame in the doorway. Framed behind the glass of the door through the smoke was the spectre like, frightened face of Jarnail Kumar the owner.

Allison pointed to the corner of the picture by the front of the fire engine, "Who's that?"

Mark stared hard, "It looks like Rosie."

"With that head of hair, I'm damn sure it is."

"Don't you find that odd?"

"They may have been working on the story together."

"Possibly. That can be checked. Make a note of it will you? Who's the photographer?"

Mark turned the pictures over, "Lex Montague."

"Is it be damned? Then I think we may just tackle Mr. Montague ourselves."

*

Colette, from the Rainbow Casino, walked up the corridor towards the Intensive Care Unit brandishing a huge bouquet of flowers and carrying a basket of fruit. She spoke to the nurse on duty and was given permission to go in to Chrissy's room.

"Hey there!" she said softly to her workmate, who was wired to an assortment of machines, which gave out bleeps and burps as they monitored Chrissy's status.

Chrissy turned her head and managed a half smile,

"Colette!"

"You'd better get well and back to work quickly, the punters are missing you. Look!" And she plonked the fruit on the locker dislodging Mark Stringer's card, which fluttered to the floor. "And these," she added showing Chrissy the beautiful blooms. "I got as many scented ones as were in season. Do you like them?"

Chrissy nodded, "Thanks, who are they from?"

"Mr. Sexy, Stuart Allen and that new punter, he's an Asian guy, a big tipper."

"Oh, I know, that's kind."

"I'll get these put in water for you. I can't stay long the nurse has only given me a few minutes; more's the pity. I've got heaps of gossip but I've been told not to excite you so you'll just have to get well to hear all the juicy bits."

"I'm hoping to get out into the main ward by the end of the week," murmured Chrissy.

Colette started chatting about her colleagues at the Rainbow and what had been happening but Chrissy had a nagging something at the back of her mind, something so elusive she couldn't put it into words. Finally, Colette said, "You've not heard a word I've said, perhaps I'd better go."

"No, no it's just... there's something I'm trying to remember, keep talking, it may help."

So Colette continued to chatter in her chirpy fashion until she was interrupted by the duty nurse, Nurse Blaine.

"Time's up I'm afraid. She must rest now." The nurse eyed the flowers, "Aren't they beautiful? Your friends must think very highly of you. I'll put them in water and when I get back I'll expect you," she nodded at Colette, "to be gone."

"Right then I'll say good-bye."

"Wait!"

Colette stopped at the door.

"There's a card on the locker, can you call the number for me?"

Colette looked, "Nothing here, Chrissy, are you sure?"

"I thought there was.... not to worry, I'm sure it's not important."

"What?"

"Nothing, thanks for coming in."

"A pleasure, see you soon... in the main ward!" and with that Colette left the room. She didn't see the white coated orderly standing by the door to the stairwell. His face was turned away from her. Colette stopped and turned back.

"You'll have sister after you," smiled Chrissy.

"I just thought, about that card... it may be on the floor. I think something fluttered down when I put the fruit on the locker." She scrambled down on her hands and knees, "Yep here it is. Is this the one? Mark Stringer?"

Chrissy nodded, "Can you ring him for me? Tell him I may have something."

"Sure, will do. Now, this time I really am going. Is there anything else I can get you?"

"I could do with some decent shampoo."

"Done! Bye for now," and Colette began to make her way to the end of the ward and the lifts.

"You're off then?" asked Nurse Blaine as she returned along the corridor with the flowers. "Aren't they just gorgeous? I love scented blooms. So few of them have any perfume nowadays. It's all bred out of them."

A male doctor who was on the brink of entering Chrissy's room ducked back inside the stairwell as he saw the duty sister coming back along the corridor.

"I'm just off to get Chrissy some shampoo, if that's okay? Is the shop downstairs?"

"It is, but she won't be in any state to wash her hair, not for a while."

"I know. It's just a psychological thing to make her feel better. I promise I'll only drop it off. I'm not staying."

"All right. It can't do any harm." And so saying the nurse marched briskly on her way.

The intruder stealthily tiptoed out and watched through a crack in the door. He could just hear the pleasantries exchanged between Chrissy and the sister. He retreated back into the stairwell and waited patiently for his opportunity. He secured his white clinical facemask and tucked his hair into the sterile, surgical hat. He put on the heavy framed, plain glass spectacles and buttoned his white doctor's coat and attached his false name lapel pin. Then, donning his latex gloves he took a hypodermic syringe from his pocket and removed the sheath. His eye was fixed on the door to Chrissy's room.

He had grey, watery blue eyes, with sparse lashes. They were cold and dead like those of a fish on a slab; the eyes of a killer; the same eyes, which had peered through the balaclava and had murderously attacked Mike and viciously wounded the valiant canine and Chrissy. He had been hired to do a hit and he had never failed yet. His reputation was at stake. He took great pride in his work. Killing was something he enjoyed and Vencat had always been a good customer although he'd never met the man. Instructions had always come by telephone and the money wired into his offshore account. His ability to melt into the background and his ingenuity in style had earned him the nickname, 'The Chameleon'.

He knew the police were scurrying around, starved of clues in the Friel killing of the undercover cop. He knew that they had nothing on the murder in Bristol Road. Chrissy was still his mark and a loose end, one that was just about to be tidied.

He waited. The voices stilled. The nurse purposefully left the room. He waited. The time was right. The time was now. He slipped out from his hiding place and silently entered the room of his prey.

Chrissy lay on her side, tired from her visitors; her eyes closed peacefully. She was blissfully unaware of the danger closing in on her.

He assumed the authority of a health professional and zoned into her bed. He grasped her arm. Chrissy stirred. He spoke calmly. His voice was light and high, disguised and belying his intention.

Chrissy sleepily lifted her lids and saw those eyes, which held no emotion, those eyes, which dealt in death and she knew. She started to cry out, but the hand of the killer stopped her mouth. He held the struggling Chrissy and tried to inject something into her arm.

"Right, that's my good deed done. I'll be off now," said Colette as she breezed in, "What's happening here?" Her tone took on a shrill urgency, "Nurse!" She screamed at the top of her voice.

The Chameleon jumped at the sudden intrusion and panicking he pushed past Colette into the corridor and dropped the syringe as he fled. Colette screamed again at the top of her lungs and nurses came running from every direction. She pointed at the fleeing man who scrambled his way to the stairwell pursued by two orderlies.

"Are you okay?" asked Colette

"Thanks to you. Why did you come back?"

"I was going to get your shampoo but forgot to ask which sort you wanted."

"Medicated," answered Chrissy with a smile. "Ironic, isn't it?"

"You nearly got that and more."

"But, not in a shampoo!"

"The police are on their way," the duty nurse informed them. "They want to speak to you. You can wait in my office."

"Can't she stay with me?" pleaded Chrissy.

"We need to check you over first, make sure none of that stuff, whatever it is, got into you," said the nurse apologetically.

"Do the business," said Colette. "I'll be back. Promise," and she left her friend being ministered to in safety.

*

Ajay scrambled along the wall by the reservoir waving his ruler like a sword in the air. He'd finished Stamp Club and had gone off with his newly made pals to look for lizards and frogs. He didn't know what he'd do with them when he found them. And he didn't like the idea of sticking pins in them to make their eyes pop out. That seemed too cruel for words. He liked frogs and if he caught any he'd keep them as pets for a while. He even knew what he'd call them, Flip, Flap and Flop, if there were three... He could keep them in the bath, or in the old tin bath in the yard outside the shop if his mother didn't approve of frogs indoors. Ajay was so absorbed in his thoughts and dreams he didn't notice two older youths talking to his so-called new friends. The young men sloped away into the undergrowth and the two year six boys from Ajay's school, Wayne and Kevin, pocketed the ten pound notes given to them by the other men, and bounced up to the small boy.

"Careful on the wall Ajay! You don't want to fall in." Kevin pointed out.

"No! There's lots of tangling weeds there and kids have drowned. I should come down if I were you. It's safer on the path," added Wayne.

"Yeah, if you fall in and get wet, your mother will blame us and you won't be able to come again," emphasised Kevin.

"Okay. I didn't think of that."

"Can you swim?" asked Wayne.

"Not very well, but I'm learning. Ghita is teaching me."

"Lucky you, to have a sister who cares so much. All mine does is slag me off. We fight nearly all the time," continued Wayne.

"There doesn't seem to be much in the way of frogs here. Let's try the canals." Kevin suggested with determined look in his eye.

"I don't know." Ajay hesitated, "It's getting late and no one knows where I am."

Wayne and Kevin looked slyly at each other. "Come on.... just for another half hour. Then we'll pack up and try again next week. That's if you want to stay friends..." said Wayne.

Ajay looked at them both with his face shining. He didn't want to let the boys down and he nodded vigorously. He would fix it with his mother afterwards and with Ghita. He'd skipped off without waiting for her as he had promised. "Okay." Ajay beamed.

"Right on!" shouted Wayne and did a high five with Kevin. The three left the reservoir and made their way towards the bridge spanning the canal. Ajay whooped and dragged his ruler along the railings. It made a satisfying click, clack, rat-a-tat of wood on metal. Ajay didn't see his so called friends drop back and the two men emerge from the bushes by the bridge and fall into step behind him. Ajay was singing happily when he felt strong arms lift him up. Surprised he turned his face to see Tough Nut grinning coldly at him.

"Want to find some frogs then? Maybe, you'll have more luck in there... swimming with them!" Tough Nut hoisted Ajay over the railings and dangled him above the murky canal water.

"Someone's coming!" hissed his sidekick.

Tough Nut tossed the now screaming small boy like a sweet wrapper into the gloomy depths and he and his accomplice ran back the way they had come. Wayne and Kevin looked on in horror.

"I th... th...thought they were just going to give him a scare... frighten him a little," stammered Kevin. "Ajay can't swim. He'll drown. We've got to do something. Go in after him, Wayne."

"I can't swim neither," muttered Wayne. "You go!"

"Me? I'm no good in the water... what'll we do?"

"I'll call the cops and we'll have to run or we'll get the blame. Come on!"

Wayne sprinted for the phone box. Kevin dithered on the spot, looking at the floundering child in the water. Wayne glanced back. "Hurry up! Come on."

A mother and daughter were coming across the bridge. Kevin made up his mind, "Go on. Make the call. I'll be there in a bit," and he dashed down the steps at the side of the bridge looking for something, anything to throw to the panic stricken child who was gasping and spluttering for air. But there was nothing there and nothing he could do to help. Kevin watched the small boy disappear under the water. He burst into tears and ran back up the steps to the bridge and screamed for the woman to help. The sound of a siren could be heard in the distance. Fearing he would be in even more trouble Kevin fled.

*

"Are you sure?" Allison's gravel tones questioned.

"Positive. He may have changed his face but he can't change his prints. Bartlett Sharma is Vencat," Stringer replied.

"Pick him up. There are a few questions I'd like to ask him."

"Brand's onto it. Got a team going over the place Vencat rented. Gibson is singing like a canary. It's just a matter of time."

"We've lost him before.... I have an idea." Allison switched the intercom, "Maddie, get Brand on the phone."

Allison's secretary put the call through.

"Brand," came the business like tones.

"What's the story on Sharma?" asked Allison.

"According to my sources he's away for the weekend. Gone to Devon."

"Forensics have picked up enough evidence to prove that Sharma is Vencat and that he was responsible for the attack on Rhonda that took place here."

"Is there a problem?" asked Brand.

"Not really, we never got to the bottom of the Devon link, did we?" mused Allison, thinking aloud.

"No, I got no joy there at all. Everyone was very tight-lipped with me. I put it down to Devon mentality. At first I thought he was maybe going to use the coastline for smuggling but that didn't make much sense. Queen Bee couldn't help much either."

"Queen Bee?"

"Hayley Roberts, local woman who seems to know everything."

"Ah yes! Friend of Rebecca Mills. Helped us out on the antiques' fraud case."

"That's the one."

"I know we have plenty to charge him with but I'm still interested in what he's got in mind. It must be something big to make him come back to Britain. Instead of nabbing him on his return to Brum, have another crack at things in North Devon," ordered Allison.

Brand ended the call. He was on his way.

*

Susan Hardy looked up from her typing in amazement as Melody Harper breezed into her office.

"Sorry, I'm so late. Had a bit of a heavy night last night. Is Mr. Clifton in? There was no one in the office so I thought I'd better report to you."

"Melody! You're okay!"

"Why shouldn't I be?"

"Haven't you heard? He's been arrested."

"What?"

"For your abduction!"

Melody's mouth gaped open and her chewing gum tumbled out of her mouth before her tongue could field it.

"That's ridiculous!"

"Maybe, maybe not..."

Susan picked up the phone and called the police station with this information and then explained to her young colleague the history of Mr. Clifton's dubious past.

"That settles it. I'm not working for him, doubt or no doubt. It's a shame. I thought he was quite cute, but I'm not prepared to take that kind of risk. Tell Dempseys they can stuff their job. I'm back to the temp agency. What I can't understand is why no one warned me?" She shook her head capriciously and flounced out of the office her Isadora scarf flapping at her neck.

Susan left her desk immediately and went to report to Charles Payne. She was now feeling more than a little guilty over her uncharitable thoughts and felt at best she should give Tony the benefit of the doubt. After all that's what the courts had done.

*

WPC Beck strolled into the station smiling to herself and bumped straight into Pooley who exclaimed, "Where have you been? Clifton's here. Interview Room 3."

"Whatever for?" answered Kirsty Beck.

"Abduction, last night, Melody something or other."

"That's absolute rubbish...!" she retorted.

"How come?"

"... I watched Clifton last night. He did nothing wrong."

"You could be right. We've just had a report that the girl's turned up for work. I'm off to check it out. Coming?"

"No. I've got some reports to file. See you later."

"Suit yourself. I'll get Taylor."

Kirsty Beck smartened her pace and knocked on interview Room 3. She popped her head round the door. Tony glanced up, his face was furrowed in a frown and his eyes looked haunted. As soon as he saw the WPC the misery fled his eyes and he began to brighten.

"Kirsty!"

"It's all right," she soothed, then faced her fellow policeman. "What's he doing here? He's done nothing wrong."

"And what makes you say that?" demanded the interviewing copper.

Kirsty Beck hesitated fractionally before answering, "Because he was with me..."

7
Don't give up

Mrs. Kumar sat at the bedside of her young son, Ajay, in Intensive Care. Ghita was with her and anxiously watched the monitor with its fluctuating heart beat rhythm lines and then looked back at her little brother.

He looked so, so tiny, young and vulnerable. The tears were streaming down her face. In her gut she felt sure that Tough Nut had something to do with this and she was determined to find out the truth. But then, to her and her mother's horror the monitor flat lined. Ghita yelled for the nurse and the crash cart with a team of medics raced into the room. Ghita and her distraught mother were shooed out. They could only watch in desperation through the glass of the door. Tragically, the flat line tone remained constant.

The children's hospital team worked on the little boy for twenty minutes before giving up. Ajay was gone. It was now a case of murder and Ghita made up her mind there and then what she was going to do.

*

Night had fallen and the sonorous snoring of the elderly patients in the geriatric ward was music to Grace's ears. At first she had thought it was an imposition being placed with the elderly, now she realised it was pure good fortune. The old woman she had swiftly dispatched the previous night had since been discovered and luckily no suspicions had been aroused. The doctor had proclaimed a heart attack.

Grace felt invincible. She only had to wait for the copper outside her bay to drop off to sleep, as he did every night, and then she could get to work. She was already wearing her under garments and as she lay there with her eyes closed, and feigning sleep she listened impatiently for the policeman to put down the evening paper he always read each night until his eyelids became too heavy and he succumbed to slumber. Oh, how she wished she had some of her opiate mixture to put in his tea. That would ensure he wouldn't awaken.

The welcome rustling of a newspaper assailed her ears as the policeman straightened the pages and folded it up. Grace held her breath and mouthed a silent prayer. She peered at the luminous dial on her wristwatch. The night nurse would soon be making her pot of tea, just half an hour longer. She was so excited, but resisted the urge to sing or chant her verses of praise. Those would wait until she was free.

*

Holly was sitting reading to Paul's father, Bernie, who could no longer enjoy the pleasures of literature for himself, as cataracts had formed across his rheumy eyes and he was a victim of hospital waiting lists.

"I should think that's enough now, Holly," Paul remonstrated, "You've been reading for nearly two hours. It's a wonder you're not hoarse."

"If she's content to read then let her be," the old man selfishly exclaimed.

"Actually, I think I will take a little break, " affirmed Holly. "I need a drink and my neck is a little stiff.

"If you're making a drink, I'll have one too," grunted Bernie, "then when we've wet our whistles, you can sit at my feet and I'll give your neck a rub. I may not be worth much for anything else, but I've good strong hands. My Elsie swore I could stroke away a headache and banish pain from anywhere I laid my hands."

"That's too good an offer to miss," smiled Paul. "He does little enough for anyone else. Go for it."

Holly sighed gently as she put down the tome she was reading, a book by James Patterson. She'd not read the novelist before and had to admit that she was enjoying the story as much as the old man. The brevity of the chapters meant it was easy to pick up and put down, and even she wanted to see how the detective Alex Cross was going to proceed.

"So, what do folks want? Tea, coffee or something stronger?"

"I'd love a cup of tea with perhaps a tot of something in it," Bernie mischievously requested.

"Done." She smiled at the old man. "Paul?" asked Holly.

"Tea for me, and then a large red wine I think."

Holly rose from her seat and went into the kitchen. Her brow furrowed as she saw some dishes in the sink.

"Paul! If I'm doing this, at least you can do the washing up. After all I did make lunch."

"Okay. Okay. And I will prepare dinner. I promise." he called back.

Holly walked to the window and stared out at the cobbled yard at the back of the house and the garden with its meagre vegetable plot. At first, she thought her eyes were playing tricks on her but staring harder she was sure she saw an animal disappear under the cover of the red currant bush. It looked like a cat but larger and all the stories of the beast of Bodmin and Exmoor and from other places in the South West tumbled through her mind. She shouted to Paul, "Here a minute."

Paul noticed the change in her tone and hurried to her side. "What is it?"

"There in the garden, under the bush. It's too big to be a cat. What is it?"

"I don't see anything," said Paul as he peered out of the kitchen window.

"I can't see it now, but it dived under there."

"I'll have a look."

"Be careful!" Holly watched nervously as Paul went through the yard to the garden wielding a spade. He poked around the shrubs and bushes but there was nothing. Holly felt her skin begin to itch as if a battalion of marching ants were striding up her spine. It was a sign. She was sure. But a sign of what?

*

Mrs. Clifton tiptoed out of her bed and, remade it using some of the many pillows to tuck under the covers making it look as if she was still asleep there. She removed her nightdress and placed it over the supposed sleeping body. Gingerly taking out the bag of clothes she had stolen the night before she moved to the edge of her bay and looked along the corridor. Everything was still. Grace eyed the sleeping policeman warily and moved past him to the lavatory by the ward exit and slipped in. She didn't close the door as that might attract attention and so, she struggled in that confined space to dress herself. She shoved her badly permed, grey hair under a hat and masked her face with a scarf. Grace's cobra hooded eyes gleamed fervently in the dim light and she manoeuvred her way out of the toilet and through the double doors, which swung lightly on its hinges. The policeman stirred in his sleep, his eyes flickered open momentarily and he saw the door swing back and for, but nothing registered and his eyes closed once more.

Grace didn't trust the lifts. She now had no need of the doctor's white coat she'd planned to take. Grace crept to the stairs and quietly, pattered down them watching and listening every step of the way. Ignoring the exit to the ground floor level she made her way into the basement, along the maze of corridors to a lower entrance past the still and empty, Out Patients Department to liberty.

*

Allison groaned at the mounting pile of paper work on his desk. There were just too many cases on his load and everything seemed to be happening at once. It was the third night this week he had stayed long into the small hours ruminating over notes and reports with only his Mars Bars for company. Mark had his own problems at home. Although, his second child, Catherine was angelic, the older toddler son, Christian was a handful and Debbie was pregnant again but at least this pregnancy seemed less fraught than the last. However, Mark wasn't taking any chances. His mother-in-law, Jean, who willingly helped out was on holiday, which meant Mark was sticking strictly to working hours so he could be at home as much as possible.

Allison took a Mars Bar out of his drawer and ripped off the paper, walking to the window he viewed the scene at the General Hospital. It all seemed quiet tonight, nothing to distract him or interest him. He munched satisfyingly on his chocolate bar and started to run through the cases in his head; the unsolved murder of Friel, an undercover cop trying to flush Vencat into the open. Vencat's battering of the beautiful Rhonda. Allison was sure Brand would track the villain down in Devon and discover what the drugs baron was planning. Then there was the attempted murder of the casino worker Chrissy and the murder of her boyfriend, Mike. Allison believed this was linked to Vencat, as well. Also, there was his daughter's friend Rosie being stalked by some maniac, but he reasoned with himself she was safe, at least, for the time being, staying with her cousin in London. What else? He scratched his grizzled head, Tony Clifton was being watched and his loopy mother secure in hospital, for the moment anyway. He didn't foresee any trouble there. The racial tension in Handsworth was being handled by another division and would remain so unless the locals rioted again or worse.

Allison moved back to his desk as he finished his treat and checked through the rest of the files and started to put them into some sort of order for delegation. He was just beginning to prioritise his labour for the next day when the phone rang.

"Allison," he responded gruffly.

"Chief? There's been another attempt to kill the Black Jack dealer, Chrissy Stephens," announced Pooley.

"What?"

"Some bloke dressed as a doctor tried to inject her with something. The lab and Forensics are checking it now."

"Is she all right?"

"A bit shaken. I've taken the decision to have her moved."

"Good man. What about the perp?"

"He got away, but two orderlies chased him and have given a reasonable description. They're working with a police artist on a computer now. They think they saw him driving away in a blue Subaru Imprezzo."

"Licence plate?

"'Fraid not."

"There can't be too many of those in the area. Bit of an expensive car. Get in touch with the dealers, get a customer list." Allison replaced his handset and rubbed at his sand paper chin sprouting bristles that Bob Geldhof would have been proud of.

The phone jangled again making him jump. "Yes?"

"Handsworth local division here."

"Well?"

"The little lad from Darleston's, Ajay Kumar? He's died. It's now a case of murder, too big for us to handle."

"You better tell me about it and get someone to fax through a report."

Allison listened to the distressing tale of the attack and gritted his teeth. What was the world coming to?

*

Mrs. Clifton scurried out into the staff car park keeping her face well shielded from the Close Circuit Television Cameras. Where would she go first? Not home, they would expect that and besides Tony would be watched but she did need to contact him. Not yet, anyway. She'd think about that later. Gillian or Holly or whatever she called herself, she was the one to blame for this mess, helping the police with her premonitions. Well, now Holly would need to protect herself. The girl lived in Worcester and Worcester is where Grace was headed.

*

Brand was sitting comfortably enjoying his morning coffee in the lounge bar of the Hunters' Inn in Newton Tracey, Devon. He was being well looked after by his delightful hostess, the landlady of the pub, Karen. She had sparkling eyes and a personality to match, he promised himself a little trip here when he was on leave to really enjoy all that North Devon had to offer. His wife, Lucy would love it, as would the children. Karen had just gone to replenish his cafetierre and Brand was listening to the conversations of those around him. He heard a gnarled, weather worn man mention Joel Macready. Brand leaned forward in his seat, straining his ears, but averted his eyes from the man, trying not to look interested.

"Rumour has it, Joel has come up on the lottery."

"What makes you say that, Jim?" asked a portly gent leaning on the bar.

"He's been flashing money around, bought everyone a drink a couple of nights ago."

"Joel?" said the portly man with incredulity.

"Joel." affirmed Jim.

"That's hard to believe. Him buying a drink is as rare as hens' teeth."

"Exactly. Do you get my drift?"

"Well, I heard he was into some rich deal," interrupted a lean faced man with a slight stutter.

"What do you mean?" questioned Jim.

"According to Bob Challacombe, Joel's doing a bit of business under the counter."

"You mean illegal?"

"I didn't say that... I know nothing about it, but Don Richards knows a thing or two."

It was then Karen returned with Brand's coffee and the conversation at the bar turned to general chitchat and inconsequentials and the chances of a local jockey in the first point-to-point races of the year at Chapleton.

Brand inwardly digested what he'd heard and made a note of the name, Don Richards. He'd pay Queen Bee a visit and see what she could tell him about the man.

*

"You look like crap," said Mark as he viewed his chief across the desk. Allison was in the same clothes as the day before looking grubby, crumpled and tired. He hadn't been home and he needed a shave.

"Don't sugar the pill, Mark. Why don't you say what you really think?" growled Allison. "I'm going to freshen up. My mouth feels like a chicken coup." He reached in his drawer for his toothbrush and shaver and lumbered to the door as the phone jangled for attention. "Get that would you? Give me a few minutes." The chief left his office and Mark picked up the phone.

"Stringer.... What? We'll get right on it." Mark scribbled something on a piece of paper. The phone rang again, "Yes? Stringer here... I see. What's your number? Hold fire until I've spoken to the chief." No sooner had he replaced the receiver than it rang again. He exclaimed, "What is this? The hotline for place your bets? ... Yes? I don't believe it. How? ... You better get someone down to Golden Hillock Road now. I don't know but it's worth a shot." Mark rubbed his eyes. He couldn't concentrate, too much was happening at once.

To Mark's relief Allison returned looking slightly better for his wash and shave. He caught Mark's frazzled expression and asked, "What's the problem?"

"I don't know where to start, the phone hasn't stopped since you left. Bad and good news I'm afraid."

"Let's have the good, I could do with a bit of cheering up."

"It's not that good, but it is a break... The attempt on Chrissy Stephens, the guy dropped a syringe. It contained enough insulin to kill her."

Allison raised an eyebrow, "The same with Friel."

"Exactly! Whoever killed our cop also attempted to kill Chrissy and there's more, during the chase his surgical hat came off, and with it a few strands of hair."

"DNA?"

"Right! And one of them is not human but belongs to a cat, a white cat."

"And the bad news?"

"Mrs. Clifton escaped this morning."

Allison groaned and rolled his eyes. "Anything else?"

The young lad who was a witness to Ajay Kumar's murder is too frightened to speak. Children's Services have taken him home."

"Have someone get down to Golden Hillock Road now."

"Already done."

"Good. Better get someone to the granddaughter's house, somewhere in Worcester, I think. Call the local force."

"Sir."

"We had better get over to the hospital. I want to speak to the copper who was on duty."

Mark didn't envy whoever it was. They'd be in for a roasting.

*

Young Kevin Dobson sat miserably at the tea table. He wasn't hungry but he was frightened, very frightened. There was a knock at the door. Kevin's mother screeched at him, "Get that will you, Kev?"

Kevin pushed his plate away and hesitated.

"Kevin!" came the shrill tones again as another more insistent knock was heard.

Reluctantly, Kevin left his place and went to the front door. It was his friend, Wayne, looking ashen faced and trembling.

"Who is it?" Mrs. Dobson rudely shouted.

"It's all right, Mum, it's for me."

"Don't you go disappearing now. You're in enough trouble as it is."

"It's okay, Mum, it's Wayne. I'll only be a minute," and he slipped quickly out of the door before his mother had a chance to haul him back.

The two boys ran swiftly to the park and the safety of its shelter.

"What happened? Where did you go?" asked Wayne.

"I didn't tell on you if that's what you think. I tried to help Ajay. But I couldn't, there weren't nothing to help him with. It was horrible he was spluttering and coughing and then I couldn't see him anymore. He just sank. I yelled at some woman on the bridge for help but she couldn't do nothing. Then the ambulance come and some bloke dived in and fished him out. Police come after that and they carted me off."

"What then?"

"They kept on at me asking questions, but I told them nothing. Never mentioned you. Why?"

"My cousin came over and threatened me, said if I said anything to anyone about what his mates had done they'd do the same to me and you."

"What we gonna do?"

Wayne shrugged, "Keep quiet, I suppose. What can we do?"

They looked at each other, their fear uniting them in silence.

*

Brand sipped his coffee and helped himself to another slice of lemon drizzle cake. This Queen Bee, Hayley Roberts, could certainly cook!

"So, what exactly do you want to know?" asked Hayley, eagerly. She enjoyed a bit of gossip and loved to be in the know.

"What can you tell me about Don Richards?"

"Not a very nice man. Certainly he can't be trusted. He was in a spot of bother last year with DEFRA, fiddling his IACS forms."

Taking this as the green light to tell what she knew, Hayley steamed on with relish. "Claiming for bits of land that weren't his. And he was caught fiddling his cattle movement books. He paid quite a hefty fine, if I remember. But it won't stop him from doing it again. It was rumoured he was involved in some scheme to allow cattle from BSE infected herds into the food chain. In cahoots with an abattoir, they said, but I'm not sure of the truth. I also heard that he was trying to get some new business deal with some rich chap from Birmingham, but I couldn't say what it was."

"Any chance of finding out?"

"Milly Truscott from the Ladies Circle. She's a friend of Angela Richards, Don's wife. I feel sorry for her. She's a nice lady, nearly died of shame after what he did. Trouble is, he's too free with his fists, is Don, and she's afraid of him."

"Does she trust you?"

"Of course," grinned Hayley, "Doesn't everyone?" She winked at Brand, "I know where you're coming from.... I'll see what I can find out."

*

Rosie was enjoying a glass of wine with her cousin, Linda, when the phone rang. Linda answered, "Hello?"

"Hi! Is Rosie there? It's Lex from work. Lex Montague." Linda popped her hand over the mouthpiece and turned to Rosie. "It's for you. Lex Montague from work."

Rosie was surprised but nevertheless took the phone, "Hi Lex! What can I do for you?"

"Hey...! Good to hear your voice! Listen, there's a break in the racial tension case. Thought you'd want to know. After all it was your baby."

"Why? What's happened?"

"The youngest child of the Kumars. Remember Darleston's newsagents?"

"What about him?"

"First they thought it was an accidental drowning. It wasn't. He was murdered."

"That's awful, what else?"

Lex went on to tell her what he knew. "So, is that enough to bring you home?"

"Maybe, I'll let you know."

"Okay. It's your call."

"By the way, how did you get this number?"

"What? Oh, Brian gave it to me."

"Brian?"

"Brian Bates."

"I see... thanks for letting me know. I'll call you." Rosie replaced the receiver thoughtfully. "How the hell, does Brian have this number?"

Linda pulled a face, "No idea. P'raps you ought to ring Popsie."

"That's just what I will do."

*

Mrs. Clifton smiled secretly to herself, she was doing well and she knew it. She'd got herself out of the hospital without anyone seeing, into the town unnoticed and using the old lady's credit card had accessed enough cash to get her around. She'd checked in at a family hotel on the Hagley Road run by Greeks. It wouldn't be long before her face would be staring out at her from television screens and she knew she had to alter her appearance. She'd done it before. She could do it again. They'd be looking for a white woman.

Grace wondered how she would look in a sari?

*

"Brand? I'm with Angela Richards now, can you come over?" Brand didn't need a second bidding. He drove the two miles to Hayley's farmhouse and knocked on the door.

"Come in! We're in the kitchen," called Hayley.

Brand entered the hall, went down the tiled passage way and the two steps into the quaint, but dark kitchen. Hayley was at the worktop making a pot of tea. Seated at the table was a dark haired woman in her late thirties who would have been attractive if it wasn't for the black eye, split lip and bruised cheeks.

"I've taken her in. She's not going back to that monster again. He'll have to get through me first."

Brand didn't doubt that. Hayley Roberts was a formidable woman, not only in size but also in personality and manner. He didn't believe this Don Richards would want to confront her.

"Angela, this is the gentleman I told you about," said Hayley taking charge. "Tell him what you told me."

Angela nervously glanced at Brand and continued twisting the handkerchief in her hand.

"It's all right. Take your time. You're safe here," soothed Brand.

"But for how long? If Don finds out I'm here and that I've said anything he'll kill me."

"I doubt that very much," came Hayley's crisp tones. "Because after you've spoken to Brand here, we're going to do your husband for assault and slap an injunction on him. He won't be able to go near you, let alone hit you again. And if you still feel unsafe I've plenty of friends you can stay with for a while up country who owe me a few favours."

Angela hesitated again before gratefully accepting the cup of tea Hayley offered. She took a sip and started to talk, slowly at first. But then her speech seemed to gather momentum and an avalanche of information bombarded Brand's ears.

"He's always been difficult, Don. It started when we found out we couldn't have kids, blamed me, of course. That's when he became free with his fists. I got used to not saying anything, never spoke unless I was spoken to and tried to stay out of his way, especially after he'd had a drink. It got so that even when I was in the same room with him he'd forget I was there as if I'd melded into the wallpaper or something. I suppose that's how he got careless. I heard him on the phone a few weeks ago talking to Joel Macready. Don was cursing about his losses with foot and mouth and said he was getting out of cattle and going arable. He was asking

Joel's advice and his plans for crops this year. I heard him say, 'Hemp? What market is there for hemp?' and then he started to chuckle. 'Proper job,' he says. 'What a scheme! I could do with some of that. Do you think you can get me in?' He went on asking questions. The way he was talking I knew it was something illegal. I've been down that road before. I tried not to listen but I couldn't help it. It seems Joel had some deal with a foreign gentleman to grow cannabis amongst his crop of hemp and was being paid a packet to do it. The mistake I made was asking him about it. I pleaded with him not to get involved and got a beating for my trouble. He thought that had bought my silence but when he heard me on the phone to Hayley arranging to meet her, he did this. He thought I'd cancel, be too ashamed to let anyone see me like this. He's intimidated by Hayley, reckons she's nosey and was worried I may let something slip. There, I've said it," and there was almost a hint of pride in her voice.

"So, what do you think?" asked Hayley, leaning forward, her eyes bright, keen and inquisitive.

"Hayley! You're a star! This is just what we needed. I just need to know where Vencat, the foreign gentleman," he explained to Milly, "is. He's calling himself Sharma now, Bartlett Sharma."

"That's easy... Go on Angela," prodded Hayley.

"He's at the Fox and Goose in Torrington. Having dinner with my younger sister. Don fixed her up with Joel's foreign friend in hope of getting a slice of the action, at least that's what he said."

"Then I'd better get to her and fast before she becomes another victim." He looked at Hayley and Angela's puzzled faces. "He likes to hurt women and what your husband has done to you is a walk in the park compared to what he does." Brand immediately put a call through to the Devon and Cornwall police.

"The coppers are on their way. Now, how do I get to the Fox and Goose?"

*

WPC Beck had enough of the questions. As she explained, it was part of her duties to shadow Tony Clifton.

She'd seen him talk to Melody Harper and she saw Melody leave with her friend. So, when Tony recognised her in the club it seemed sensible to strike up a conversation. In fact, she'd spent quite a pleasant evening with him. She found him not only charming but excellent company and when he hadn't wanted to go home alone that night, she'd put a call through to Pooley telling him that Clifton was under close observation but omitted to say she was taking him home to her flat. This did not go down well at all.

"Don't you realise the risk you were taking? He could have killed you?"

"I doubt it. Too many people saw us together and besides I don't think he is a killer."

"That's it. I'm taking you off surveillance. Don't see him again."

"Sir, you may remove me from this duty but you can't stop me from seeing who ever I want in my own time." WPC Beck could be quite feisty when she wanted to be. A part of her still had that rebellious streak she'd sported in her teens, forbid her to do something and it instantly became more attractive.

*

Ghita sat up in bed. The chanting was back. She could hear the chorus of voices getting louder as they approached. This time she was ready for them. This time she was prepared. She drew back her curtains and the faint orange hues from the corner street lamp mingled with the silver moonbeams, which streamed through the window and pooled in a watery glow on her bedroom carpet.

Ghita gently eased up her sash window, opening it wide. It glided up efficiently and without a sound. She foraged in her wardrobe for the box, the box that contained revenge in a bottle. She scudded the carton across the floor to the window and picked up the cigarette lighter she'd hidden in her desk drawer. She had to time this just right and stepped from view to be cloaked in the shadows of her room.

The slurs and slanderous obscenities grew louder. "One Paki less, who's next? You guess!"

Ghita's heart was pounding but if the gang could have

seen her face, they would have been afraid, very afraid. Her resolve was clear. She waited until the scumbag rabble was assembled. She was tired of their giggles and abominations. She lit the rag protruding from the neck of the petrol filled wine bottle and stepped into view. Tough Nut and his mates began to jeer as soon as they saw her but their scorn and derision abruptly ended as the Molotov cocktail was hurled out of the window and into their midst. Ghita savoured the moment and the next few moments were as if in slow motion. Too late they saw it coming and it was too late for them to move. Their cries of fear and the look of their open-mouthed terror struck faces would live satisfyingly in Ghita's memory forever. The glass of the bottle shattered on the unforgiving pavement and exploded into a frenzied fireball scattering the youths away from the shop. Tough Nut was screaming as he ripped off his flaming balaclava ski mask. Lights were switched on in the houses opposite. Ghita firmly closed her window, redrew the curtains and returned to her bed. She had done what had to be done.

*

Mrs. Clifton's cobra hooded eyes narrowed cunningly. She had safely purchased some brown skin dye, a dark wig and a colourful sari with a matching scarf. The delightful, Indian, female shop assistant in the specialist boutique in Small Heath had been only too pleased to show her how to wear it. She disappeared into the ladies lavatories in the park as an elderly woman with a stoop, and emerged some time later, as a grandmotherly, gentle Indian lady. Her brittle, permed hair was out of sight, tucked under the wig now greased and shining. Her head was covered with the matching scarf, which draped back across her shoulders. She even had a false nose ring clipped to her nostril, shining dangling multi bell earrings and a score of bangles adorning her arm. Now, she looked the part she could be on her way. Grace caught the bus into Digbeth and purchased a ticket for the Worcester coach.

*

Brand arrived at the Fox and Goose ahead of the Devon and Cornwall police. He took a moment to check the back car park and saw Vencat's BMW Z3 smartly parked next to a battered Ford Fiesta. Brand could hardly believe that Vencat was at long last to have his come-uppance. He was sure the villain would be put away for a very long time. The height of the entrance to the Fox and Goose was very low and Brand carefully observed the notice "Duck or Grouse" and did as he was told, although he was not a tall man he felt even he may have bumped his head. He slipped quietly into the bar and glanced across at the restaurant area. Vencat was there entertaining the attractive sister of Milly Richards. Brand noted the table and retreated outside. Vencat was sublimely oblivious that dessert for him would be a police cell.

Brand placed a call through to Birmingham and updated the chief on what was happening. The pleasure he heard in Allison's voice, when he gave his update, left Brand with a warm glow deep in his stomach.

Four police cars arrived in swift succession with lights flashing but no sirens, there was no sense in alerting Vencat; he'd been difficult enough to track down and even when he had been caught before he had managed to effect a daring escape and had remained at liberty for far too long.

"Brand," he introduced himself to the local constabulary. "Our man is inside, third table to the right of the dividing balustrade. The woman he's with is a local and knows nothing about him."

The officer in charge nodded in acknowledgement and engaged his men, "On my word, go in and take him down."

The police were all armed and wearing bullet proof jackets. The pub was besieged. The doors to the bar burst open and they homed in on the startled Vencat and his dinner date. The lucky lady was jostled away to safety. Vencat shouting his innocence was floored, cuffed and taken away to Barnstaple police station where there was paperwork to fill out before he could be released into the custody of the West Midlands force.

Sleepy Torrington had never seen anything like it! It would be the talk of the town for months, perhaps even years to come.

Brand was almost satisfied. There were just a couple of things he had left to do.

In the company of uniformed police, and a local agronomous, Peter Snell, a crops expert, they walked the hemp fields of Joel Macready. Peter had soon delineated where the legitimate hemp ended and the illegal crops began. Joel Macready was arrested and taken away. He wasn't too worried. It was his first offence and he still had his initial payment, a payment, which would keep the bank happy in the months to come.

Brand made his way back to Newton Tracey and Hayley Roberts' farm.

"How's Angela?"

"She's better. Just taking a long, soothing bath," smiled Queen Bee.

"What about her husband, Don Richards?" enquired Brand.

"Dealt with. He's been done for assault. I'm taking her to meet my solicitor tomorrow so she can file for divorce. In the meantime she stays with me."

"You seem to have it pretty well wrapped up."

"You know me, I'm not one to stand by idly. I'm a get in there and act, kind of woman," and she winked at Brand.

Brand certainly did know her by now, formidable she may be, but with a heart of gold, Devon gold and he told her so. She even found some modesty from somewhere, which made her blush.

The news of Vencat's arrest made the national papers and news and one person took it seriously, very seriously indeed. With Vencat in prison his identity was in jeopardy. He knew that Vencat would do anything to make things easier on himself and that was one risk 'The Chameleon' was not prepared to take.

8
Walk on the wild side

Tony was beginning to feel good. After his initial brush with the law when he was wrongly accused over Melody Harper's disappearance he felt that he had someone on his side. That someone was Irish colleen, WPC Kirsty Beck.

The staff at Dempseys were treating him with more respect, too, as more and more of them believed Tony had been incarcerated wrongly. Furthermore, his singing career was getting back on track. Amy, sweet loving Amy who had died at the hands of his mother would have been proud. He could almost feel her near him and he silenced the sob threatening to rise from his throat. If Amy was watching, and he was sure she was, then she was looking out for him, as a guardian angel, a guardian angel who had led Kirsty Beck to his side.

Tony raised his glass and toasted her, "To you and me and Amy."

"Amy? Is that the lass, who …?"

"Yes." Tony cut her off, "Sorry, it's still too painful for me to talk about... But, I will... when the time is right. I just have a hunch that Amy's been instrumental in bringing us together."

"I don't know about that. It was my job of work... but if it makes you happy to think that, then ..."

"It does."

They chinked glasses and continued with their meal. Tony's first set at Chaplins wasn't for another hour.

"So, tell me, how do you feel about your mother now?"

"I'm just delighted she's locked away and can't harm anyone ever again."

Kirsty looked mystified, "Haven't you heard?"

"Heard what?"

"Heavens above Tony, don't you know?"

Now it was Tony's turn to look puzzled, "Whatever are you talking about?"

"It was all over the news and in the papers. I was sure you'd have seen it. Your mother's at large. She escaped from the hospital. She's out there somewhere."

The vein in Tony's temple began to pulse and he could feel the blood flooding to his head. He stood up from the table and threw down his napkin. "If you'll excuse me a moment. I won't be long."

"Of course." Kirsty looked concerned as Tony headed for the dressing room.

He couldn't trust himself. He couldn't trust himself with her or anyone after this bombshell, at least not for the moment.

He burst in through the door and smashed it shut with the palm of his hand. Why? Why wouldn't she let him live his life? For the first time, in a long while, he had felt safe. She had ruined that. He didn't feel safe anymore. The gnawing emptiness that he thought was buried began to rise and he made up his mind that if he encountered her, she would pay the price; the price that all those other women had paid when he had been under her control.

He splashed some cold water on his face and patted it dry. His face had paled and his eyes had a glimmer of that haunted look, which had possessed him in the past. With shaking hands he sat at the mirror and carefully applied a little stage make up; just enough to make him appear calmer. He jumped as one of the hostesses walked in.

"Sorry, Tone, I'm busting for a pee, do you mind?"

He shook his head and his eyes followed the girl into the toilet. She cursed as her long trailing scarf caught in the door. Tony's eyes were riveted. In his mind, his mother's face came into view with her thin lips; thread veined cheeks, and those hideously unforgettable eyes. He could almost hear her reedy tones and the urge to snatch at the trailing scarf and squeeze it oh so tightly around her crepe skinned neck was becoming hard to ignore. He bit the inside of his mouth until he tasted the coppery, warm, salty blood and he felt his rage begin to subside. Tony was frightened, frightened of what he could do. He had believed that the evil side of him had been safely suppressed but now it had come back to taunt him, to

116

play with him and Tony was not sure he could control it.

The toilet flushed and the hostess emerged tugging down her skirt, "Ta for that. Are you all right? You look a little upset."

"Er, just something I ate, didn't quite agree with me," he lied. "Tell me why do you wear that scarf? When you have such a beautiful neck... such a pity to hide it. It's so long and elegant like a swan."

"Oh? Do you think so? Ta muchly," giggled the girl.

"Here, let me help you," and he slid his hand to her shoulder and caught the diaphanous silk entwining it through his fingers and pulled it free from her neck. The rush he got from the act was exhilarating, freeing. He let his fingers explore the material as he gathered up both ends and brought it to his face to smell.

"Estee Lauder Pleasures. One of my favourite perfumes," Tony said.

"Is it? I'll have to wear it again then, won't I?" She looked at herself critically in the mirror, "I think you're right. I do look better without it. You can keep it." She smiled cheekily and left. Tony crumpled up the swathe of cloth and shoved it in his coat pocket hanging on the door. He tried to still his beating heart. That was close, too close and the girl didn't have a clue.

Tony wiped his brow he was sweating; he quickly brushed his hair, checked his appearance and returned to the table. Kirsty wasn't there. He glanced around hastily and saw her at the bar talking to a man. The blood began to shoot to his head again. Red surged behind his eyes. He took a deep breath to quell the raging monster which threatened to rocket to the surface and just managed to sit back down at the table. He didn't like the thoughts he was having. Who was that man? Was this a betrayal? What should he do? But he had no more time to think. Kirsty had seen him and was returning. She looked concerned.

"Are you all right, Tony? I'm so sorry blurting that out to you. It must have been a shock. Can you forgive me?"

He gazed up at her and smiled, "Of course. It ... well... it gave me a bit of a turn." His lips were smiling but his eyes were not. There was a coldness, a deadness, which had not been there before but Kirsty didn't notice.

"Who was that man? The one at the bar?" he questioned casually.

"Don't start me off on him. It makes me mad, but I suppose I'd better tell you. It's a chap from the station pretending to be off duty. But he's not. I know he's watching us."

Tony's eyes lingered on her eyes then dropped to her neck, which he traced gently with his finger. He fixed his gaze on her mouth, "Then, let's give him something to watch" and he reached across and kissed her passionately on the lips.

If Kirsty tried to resist, it wasn't for long and she relinquished herself to him. Tony felt better. This was right after all... Wasn't it?

*

Mrs. Clifton was not having much luck. She'd had trouble finding somewhere to stay and the room she'd booked was only available for one night, last night, but she made up her mind that she would solve that problem later. God always looked after his own, of that she was sure.

Grace made her way to Holly and Paul's residence but the car was gone from the garage. It was just bad luck. So, she decided she would make her own luck. Everything happened for a reason and perhaps this was an omen, presenting a window of opportunity for her to better acquaint herself with her granddaughter. After all, didn't they say forewarned was forearmed?

Grace had taken great care not to be seen approaching the house. It was fortunate that the house was set on its own, and away from prying eyes. Furthermore, she had waited and watched and only when she was certain there was no activity inside did she boldly knock on the door and ring the bell. She even shouted through the letter box and when she heard nothing she tried the garage door... Careless! The lock wasn't fully engaged and with a little bit of jiggling, poking and prodding with the knife she had surreptitiously slipped into her bag from the guest house she had stayed at, she gained entry to see that the car was most definitely gone. Hidden in the garage with the door firmly closed she was able to take her time in trying to open the connecting door to the house. There was a satisfying crunch as the wood around the lock splintered and Grace was able to force an entry.

She went through the utility area and started up the back stairs to the living quarters breathing in the perfumed air from strategically placed pot pourri. She opened and lifted her arms letting the feel of the house with its very special atmosphere lightly massage her senses and Grace could hold back no more. Accompanying herself with a verse from, "He who would valiant be," she beetled through the rooms on the first level, down the front stairs to the door where a week's mail had piled up. She sifted through it eagerly before placing it on the hall table.

Grace remounted the stairs her heart full of joy, her thin nasal tones blared out as she recited from the book of Ecclesiastes, *"I have acquired great wisdom surpassing all who were over Jerusalem before me. For in much wisdom is much vexation and he who increases knowledge increases sorrow..."* Oh how true were those words. Grace slithered to a halt as she heard the phone and the responding answer phone kick in.

"Holly, Paul it's me, Colin. I don't expect you're back yet and I don't know how long your dad will need you to stay in Cornwall. If you're not aware, Grace Clifton has escaped. I just wanted to let you know, be careful."

Colin, whoever he was disconnected the call and the tape machine adjusted itself and sent out an irritating peep that there was a message waiting. Well, she wasn't going to listen to that and she deftly erased the message. The house was quiet once more. So, Holly and Paul were in Cornwall and staying with dad!

She picked up the address book by the phone and her bony fingers raked through the names, she knew from the letters what they called themselves. She was looking for an address in Cornwall. Nothing. Mm, of course! They wouldn't have written his name! It would be under 'D" for dad. She hastily turned back the pages. There it was, dad, his address and phone number. Cornwall, that was a little far for her to go. But at least she didn't have to worry about finding somewhere to stay. She would stay here. After all, she was family.

Her face shone with a fervour which would have alerted any sane person and told them that Grace Clifton was not of sound mind. She giggled. It wasn't pleasant.

What fun she was going to have!

*

Vencat sat sullenly in the primitive holding cell, his bail denied, awaiting news of his proposed transportation to Winson Green prison where he was to be held on remand, until his trial. The indignity of being stuffed into the back of a police car and driven to that back water of a police station in Devon, where he was made to wait for hours before he could speak with his lawyer, did not sit well with him. Nor, was it the most comfortable ride back to Birmingham where he faced a catalogue of charges. He had bounced around in the back of the car and frequently felt sick as the car lurched along the Devon Link Road and speeded onto the M5.

Vencat's mind was spinning with schemes, plots and lies, anything to make his life a little more bearable. Of course, he could think more efficiently if the drunk in the next cell would shut up with his snores and burbling. Almost as if the man had heard Vencat's thoughts, a peaceful hush descended.

Vencat gazed with disdain at his surroundings. All of the boxed cells with sliding viewing panels in their heavy metal doors had been removed. Vencat was a late arrival and like the drunk next door had been forced to suffer in one of the few remaining old fashioned barred cells, open to the world with no privacy. He looked in disgust at the Armitage Shank lavatory pan minus its seat. He couldn't even urinate without being heard, or if a copper came by on patrol, he would be seen. He wrinkled his nose, the stench of disinfectant mixed with urine and stale vomit made him want to retch.

"Mr. Vencat?" The voice made him jump. Vencat turned his head and saw he was being addressed by the drunk in the cell next door.

"Who wants to know?"

"We need to get you out of here."

Vencat was immediately interested, "Who are you?"

"Doesn't matter. A friend sent me."

"You'll be well rewarded. What's the plan?"

"We need to make it look as if you're ill. You'll have to get into bed and look unconscious. Then when they come for you they won't be able to wake you and they'll take you to hospital. That's when you'll be sprung."

Vencat hissed back, "That's ridiculous. How can I fake unconsciousness?"

"That's where I come in." The man lifted his foot and switched back the heel on his shoe and retrieved a small, plastic bag with two red and yellow capsules."

"What are they?"

"Sedatives. Got a kick like a mule. Two will put you out for twelve hours flat. End of story, you'll wake up in hospital. The rest is easy.

"How do I know you're telling the truth?" Vencat asked suspiciously.

"What other option do you have? Trust me."

"I rarely trust anyone. Who sent you?"

The man plucked a name out of the air. He had done his homework. "Stuart Allen ring any bells?"

"Stu sent you?"

The man nodded. Vencat held out his hand. "Pass them across."

The grizzled chinned drunk slipped the small packet through the bars, which Vencat retrieved and opened. He went to pop the capsules in his mouth.

"Wait! Get into your cot first. These things are quick acting, we don't want you collapsing on the floor or they'll suspect me. I need to get out of here before you so I'm in the clear."

Vencat hesitated, but felt he had little choice, so he got into the basic bunk and lay down.

"Face the wall. Then pop them."

Vencat did as he was told. He lay on his side away from the corridor and swallowed down the capsules. He closed his eyes and waited for sleep. But it wasn't sleep, which overtook him but death. Vencat felt his lungs stop breathing.

He opened his eyes but he couldn't move. His mouth gasped for air as his heart beat began to accelerate at an alarming rate. With a shuddering groan his life's spirit left him and the tortured expression of greeting damnation was imprinted on his face forever.

Satisfied, the drunk started clamouring and shouting, "Oi! Bobbies, coppers, let me out." He rattled his tin cup on the bars and a few of the other inmates yelled for him to pipe down.

The door to the cells' corridor opened and the duty officer came in. He addressed the drunk. "All right, Walter. Keep it quiet. Did you think we'd forgotten you?"

"I've slept it off good and proper, Sir. I need to get home have a swill and change my clothes. Can I have my belt back now? Can't keep my pants up else."

The duty officer smiled leniently and unlocked the cage. "I don't want to see you in here again. Right?"

"Right." Walter hung his head and shuffled out. He collected the few personal belongings checked in when he was arrested for being rolling drunk in Steelhouse lane.

"Next time you decide to get a skin full, don't fall down outside the cop shop! Bad planning that!"

"Yes, Sir. Thank you, Sir." Walter left the station, trundled down the steps and took a big gulp of air. He lost himself quickly in the city streets. Ensuring no one was watching he headed for the municipal car park near the UCE halls of residence. He quickly located the people carrier with its tinted windows, removed the key from under the wheel arch on the front passenger side, and jumped into the driver's seat where a transformation took place. He removed the cotton wadding from his jaw line and cheeks. He pulled at the spirit gummed side burns and cleansed his face with a wet wipe. An electric razor, from the glove compartment, removed the stubble on his chin and neck. He reached in the back for a small bag and discarded his stained jacket and grubby shirt revealing lean toned muscles. A squirt of deodorant, splash of after-shave, a change into neatly pressed trousers and polished shoes and it was good-bye to Walter the drunk and hello astute businessman. The Chameleon was delighted, a perfect plan, perfectly executed. It had gone better than he'd dared to hope. His identity was well and truly safe. For now.

*

Mrs. Clifton wandered through her granddaughter's house. She peeped in the medicine cabinet, poked through cupboards, pried in drawers and nosed her way through the entire place. Nowhere and nothing was sacred. She even snooped through Paul's studio; examining the finished and unfinished canvasses stacked around the room.

Grace selected a fresh canvas, mounted it on the easel after discarding the work that was in progress. She began to daub it haphazardly with oils, favouring the colours red and black. The resulting frenzied mess left Grace feeling alert and all-powerful. She continued the mood by systematically desecrating a number of the completed paintings. Like a street graffiti artist she left her own indelible marks on the walls of the studio and she relished it. But her tour of destruction wasn't over.

She rampaged through Paul and Holly's bedroom, attacking their clothes with a pair of scissors and smashing the delicate perfume bottles, which adorned the dressing table, and secreting the glass in the couple's bed. The teddies and cuddly toys, which sat on the wicker chair in the corner of the room, watched her. She felt their accusing stare and deftly blinded them, one by one. She enjoyed the ritual as if they were alive. The spare room was exempt, after all that's where she would sleep. She would turn her attention to the living room and kitchen when it was time to leave. Feeling sated, she sang a hymn as she made herself a cup of tea before settling on the couch to watch the local news.

*

Holly jumped. Her stomach began to churn as if she was on a whirling fairground ride. She felt herself spin across the floor and stick to the bedroom wall as if a centrifugal force was immobilising her. The rugs, which were scattered on the pine floor, flew up and adhered to the floral wallpaper as if plastered there. The room seemed to hum and drone with an alien whine. The bed shifted, turned on its side and slammed

123

against the wall. The small items of furniture gravitated to the sides of the room leaving the centre clear. A twisting mist rotated in the centre of the room and Holly couldn't move and couldn't speak. The room felt like a giant rota. She felt pinpricks of ice stabbing across her body, which grew into ball bearing sized pins and needles but with a difference. She began to bleed.

Paul and his father heard the sounds of the scraping furniture being tossed about above them and looked at each other.

"Holly! Are you okay?" yelled Paul through the stair door and up the winding wooden steps. Not hearing her answer he tore up to their room and was shattered by what he saw. The room was a mess with the furnishings flung to the sides and a grainy cloud filled with floating particles of black and crimson spun in the middle of the chamber. But most frightening of all was Holly. She was stuck two feet above the skirting board her head nearly touching the ceiling. Her hair fanned out from her head and her arms and legs were held in a perfect crucifix position. Blood seeped from the palm of her hands and from her feet as Christ's had on the cross. Perfect stigmata. Then as violently as the psychic storm had started, calm returned. The rugs and mats floated down, the bed crashed back the right way up. The rushing wind dropped to a whisper and the floating mist dissipated. Holly slumped to the floor. Paul flew to her side and helped her on to the bed where Holly whispered, "Phone the police, call Colin. She's in our house." Then she slipped into unconsciousness.

*

Allison grabbed a Mars Bar from his drawer and slipped it in his pocket. He was on the point of leaving his office when the phone rang. He answered it gruffly. He was exhausted, and looking forward to a long hot bath, a home cooked meal and a drop of Scotch, "Yes?"

"Chief? Colin Brady. I've just had a call. Holly says Grace Clifton is in their house."

At the same time Mark burst in, "Sir, Grace Clifton..."

"I've heard.... Thanks Colin."

124

"You'll check it out? I'll meet you there."

"On our way," affirmed the DCI.

Allison and Mark were almost out of the building when the duty officer came speeding after them as if the furies from hell were on his tail.

"Sir! Sir! Thank goodness I've caught you." he muttered breathlessly, "Sarge said to tell you, Vencat is dead."

"What?"

"The black Mariah came to take him to Winson Green. We couldn't wake him. His face was horrible, could be suicide."

"Can't stop now. Leave a full report on my desk. I'll see to it when I get back. Why, oh why does everything happen at once and all on my watch?"

Allison and Stringer made their way to the police car park.

"Have you organised back up?" growled Allison.

"Local force is on their way."

"Mm," grunted Allison ungraciously. He rubbed a hand over his blood shot eyes, "You drive. I'm in no fit state."

"What do you make of the news on Vencat? Do you think it is suicide?" queried Mark.

"It's too early to speculate. I prefer to wait till we have all the facts. The only good thing is he's saved the taxpayers a packet. No trial fees and no board and lodging costs care of her majesty's prison."

"I suppose."

"The problem is if we can't question him, I wonder if we'll ever get to the bottom of Friel's killing and the attempt on Chrissy Stephens. There has to be a link. Vencat was at the root of that and a lot more."

"Maybe the autopsy will give us something or Forensics."

"Like I said it's too early to speculate."

The two fell silent as the car purred its way up Broad Street under the underpass and out on to the leafy tree lined Hagley Road. Mark drifted away to more comforting thoughts of home and Debbie.

"Keep talking Mark. I need to stay awake. If I take a nap now I won't be fit for anything."

Mark rescued himself from his daydreams and searched for another topic of conversation. Everything seemed to come down to work.

"What's the latest on Holly, Sir?"

"Colin told me she's finally given in to her legacy and has been undergoing training to help her deal with this gift."

"Didn't even know there were such things."

"Neither did I. Never been one for all that paranormal rubbish. Too many charlatans out there ruining people's lives."

"But, you have to agree she has something special."

"I do. And I'd use her again if I had to. She could be extremely useful to us. Extremely useful." Allison had the germ of an idea forming. "There's a number of forces around the country who use psychics, maybe we could put her on the pay roll!" He laughed as if negating the validity of his statement, but Mark sensed that the chief wasn't making fun of the idea.

"Did any leads turn up over the little lad's murder, Ajay wasn't it?" questioned Mark.

"Not that I've heard. Children's services are still trying to prise the truth out of the young lad who was with him. Interestingly enough, there was a disturbance outside Darleston's not so long ago. Youths armed with petrol bombs, in an attempt to intimidate the Kumar family, which went horribly wrong. They got their fingers burnt instead. The ring leader and some of his cronies are in hospital with second degree burns."

"Is that right?"

"That's the story."

"You don't sound convinced."

"I'm not sure... I've got an open mind."

Allison groaned as their car was forced to slow, caught in a tail back of traffic. He reached in his pocket for his Mars Bar, "Do you mind?" he asked.

"Go ahead."

"I think I need the energy boost," grunted Allison as he sunk his teeth into chocolate heaven. "Slap on the siren, we need to get moving."

9
Instant replay

Grace felt, that at last she had a real understanding of her granddaughter. She appreciated Holly's choice in food when she made herself something to eat. She relished fingering Holly's belongings, an act, which connected them. Her miserable lizard lips pursed in content with the damage she'd inflicted in that home where love sickeningly seemed to pour out of the walls.

She took great pleasure in using Holly's toiletries after luxuriating in a soothing bath. Grace lit several scented candles. The perfume was both relaxing and titillating, which led her to thoughts of her son. Oh, how she wanted to hold him. She finished reapplying her body dye and donned her sari. Grace wondered how Tony would respond to the little Indian lady she had become and she smiled to herself. The smile was more of a lascivious leer than motherly love, a smile, which froze on her lips as she heard the sirens. Mrs. Clifton knew. She knew she had to get out before the flashing blue lights, which accompanied the wailing din, drove up the gravel drive. Tearing out the Cornish address and phone number she grabbed what she needed and fled.

*

Tony had just finished his third and final set. The applause was strong. He was establishing himself on the club circuit once more. Things were definitely going right for him. He looked around for Kirsty and saw her walking out to the foyer. His eyes lingered on her shapely legs until they turned into the cloakroom. He licked his lips and relaxed. After all she was only going to the lady's room.

Kirsty took out her mobile phone when she was in the privacy of the loo. She needed to report in but the signal wasn't strong enough to maintain a conversation so she sent a text to Pooley's mobile, which succeeded in getting through the second time of trying. Kirsty was getting into difficulties, emotional difficulties. She'd volunteered for this job of getting to know Tony, winning his confidence and watching him. Few at the station were aware of this. The less other officers knew, the better her chances but she was having a tough time of it with the rest of her colleagues. They were unaware that Pooley's dressing down was for their benefit. Some of them were downright rude and she would be glad when the assignment was over, wouldn't she? Then again, something was happening to her. Something she hadn't bargained on. Kirsty Beck was succumbing to Tony's charm. She liked him. She enjoyed being in his company and more especially she had enjoyed being kissed by him. She had been totally unprepared for the fluttering and stirring inside her, which his kiss had aroused. Kirsty applied a fresh coat of lip-gloss and fluffed her hair. She hoped she wasn't falling in love. With a last look at her reflection in the mirror she left the ladies' cloakroom and went back into the club to their table.

*

Greg Allison and Mark Stringer arrived at the house in Worcester. Local police already had Holly and Paul's home cordoned off. An examination of the house revealed the vandalism wreaked by Mrs. Clifton but no sign of the old woman.

"She can't have gone far," said the sergeant in charge. "The tele was on and a left half a cup of tea is still warm. I've got men searching the area now."

"Have you taken the cup? To see if it really is Grace Clifton?"

"Bagged and on its way to the lab now."

"Mind if we see for ourselves?" asked Allison perfunctorily as he entered the building.

"Be my guest," replied the sergeant but his answer was hardly necessary.

Mark Stringer and Allison went through the rooms and saw the havoc that had been created. They were particularly fascinated by her destruction of Paul's artwork. "Ought to let Colin have a look at this. Give him a ring," ordered Allison.

Mark unclipped his mobile from his belt and placed the call.

Allison winced as he saw the eye-less toys in the bedroom and the viciously slashed clothes. But it was in the bathroom he took a keener interest in his surroundings. "Mark what do you make of this?" He pointed at the brown stains in the bath and similar splashes on the washbasin.

"Looks like some sort of tincture or dye. Maybe, it's for the hair or Holly likes to use a fake tan or skin make up, maybe. Or even, Paul."

"Maybe, but I hardly think Holly or Paul would have left the bathroom in such a state. Not like this." Allison rummaged in the wastebasket and removed a few sodden cotton wool balls, which stained his fingers brown. "How long have they been away?"

His question was left hanging in the air as he picked up a crimson lipstick, cap off. "Now, what does that remind you of?"

"Dunno, Marilyn Monroe?" replied Mark feebly.

"Remember how Mrs. Clifton escaped last time?"

"Dressed as a man. Toothbrush moustache and all."

"So she's good at disguise, inventive. Now, what do you think?"

The lights went on in Mark's head, "I see... she's changed the colour of her skin."

"And the lipstick?" prompted Allison.

"The little red dot the women wear in the centre of the forehead. Eye of Shiva or something."

"Or to show their fertility."

"She got that wrong."

"Certainly did, and probably wouldn't know it. I think we're looking for a little Indian lady, don't you, Mark?"

*

Rosie had had no luck in contacting Greg Allison, she always seemed to just miss him and even though she had left a message with Mary, Allison's wife, he'd not got back to her.

"He's a busy man," Linda pointed out. "And he thinks you're safe and sound here."

"I know. But I don't feel so secure now. What if the nutcase has followed me?"

"If he had we'd know about it. It's one thing to terrorise you with a phone call but quite another to come all the way to London. If it is someone who knows you then coming here will firmly point the finger of suspicion at them. Come on, relax."

"I suppose you're right but we could work a double bluff."

"What do you mean?"

"If anyone rings, you could make excuses for me. I'm in the bath, shopping, asleep... anything."

"And what about the police? And the call monitoring?"

"We already know the perp's using some sort of gadget on his throat to distort his voice, so we won't get to hear his real vocal tones."

"Don't be too sure, technology can do amazing things these days. What if the police demand to speak to you?"

"Tell them I've gone off to Wales to see Aunty Joan. Done a disappearing act."

"But she's dead. She died three years ago."

"No one else knows that. I wasn't at the Post when she died. I was still at uni."

"And the police surveillance?"

"We'll think of something."

"But why?"

"This story on racial violence is mine. I'm not letting Audrey or anyone else steal my thunder. It's important to me."

"As important as your life?"

"Now, you're just being melodramatic."

"But, where are you going to go?"

"Home."

"Don't be stupid! That's too dangerous for words."

"Not the way I intend to do it."

"But how?"

*

The autopsy on Vencat revealed a combination of digitoxin, verapamil and a diuretic. Together they caused a massive loss of potassium and magnesium and an increase in digitalis toxicity, which caused the kidneys to shut down, increased heart rate and subsequent heart failure. Hurst, the pathologist thought suicide was unlikely; there were easier ways to go.

"This is interesting. Forensics found a small plastic packet with traces of shoe polish and...."

"Yes?" queried Mark.

"There was a small hair attached to the packet, a white cat's hair," smiled Allison.

"Is it the same as the one found in the surgical hat?"

"Identical."

"Then whoever murdered Friel and then tried to off Chrissy..."

"Helped Mr. Vencat meet his maker," finished Allison with a grimace. "Vencat didn't take this medicine by choice. Who had access to him? Or more to the point who was in the next cell?"

"I'll get the charge book." Stringer moved swiftly from the office leaving Allison time to reflect as he gazed at the comings and goings of the General Hospital opposite. He comforted himself in his observations by letting his taste buds loose on his favourite delicacy. Allison had just swallowed the last heavenly mouthful of his beloved Mars Bar when Mark returned, "Some chap called Walter Whitworth found rolling drunk in Steelhouse Lane."

"Known? Previous?" grunted Allison as his tongue swept across his teeth cleaning off the remnants of chocolate strands and caramel.

"First timer. Put in a cell to sleep it off. Just got a caution."

"Address?"

"Flat 17, Leon Machel House, Lizard Walk, Yardley."

"Never heard of it. Check it out and get him in."

"Sir. Oh and by the way, Maddie complained that you haven't been picking up your messages."

Allison groaned and held up his hands in surrender. "I know! I've just had so much on my plate I thought what I don't know can't hurt me."

"Except that Rosie has been trying to call you. She wouldn't leave a message."

Allison frowned, "It must be important. Ask Maddie to get her on the line."

*

Mrs. Clifton was confident, so confident she was no longer worried about returning to Golden Hillock Road. In fact, she believed her timing was excellent. The police would be scouring Worcester and the surrounding area. They would never believe in a million years that she would return home under cover of darkness and away from prying eyes. Her disguise was so good even she didn't recognise herself!

Grace managed to catch a night service Midland Red bus that would take her to Digbeth; from there she could walk to a bus stop where she could take another bus to Spark Brook. She sat downstairs on the long seat near the driver and doors and inspected those around her. There was a young couple involved in each other on the back seat. She shuddered thinking it was such shameful behaviour for ones so young. It was as much as she could do to prevent recriminations pouring from her lips and many came to her mind. She wanted to quote from the gospels but knew that such an act would shatter her disguise. What would a good Hindu woman be doing quoting verses from a Christian Bible? Further along inside the bus was an old man nodding gently to the rhythmic rattle of the diesel engine. Opposite her was a woman Grace estimated to be in her early forties. Although smartly dressed she had a hooked nose, which gave her a predatory look and an overly painted face. Secretly the words Jezebel and harlot sprang into her thoughts. Mrs. Clifton suppressed the urge to spout her religious admonishments but as the journey progressed she grew more disconcerted at the insolent, rude way the woman stared at her, as if she, Grace, had no right to be on the bus breathing the same air. Prejudice that's what it was and that was something Grace had never experienced firsthand before. She had always prided herself on her tolerance and understanding. Everyone was God's creation and at least in that belief she was correct.

The tired drone of the bus's engine coughed and stuttered into silence. The person who had been glaring so rudely at Grace rose from her seat and made sure she stepped in front

132

of Mrs. Clifton. Grace suffered the insult by treading clumsily on the heel of the woman and feigned an apology to which the woman acidly replied that it was no more than she'd expect. Grace narrowed her beetling brows. It was difficult not to retaliate but she didn't want to draw attention to herself so she slunk off the bus and made her way to the night service bus stop. Now, she had to be careful. If she was going home she couldn't be seen entering and had to plan her route carefully.

Grace alighted at Small Heath Park and looked down the dusty litter strewn street. Nothing much had changed. Few people were about and there was little traffic. Grace approached her house in Spark Brook from the back. It would mean trespassing through someone else's garden and clambering over the wall. She hoped there were no dogs out and no one peering through their windows.

Mrs. Clifton went quietly up the path of the house, which backed onto hers and gingerly opened their back gate. She picked her way through the uncared for garden with its coarse grass and weeds and stepped on an old compost heap to help herself over the wall. She slid down the other side grazing her knees in the process, stifling the small sound of annoyance, which threatened to burst from her. A ferocious barking damaged the quiet of the night. Lehmber Singh, her next-door neighbour, had in his wisdom invested in a large dog to protect the family home. His family would not be afraid again if Tony should go on a wrecking spree. Grace ducked down behind the raspberry cane and stayed completely still and waited for the barks to subside, but they didn't. The lights went on in an upstairs window and she heard the sash of the window going up and Lehmber's voice.

"What is it boy? Who's there?"

It was now apparent that the dog was out in the yard below and it whined softly in response to his master's voice. Grace held her breath. She needed to walk down the garden to the shed and retrieve the back door key, which would let her in safely. She didn't know if the dog was tied up or roaming free and she didn't want to find out. How could she get there without attracting more interest? Grace felt the earth around her lightly with her fingers and her hand closed on a piece of slag. Using all her strength she tossed it over the wall and across the Singh's garden where it landed with a thud after scraping down the far wall. A small animal disturbed by the stone scuttled through the grass and two marauding cats out hunting pounced and began their own fight, howling and screeching as they spat and clawed each other. This was her chance as the dog bounded to the wall and joined in the hullabaloo.

Grace dragged up the ends of her sari and like a child about to play jump rope stuffed it in her knickers and moved swiftly down her yard and into the shed. The cats' commotion and caterwauling outside distracted the dog long enough for her to find the key and unlock the back of the house. She heard another neighbour shouting, "Shut that dog up!" and Lehmber apologised and remonstrated with 'Soldier' to be quiet.

Grace gently closed the door. She was home and safe. She chuckled to herself, no one would think of looking for her here. She wondered if her son was home and felt an urgent stirring inside her. Would he have been disturbed by the dog? Would he be awake? What a wonderful surprise he would have.

Grace picked her way through the kitchen and into her living room. Something crunched underfoot and she picked it up. It felt like broken china. She stepped out into the hall and stairs and wished she had a light. Torch, there was a torch in her bag but she had left that in the shed. That could be a mistake. She would have to retrieve it or get Tony to retrieve it for her. She tiptoed quietly up the stairs and opened his door. Silence. There was just the light of the moon leaking through the curtains and spilling on the floor. His bed was empty. Grace glanced in the spare room. Nothing. A further examination of the bathroom and her own bedroom told her she was alone in the house. Well no matter. He would come home sometime and when he did she'd be here waiting for him. The thought filled her with a delicious quivering deep in the pit of her stomach. She returned to her room and settled down to sleep.

Rosie wet and scrunched up her now damp and abundant hair forcing it under a baseball cap. She donned a pair of tinted glasses and peered at herself in the mirror. Dressed, as she was now, in jeans, check shirt and waistcoat, and without make up, she looked more like a boy or art student than a professionally dressed reporter.

"What do you think?"

Linda stared critically, "I don't know..."

"Come on! My own mother wouldn't recognise me."

"Maybe. But we're not talking about your mother. We're talking about a nut case who is out to get you. And how are you going to dodge them outside?" Linda jerked a thumb at the window indicating the car parked across the street watching the house.

"I won't go out that way. They're not looking to follow me. They're there to stop someone coming in."

"I don't like it."

"Look, whoever is stalking me knows I'm here. It's dead easy to find me. I've got a new sim card for my mobile to keep in touch. You've got the number."

"And at home?"

"He won't be expecting me to return and anyway I'm ex directory now."

"Hmm! So if anyone rings I pretend you're still here?"

"That should confuse them."

"What about the police?"

"I'll cross that bridge when I come to it."

"Rosie, please think again."

"Thinking's done. It's now time for action. I refuse to run scared anymore."

The telephone rang. Linda looked at her cousin.

"Go on answer it," prompted Rosie.

Linda tentatively answered, thrust the phone towards her and beamed, "It's for you... Popsie."

Rosie grabbed the receiver, "Hello?"

"You've been trying to call me?" came Allison's gravel tones.

"Yes, no. It's all right..." she paused.

"Is it?" Greg said in a measured but suspicious manner, "What are you up to, Rosie?"

"Hang up and I'll call you back."

"Why?"

"We don't know who's listening."

She ended the call and picked up her mobile.

"Hello? Popsie?"

"I'm listening."

Rosie frowned, hesitated and nudged by her cousin suddenly blurted, "I want to come home. I know that sounds stupid but I can't stay away forever. I'll lose my job. Besides the growler knows I'm here."

"Growler?"

"My and Linda's name for the freak. You've changed my locks and phone number it should be better. I can still work, follow up my stories and e-mail them to the paper. It's important to me. Linda will pretend I'm still here. It could work."

Allison recognised the stubborn note in her voice he'd heard it too many times before. Rosie explained her plan. There was a silence.

"I can't let you do it. I haven't the men to watch your flat."

"But no one will know."

"I'll know and I'm not putting you at risk."

"But... You can't stop me."

"I know and I'm going to regret saying this... if you come back you'll stay with us. Me and Mary."

"But my things and everything I need are at the flat."

"Tell me what you want and Mary will collect them. It's the only way I'll agree..."

Rosie sighed, "Okay. Have you got a pen?"

*

Holly reluctantly waved good-bye to Paul's sister, Eleanor and his father, Bernie. The cosy fisherman's cottage had been sanctuary for a while and she had enjoyed the comfort and serenity that village life provided. She sat in silence as Paul carefully picked his way through the narrow winding streets until they reached the trunk road.

"You all right?" he asked.

"Just wondering what we're going back to. Colin said the place was a mess."

"Material things; that's all. They can be replaced."

"And the paintings?"

"We may be able to clean them up, if not I'll have to start again. It'll keep me out of mischief that's for sure."

"Why Paul? Why is she so determined to strike out at me?"

"Who can say? I don't think anyone would understand the workings of her mind. She is insane. But don't think about that. Think how far you've come."

"What do you mean?"

"The courses you've done developing your skills. Meeting your grandmother, Hilda Fisher and learning all about your mother, Ellie."

Holly sniffed, "I suppose I have... but I don't want to meet Tony Clifton or his hideous mother."

"I know. We'll talk to Colin when we get back. Deal?"

Holly turned her huge dark eyes on Paul, "Deal," she agreed.

*

Tony turned into the arcade. He knew he shouldn't be there. He was trying to fight this gambling compulsion, wasn't he? He watched the guy in the change booth chatting to some young girl. She had her back to him but it was the fluttering scarf at her neck, which caught his eye. He struggled with his feelings, which threatened to consume and overtake him. His hand went to his mouth and he bit it hard. He felt no pain. But he needed to feel pain, something, anything. The girl turned her head and he was surprised to recognise her. It was Melody Harper. A black scowl crossed his handsome features and he turned away but not before another movement caught his eye. There was a man standing by the rifle range. Tony knew he was watching him, another copper keeping tabs on him. He had to get away. Not home, he didn't want to go home, yet. He hadn't been home for two days, preferring to crash on musician, Skip's floor. Tony felt his blood trickle down his chin and tasted its warmth. He grabbed his hanky from his suit pocket and wrapped it around the bite. What was he thinking of? ... Nothing. He couldn't think straight. He had to get out of there, but it was too late. Melody had seen him. Her face paled and she whispered something to the guy in the booth and pointed in his direction.

Tony slammed his hand into the nearest machine. The few punters who were there hardly raised an eyebrow. Tony felt the pressure build in his head. He gurgled in distress and turned on his heel and broke into a half run, away from the machines and Melody's accusing stare. He walked on mindlessly, seemingly unaware of the copper on his tail and disappeared into the comfort of the park, seeking out a friendly tree to lean against and recover his composure.

Young Gary Watson, the copper from CID assigned to follow him got caught up in a crush of young people exiting a pub. Streamers popped from party poppers and silly string was sprayed, along with a squeaky trumpet fanfare from feathered party blowers. Gary looked wildly around. He hadn't seen where Tony had gone. His eyes searched up and down the road. He turned into the park and ran through the gate. Nothing. Gary dashed back into the street and began diving in through the entrances of pubs along the way to try and catch sight of his quarry. He swore in frustration and dialled in, "Sorry, Sarge, I've lost him." He winced at the crude invective, which blasted down the phone.

If only he'd ventured further into the park he would have seen Tony leaning comfortingly against a broad trunked oak tree away from the roadside entrance. Tony seemed transfixed and then a subtle change came over him. He straightened up. His twisted mouth evened out into a cruel hard line and with his head held up he made his way to the Gents' toilets at the edge of the park. He needed to think. He needed comfort, which only his mother or Amy could provide. But Amy wasn't there. Amy was gone. He would never see her sweet face again because of the spiteful, vicious actions of his mother. But there was someone who could help. What was her name? She had been kind to him. She could take Amy's place. Tony smothered a sob with his hand

and noticed the white handkerchief wrapped around it. Why? What had happened? A voice broke into his thoughts. A disreputable looking old man was zipping up his flies at the urinal and he asked in a thick Birmingham accent, "Are you all right, Mate?"

Tony nodded.

"You don't look it. Had a bit to drink, have you? Why don't you come home with me? I'll look after you."

And like a small child Tony allowed himself to be led outside and walked with the old man who continued to talk comfortingly and soothingly to him.

*

Rosie packed her bag and stepped lightly down the stairs. She faced her cousin, Linda in the hallway.

"Thanks. For everything."

"I wish you weren't going."

"I'll be fine. I'll ring as soon as I'm on the train. Popsie's wife, Mary will meet me at New Street."

"What if he's out there? Watching?"

"He's not. It's just the cops. And anyway, I'm going out the back way." She stuffed a stray lock of hair under her cap and pulled on her jacket. "Bye!" She gave her cousin a hug and went out to the kitchen and the back door. "Don't worry. This is the easy bit."

Linda opened the door and there she stayed looking down the garden path and the gate until long after Rosie had gone. She had this uncomfortable feeling, one she couldn't shake off. Something wasn't right. And she had every reason to feel this way. But it wasn't Rosie she should worry about, but herself.

10
It's all in the game

The photographer from the Birmingham Post and Mail had arrived on a morning train and easily found where Linda lived. He had settled himself at a window table in the corner cafe on her road where he could watch the house with impunity. He had noticed the unmarked police car sitting outside Rosie's hideaway but there had been no movement from the house. He still needed the power rush he got from contacting and terrifying Rosie, but he wasn't foolish enough to attract attention. Besides, he only had a couple of days off and then he had to get back to work. He had this urgent need inside him to hear Rosie's voice, to hear her fear, and he imagined how exquisite it would be to have her completely at his mercy. He was aware of himself going hard and the urge was becoming stronger. He drained the last of his coffee and moved from the window to the cafe's public phone by the toilets. He waited a few moments until he felt sure he was unobserved and dialled Linda's number.

The ring of the phone made Linda jump and she hesitated before picking up the receiver.

"Hello?"

He said nothing.

"Hello! Who is this?"

He enjoyed the overtone of panic, which was creeping into her voice. But it wasn't Rosie. He needed to hear Rosie speak. So, he made a decision.

"Hello...? Sorry, I didn't mean to alarm you. There's something wrong with this phone. Can I speak to Rosie please?"

The relief Linda felt when hearing a normal male voice was apparent.

"Who's calling?"

"Just a friend from work. Is she there?"

"Sorry, she's just gone in the bath. Can I take a message?"

"No, it's okay. I'll ring later. Tell her it's her favourite partner in crime. And I've got some exciting news. I want to tell her myself. You understand?" and he hung up.

Linda replaced the phone in its cradle. This was going to be tricky. How could she get over this? She switched on the answer phone and pressed the re-record message button.

"Hi, you've reached Linda Gilchrist. Sorry I can't get to the phone right now but I'm away for a few days with Rosie to visit Aunty Joan. If it's urgent call me on the mobile. You know the number."

The message played back to her. That should do the trick. She could monitor all calls. No more awkward callers. Anyone genuine would ring her cell phone. Linda drew the curtains in the front room although it wasn't late or dark. She turned on the television. The harmless chatter from the talk show was comforting and made her feel less alone. She switched on her mobile and went upstairs to the bathroom. A good hot soak was just what she needed. While she was running the bath she telephoned Rosie.

"Partner in crime?" questioned Rosie. "Who the heck is that? What did he sound like?"

"Normal. Not scary at all."

"It'll be Lex or Brian mucking around. Did you 1471"

"Didn't think of it. I'll do it later. Where are you?"

"Just going down to the underground now. I'll call you from Euston."

"Right. Take care!"

"I will."

Linda crossed into the bedroom and pulled the curtains together. She noticed the car had gone. Police resources were precious and now Rosie had gone they wouldn't need to watch the flat anymore. She supposed Popsie must have told them. She tossed her fiery chestnut tresses, so like Rosie's. Their mothers weren't twins for nothing. There was more than a passing resemblance between the two cousins.

The departure of the police car and surveillance team had not gone unnoticed and Rosie's stalker had seen the burnished head of hair at the window before the curtains had been pulled. He wondered if he could take two women. He would never have a better opportunity. But he couldn't gain entry from the front of the house. The back entrance would be a better prospect. He sauntered down the street his camera swinging around his neck. He steadied it and tucked it inside his coat. Four houses along was an alley, which led to the back gates of the gardens of the houses in the road. His footsteps echoed metallically in the brick walled entry. It was still quiet. Children were not out of school yet and people were still at work. He pulled the hood from his anorak up over his head and his face almost disappeared from view. He counted the houses. How fortunate, the back gates were all neatly numbered. He lifted the latch and slipped into the garden, which only half an hour before had been Rosie's escape route.

Linda had poured in her aromatherapy bath essence and was now luxuriating in the soothing foam. She had Radio Two blaring out keeping her company. Linda laughed at the factoids and enjoyed the banter between the DJ, Steve Wright and his regular friends on the show. The non-stop oldies had been compiled by someone in Reading and Linda made a mental list of what she would include if she ever got round to sending in a list. She was too busy singing along with Kylie Minogue to hear the glass break in the panel on the back door, let alone the sound of the door opening and softly closing again.

Linda ducked down under the suds soaking her hair. She blew a couple of bubbles and emerged through the water and reached for the shampoo. The cleansing gel frothed through her hair and she ice cream coned it in a pile on top of her head and reached for the shower spray.

The intruder tentatively stepped onto the first step of the staircase, which squeaked crazily. The groan of the wood seemed exceedingly loud and he paused afraid he had been heard. The television droned on in the living room. Linda was obviously engrossed in Channel Four's Richard and Judy, or Oprah or some such other magazine programme. He could hear the music from Radio Two leeching from the bathroom and he carefully continued ascending the stairs. The bathroom door was ajar. He caught his breath as he glimpsed the back of her wet body with soapsuds dribbling towards the dimples just below her waist. She was kneeling up, using the shower spray to remove the traces of an exotic smelling shampoo, which excited his senses. Linda started to hum along with a song from Madonna as she washed her hair for a second time. He stood there mesmerised. He drank in the scent of her, the perfume, and the steamy heat. His eyes ran over the curve of her back to her waist and the gentle roundness of her hips and he shuddered in ecstasy. He could feel himself becoming more and more aroused. She reached for the shower spray once more and he could bear it no longer. He pushed open the door violently and moved behind her quickly, snatching the shower spray from her hand. The spiral metal links looped tightly around her neck and her feet scrabbled uselessly underneath her as he twisted her head back and forced her under the foam. Her fingers reached out and plucked at him, scraping his face. He retaliated by pushing her down even harder. The bath water slopped over the side and soaked onto the mat. He held her underneath until she stopped kicking and a burst of bubbles escaped through her mouth. Her hair floated like seaweed, fanning out like the rays of the sun. Her eyes stared open wide in horror and her mouth shaped the sound of the scream, which was trapped in her throat. He grunted as the exertion of his will on hers reached the peak of satisfaction and he ejaculated into his pants.

Linda's face broke the surface of the water. He rose from his position behind her and saw her face for the first time. Not quite believing his eyes he pulled her up and really stared at her. This wasn't Rosie! The telephone rang and he froze expecting to hear Rosie's footsteps in the hall to answer the phone. Instead, the answer phone kicked in. Puzzled he moved to the top of the stairs and waited. Rosie's voice reverberated around the house.

"Neat message! Should do the trick! I'm safe and sound at Euston, will ring when I get home." The answer phone reset itself and beeped out that there was a message waiting.

She'd gone! How? That didn't matter. Little Minx. He knew where she was going and he would be following. Now, he needed to get out and get out fast. But first, he ran down the stairs and picked up the phone and dialled 1471. He smiled with satisfaction as the recorded voice relayed the mobile number, which he immediately programmed into his own phone. The rat would soon be in the trap! What he was forgetting was the incriminating evidence he had inadvertently left at the scene of crime. He wasn't as clever or invincible as he believed.

*

Mrs. Clifton couldn't understand it. Where was her son? He hadn't been home for days. Why? Had he got himself mixed up with some little strumpet who had turned his head like Amy? She knew his weaknesses only too well. Or was it something more serious? But she wasn't in a position to report him missing. Grace began to worry and there was nothing she could do to alleviate her anxiety. Refreshed after her sleep she cautiously made her way back down the stairs. She tried to be as quiet as possible. She didn't want the neighbours to become curious. She went into the living room and couldn't believe what she saw. Her religious icons and artefacts had gone from the walls. Her scroll box was missing and her blue willow china no longer graced the splintered, battered cabinet. Grace felt that Tony must have been dragged away or there had been some sort of fight. She hoped he hadn't fallen to temptation again otherwise her escape and all of her machinations would have been in vain. She tiptoed carefully down the tiled passageway and was horrified to see the mess of wires, which had held the lights that surrounded the wooden cross now all tangled together by the coat stand.

Grace almost began keening in misery at this sacrilegious and wanton act of vandalism, which couldn't have possibly been done by Tony. She gathered the pieces together and disappeared into her lair to repair the damage. When Tony returned home he would be welcomed properly.

*

Tony sat on a grubby stained tweed settee that had seen better days. The old man was busy making a pot of tea. He chuntered away in his thick nasal twang but Tony didn't hear. He was lost in his own thoughts. The man began to hum

144

a verse of 'Onward Christian Soldiers' and something stirred in Tony's mind. He began to take notice of his surroundings; the peeling, faded wallpaper, the torn lace cloth on the table in the window. The frayed and degrain net curtains, which were hanging off the rail in places. The room he was in was filthy. Newspapers and magazines were piled high on the floor. There was a half eaten take away meal in a tin foil carton on a tray, which had congealed and begun to sprout spores of a peppermint aero green mould. Two cats were washing themselves by an overturned wooden chair with only three legs. The place stank of cats' urine, mouldy food, rotted paper and unwashed clothes. The dirty ripped carpet was covered in fluff and had obviously not seen a vacuum cleaner in years and the thick dust layered on the mantelpiece was like a felt coating. Something scurried in the corner of the room and the walls seemed to be covered with black bugs like book lice of some sort that were in a breeding ground haven. Gradually, Tony's mind began to clear and when the old boy scuttled in carrying a tray of tea Tony's revulsion began to grow. The gent cleared his throat and spat into the empty fireplace. His shaking hands poured out the stew like brew into two cracked and chipped mugs. Tony had no idea where he was or how he had got here but the Birmingham whine grated on him just like his mother's irritating tones. The old man wore half mittens and his exposed fingers were encrusted with grime as if he had been mining for coal with his bare hands. He had an old moth eaten muffler at his neck and the wool had unravelled at the end and dangled down like heavy strands of a spider's web.

Without warning and amid the old chap's protests Tony leapt up and dashed the mug of tea from the gnarled and wizened hands. Tony pushed the old man backwards and the cats scuttled into the kitchen. Without looking back Tony fled the room and found his way outside where he took several large gulps of fresh air to try and clear the foul taste from his mouth and the stale smell that seemed to cling to him and he stumbled down the front path and back onto the road. He needed to get home to scrub himself clean and wash away this abomination. He heard a tirade of abuse screeched after him by the old man who had chased him onto the road and stood there shaking his fist whilst his other hand held a foul soiled rag to his cheek, which appeared to have a dribble of blood clearing a track through the pasty grey whiskered skin. Tony knew he had to get home no matter who was watching or following. He knew he was safe. He'd lost his tail.

*

"I don't want to stay here tonight." Holly turned her huge sooty dark eyes to Paul, "Please."

"But it's late and it's our house. We're safe here. She's not coming back."

"I just feel... defiled, raped. The place is such a mess. The thought of her poking around our things fills me with such horror. It'll be different in the morning, I know. I'll be more able to deal with it, then. Please, Paul." She looked pleadingly at him.

"I never can say no to you." He smiled and kissed her tenderly on her forehead. "Okay. Colin has the name of someone who makes it his job to clean up scenes of crime. How about we give it a shot?"

"Nah! I don't want anyone else here. The clean up is all part of the process to heal. It's just for tonight because I know we won't be able to finish doing everything. We'll need the whole day. I want to wash her out of our home. Make sure every last vibration has been scrubbed away."

"Where do you want to go?"

"I know it's a bit of a cheek but p'raps Colin and Marcie could put us up. If not there's always Redlands."

"Oooh! That doesn't come cheap! Like your luxury don't you, Girl?" Paul teased but he saw she was serious. "Right. I'll give Col a call."

Holly walked through the rooms registering all of the damage Grace had inflicted. She was especially concerned with the sightless eyes of her cuddly toys. She went to the kitchen for a dustbin bag and lovingly placed the blinded animals inside. Then she hunted on the floor for the sets of eyes scattered like tiny gemstones across the carpet. She picked up all she could see and placed them in an envelope, which she sealed and deposited into the bag with the toys, by which time, Paul was back in the room with her.

"That's okay. Marcie's making up the bed in the spare room. It'll be good to be among friends. What are you doing with that?"

"You know how bad I am with a needle? I quarrelled with one years ago."

"Don't remind me. You'd rather buy a new shirt than sew on a button."

"I'm not quite that bad."

"No. I just have to wait until all the buttons are off before you do anything!"

"Well, you know the answer to that!"

"I know... do it myself."

"Precisely!"

"You still haven't told me..." Paul complained.

"Marcie's great with a needle. With her it will be a labour of love and that's just what these need. It really will remove all of Grace Clifton's horrid energy."

"If you say so. What about these?" He pointed at the heap of ripped and butchered clothes on the floor.

"Marcie's not that in love with sewing! Those we will burn."

"Neat way of getting a new wardrobe," Paul joked.

Holly batted at him playfully with her hand. "Actually, let's get another bag and put this lot in. Stick it in the skip down the road. No one will mind. And it will give the room longer to heal."

Paul didn't argue. It made sense. He gathered everything up whilst Holly set some joss sticks burning. Sage was particularly good at clearing bad energy. That would be the first step.

*

Tony turned into Golden Hillock Road and up the unkempt path to his house. He noticed, the curtains twitch on the house next door and a dog could be heard barking frenziedly in the background. He fumbled in his pockets for his key and struggled with the lock. As soon as he pushed the front door open he was mesmerised by the fairy lights blinking on and off around the old brown wooden cross above the door in the hall leading to the passage. He stood there almost a full five minutes staring in disbelief and shock. He must be dreaming! This couldn't possibly be happening. Either that or he was caught in a time warp. Tony snapped himself to attention and shut the outside door. Cautiously, he opened the glass door to the passage and gingerly stepped inside. The cloying sweetness of joss sticks wafted up the passage and he went rigid with fear. Was there someone there? Was someone playing tricks? No one else mixed the scents of musk with sandalwood, lavender and jasmine except his mother.

He tried to call out, "Mum!" But the words stuck in his throat and came out as a whispered, throaty rasp. The door to the parlour was ajar. He peeped inside. Everything was gleaming and clean. He closed the door hurriedly; he was going mad, finally, after everything. That was the only possible explanation. Slowly he touched the sitting room door with his finger. The remaining debris from his shambolic homecoming had been cleared away. The table was laid and he could smell something cooking, cakes or muffins or something. A ripple of fear trickled down his backbone and his heart began to hammer. He heard a faint sound coming from the kitchen. The tinny rattle of a kettle being boiled. Curiously he moved towards the sound. He stood framed in the doorway and looked on in horror as he saw his mother, feet encased in pom-pom bedroom slippers and an old woollen hat pulled over her hair, preparing a tray of tea.

"You haven't got any Jaffa Cakes," she whined. "You know they're my favourite."

At the sound of her nasal moaning and the sight of her plump body corseted so that her fat spilled over the top of her stays Tony uttered a low and mournful cry.

"Shut up!" Grace hissed, "We don't want anyone to know I'm here and she turned her cobra hooded reptilian eyes on her son. Tony gasped, convinced he really had gone over the edge this time. He turned back and ran out of the house and back onto the street. He sprinted for his life and sanity and jumped onto a bus preparing to shut its doors. He sat in a daze until he reached New Street Station where he alighted.

Tony wandered around the station shopping centre before sitting on a bench close to a coffee stand near the barriers, which gave entrance to the platforms. There he sat. His mind was racing, his heart felt as if it was to burst from his chest and he began to sweat. Tony felt utterly miserable and desolate. He was sure he had been getting better. Life had begun to feel good but now this; this threatened to destroy him again. Something had to be done. He had to do something. Tony tried to reason with himself and calm his fears. He was just thinking about ringing Kirsty Beck when a young woman appeared at the head of an escalator and approached the barrier. She was dressed in jeans, check shirt, waistcoat and jacket, dragging a small case behind her. She pulled off a cap, which had contained a cascade of chestnut tresses threaded with fire, and something stirred in his memory. He remembered her luxurious head of hair and the long trailing scarf, which had been at her neck. She handed in her ticket and was met by a smartly dressed woman, in a burgundy suit, with mid brown hair swept up into a French pleat. Tony couldn't take his eyes off the young woman; like an automaton he rose from the bench and began to follow the pair through the station towards the taxi rank and car park. It was the reporter; the reporter from the Post who had so caught his eye the day he was released. Rosie! Her name was Rosie, Rosie Partridge. And he smiled.

Rosie chattered happily to Mary Allison, oblivious of the eyes, which followed her movements. Tony wandered out to the taxi rank where he watched the two women walk towards a racing green Peugeot 406. He stepped into a waiting black cab and uttered the inimitable lines, "Follow that car... discretely."

"Right oh mate! On a mission are we? Always wanted to do this."

Tony smiled grimly in response and nodded his head, a lock of his blue-black hair falling across his furrowed brow. "My girl friend," he explained, "She's with my mother. Mum and I have a special surprise party planned for our engagement but she's got it in her head that she wants to do something wonderful for me... it's all very complicated but I can't talk to mum on the mobile..."

"Cos the girlfriend can listen in," chipped in the cabbie.

"Exactly. So I have to resort to all this subterfuge... You know how it is," Tony lied glibly. He was good at that.

"Tell me about it," droned the cabbie.

*

Kirsty Beck looked at her watch. Something was wrong. She had not heard from Tony since she had left him at the club the previous night. She knew he'd been staying at his pianist friend Skip's house the last few nights but he'd said he needed to get home for fresh clothes and Kirsty just couldn't face going back to that cold, unredeeming house. He was supposed to call her when he got home and now, young Gary Watson who had been detailed from CID to tail Tony from Chaplins had reported that he had lost him somewhere on route to Small Heath Park. It looked like she was going to have to pluck up the courage to visit the house after all. She advised Pooley of what she was going to do.

"Be careful. I know you think you'll be okay but this guy is unpredictable and he's not normal."

Kirsty wanted to rebuff the comment but she knew better and kept quiet.

"Here take Gary with you, just in case."

That was the last thing she wanted, but she acknowledged the order and the two left the station together for Golden Hillock Road.

Rosie chattered happily with Mary, unaware of the black cab following at a discrete distance. They pulled into the driveway of a distinguished looking property in Gilhurst road. Mary drove the car into the garage and the two got out and made their way to the front door and disappeared inside. Tony took note of the driveway and paid off the cabbie who delighted with his tip wished his passenger well and hoped the surprise came off to his expectations.

"Oh, it will," Tony warmly replied, "I'm sure it will. And thank you."

*

"I can't understand it. Something must be wrong." Rosie exclaimed as she tried for the third time to contact her cousin Linda.

"Maybe she's out, gone shopping," soothed Mary.

"No. She'd have her mobile on."

"Perhaps her battery is down."

"Can't be. She had it on charge before I left."

"Or she's just old plain forgotten it!" Mary tried to calm Rosie who was becoming increasingly more agitated.

"I rang her from the station. I thought she left the phone message for me to hear and next time she'd pick up. She hadn't planned on going out. I called from the train and again when I arrived. Nothing. And again now. Something is definitely not right."

"I'll pop the kettle on and you can give Greg a ring. See what he says."

"I don't like to bother him at work ... but..."

"He won't mind. He's always happy to hear from you."

"Okay."

Rosie had started for the hall telephone when her mobile rang.

She called across her shoulder to Mary, "Bet that's Linda now."

She froze as she heard the distorted husky voice of her tormentor.

"Thought you could shake me off did you? Got that wrong then. Oh, and don't bother visiting your cousin again. She can't help you any more." The line went dead.

Rosie began to wail.

"How did he get my phone number? How? I've been so careful. What's happened to Linda?"

"I'll call Greg. He'll get the Met to check out your cousin. I'm sure he's just trying to frighten you."

"Well, it's working...."

"Turn your phone off. He doesn't know your number here."

"But, what if Linda tries to get in touch?"

"Here, use my mine. If you can't get through leave a message to ring my mobile. My number will come up as a

151

new number. She'll have the sense to ring that, won't she?"

Rosie nodded, her face pale with fear.

"I'll get those things you wanted after I've rung Greg. Lock the doors you'll be safe here."

Mary dialled Greg's direct line and explained the situation. Maddie answered, "Sorry, Mrs Allison he's caught up in interviews. As soon as he's free I'll get him to ring you."

"Do that. Get him to contact Scotland Yard first. Linda's house must be checked."

"Will do."

*

Greg Allison was grateful that Holly had agreed to come into the station. She was accompanied by her friend, Colin Brady, the police psychologist.

"I understand you want me to jump through some hoops," she said wryly.

"I wouldn't put it quite like that," Allison returned, "But given your skills, let's say an old curmudgeon like me who has more sceptical bones than not, is prepared to admit that you have got something, a talent, a power, or something inexplicable and we'd like your help."

"So, what do you want?"

"Two things. First, can you get a fix on Grace Clifton? And secondly, I have a particularly nasty case of racial violence, which has led to murder and serious injury. I need someone to help me get to the truth. Will you help?"

"I am amazed, Inspector that you are at last giving me any credibility at all."

"I can't do anything else, can I? Not with your track record. Just don't go broadcasting the fact, especially at the station or..."

"You'll come in for a lot of stick?"

"Something like that," muttered Allison.

Holly paused. She glanced at Colin. His expression was encouraging, "I'll see what I can do."

11
It's a hard rain

Grace Clifton wasn't used to reproaching herself, but reproach herself she did. She should have realised what a shock it would be to Tony finding her there like that as if she'd never left. She also felt that, perhaps, it had been a mistake to lose her disguise so soon. If anyone saw her they would know. Yes, she determined. She would need to adopt her disguise again. But this time she would warn Tony leave him a note. No. That could be found by someone else. Better still, she could ring him at work and leave a message. But who could she say was calling? Grace's coarse black eyebrows lowered menacingly onto her serpentine lids as she tried to solve her problem.

She slopped to the hall table with its telephone pad and scrutinised the numbers. Dempsey's switchboard, Tony's direct line, Chaplins club, Kirsty Beck.... who was Kirsty Beck? That wasn't a name she recognised. It was a mobile number. Her stomach began to knot and twist in the unrelenting grip of jealousy. Found someone had he? It had to be this woman, this Kirsty, who had taken her boy. Turned him against her. She would have to be punished. But first things first. Grace mounted the stairs softly and entered the bathroom where she threw off her clothes and began to reapply a tanning agent so that she could reassume her clever disguise. This would enable her to move more freely in the area, which was essential if her plan was to come together.

*

Tony walked down the road of the leafy suburb towards the bus shelter where he sat down. Here he could comfortably keep an eye on the house, which Rosie had entered with the older woman. But why? Why did he want to do this? It didn't make sense. He had to get a hold of himself. What on earth was he doing here? He was rambling. He knew he wasn't safe. He knew he needed help. He would just sit. Yes, he would sit a little while longer and wait. Wait, until his head cleared.

*

Holly sat quietly with Colin in Allison's office. She was quiet but nervous.

"You know what you have to do?" spoke the psychologist in soothing tones.

Holly nodded. Colin continued gently, "The phone will ring twice. That's our signal. We leave here, walk through the outer office to the corridor and sit in room 201. Through the glass windows you will be able to see the two boys with the youth worker, Simpson. The room is set up so that we will be able to hear everything that's said. On the desk is Ajay's school coat. You'll be able to feel it. It may help you to connect. Okay?"

"Okay," Holly turned her huge eyes on Colin. "Let's just hope I can help."

The phone rang. Twice.

*

Tony continued to sit in the bus shelter. He watched buses come and go. He looked at cars motoring by, some with a purpose and others more idly. Mothers with their children walked together chatting and laughing but Tony just stared. He was shocked out of his lassitude when a fire engine with sirens blaring raced along the road and around the corner. It was as if there had been an awakening and he suddenly came to his senses. What the hell was he doing here? Where was he? What had he done? Distorted fragments of his mother, an old man, Melody Harper and ... and ... the reporter, the reporter from the Post whirled and moved like a kaleidoscope in his mind. He struggled frantically to focus and bring to clarity the fleeting memories, which were blurred and indistinct. He let his head fall into his hands and sighed heavily. "Calm... I must be calm," he thought as he breathed deeply trying to still his racing heart. He glanced at his watch. It was nearly eight o'clock and he had to be somewhere at ten. The club! He needed a shower and a change of clothes. Kirsty was meeting him there later. Kirsty! He was supposed to call her. It had gone completely out of

154

his head. He took his mobile phone from his pocket and flicked through his phone book until her name came up and he hit the call button.

*

Holly was experiencing all manner of sensations from Ajay's coat. Colin, meticulous as ever, jotted down everything she said. "...He came from behind. Poor little chap didn't stand a chance. Ajay never saw his face. But I can tell you that the man concerned, the one who lifted him up and tossed him into the canal is filled with hatred. And he wasn't alone. There were two of them. The last thing Ajay heard was, 'Paki trash take a bath.' All that struggling, fighting for breath...." Holly started to cry. Colin gently removed the coat from her hands. Holly began to listen to what was being said in the next room.

"How much longer?" grumbled Wayne, "I've already told you I don't know anything. I wasn't even there."

"You can't keep us here," sniffled Kevin, "I'm already in major league trouble with my mum."

"He's not lying there. His mum is a witch," said Holly as she listened.

"A witch?" queried Colin.

"You know what I mean, she's a bully. Poor kid has an awful home life."

"What about the other one, Wayne?"

"He's not telling the truth. He was there and he's petrified. I get the feeling that neither of them knew what was going to happen. I also sense that... is it Wayne?" Colin nodded.

"Wayne knows a lot more than he's letting on. He knows the two brutes that did this. Maybe, he's even related to one of them."

Back in the next room Wayne was blubbing and complaining about being hauled in with Kevin.

"Look, Wayne," asserted Simpson. "Everyone knows you and Kev are joined at the hip. There are not many places you go and Kevin isn't in tow. That's why you're here."

"Cause I'm his best mate? I can soon change that. I want to go home."

"Not too long now, they'll be coming to interview you soon. You'll be going in one at a time of course," said Simpson.

"Aw what?" groaned Wayne.

"And Kevin will be first."

"Won't do you no good. No one's saying nothing. Right, Kev?"

"Right."

At that point a young PC came in and took Kevin out.

"I need to be in there," urged Holly.

"We're supposed to wait here," reminded Colin. "But I ought to know better with you. I should expect anything." He smiled. Holly stood up, grabbed Ajay's coat, left room 201, followed Kevin Dobson and the copper along the corridor into an interview room. Colin was not far behind.

"I'm sorry...?" queried the bemused policeman.

"I need to be here," was all Holly would say. Colin Brady nodded his head, "It's all above board. Let her stay." And he handed him a sheet of paper, which the young man perused before waving them both to a seat.

"Here, who's she? What's she got to do with me? She's not from the Social is she? My mum wouldn't like that," whined Kevin.

"No, I'm not from the Social, Kevin. But I am working with Juvenile. Okay?"

"I'm saying nothing." Kevin stubbornly folded his arms and pursed his lips. Holly pulled her chair close to the lad and touched his arm. A wave of emotion spread through her.

"You have a tough time of it don't you, Kevin?"

"Who said?" he retorted sullenly.

"Your dad leaving home and your Mum shacked up with Uncle David is it? You don't like him very much do you, Kevin?"

"I never said so.

"You didn't have to, it's obvious. He can be very cruel too. What happened to your little dog? Biscuit wasn't it?"

Kevin's jaw dropped, "How do you know about that? There ain't no one knows about that, not even mum... he said..." It was there that Kevin trailed off.

156

"He said that if you told he'd do the same to you. Ran over him with his car didn't he?"

Kevin started to cry, "He was only a little thing wouldn't hurt no one. I tried to stop him yapping but he didn't like David. Always barked whenever he was around. He tied him to the garden gate and drove out over him." Kevin wiped his nose on his sleeve. "How do you know that? You been spying on me or something?"

"No, but there's lots I know, and there's more that you can tell me."

"Can't. I'd be in real trouble, worse than with my mum."

"You and Wayne took Ajay to look for frogs didn't you? You went to the reservoir first."

Kevin started at Holly in horrified amazement.

"I know you didn't mean anything bad to happen. It wasn't your fault. Look Kevin..." Holly held up Ajay's jacket. "He was such a little boy. Did he really deserve to die?"

"Didn't know he would ... He said his sister was teaching him to swim."

"So small," Holly shook her head, "You thought he was okay didn't you? Once you got to know him."

"He wasn't half bad not for a ..." Kevin stopped himself and bit his lip.

"Not for a Paki. That's what you were going to say weren't you?" pressed Holly.

Kevin hung his head and started to cry, "Never meant it to happen, wasn't supposed to happen. Not like that. Just a bit of fun they said, a bit of a scare. Just a joke."

"But Ajay's not here to laugh about it is he?"

Kevin began to sob those shuddering sobs we can all remember from childhood and started to tell as much as he knew.

Colin looked at Holly with pride she had a tremendous gift but not just that, she was great with kids too. He touched Holly's arm and they began to leave the room while Kevin continued to report what he could to the policeman.

As she opened the door, she turned and said, "Don't be frightened; that man isn't going to do the same to you, and as

157

for Wayne. I shall tell Wayne the same thing," and she left.

They walked back up the corridor. "You did great, Holly. Just great," murmured Colin appreciatively.

"He's a tougher nut to crack," admitted Holly, "But I'll have a go." Then she reflected on what she said... "Tougher nut," she muttered, "Tougher nut. Tough Nut that's what Ajay's sister calls him."

"Calls who, what are you talking about?" asked Colin.

"I'll have the answer to that when we've talked with Wayne. Come on." Holly marched up to room 201 and pushed open the door. Wayne looked up in surprise as Holly settled herself opposite him.

"Let's talk about your cousin, Wayne. Is he such a tough nut after all?"

*

Kirsty Beck and Gary Watson were just turning into Golden Hillock Road when her mobile rang. She glanced at the screen. "Pull over. It's Tony," she ordered. "Hello? Tony? I was worried to death about you. Where are you?"

Tony craned his neck to read the road sign, "Gilhurst road."

"What are you doing there?"

"Don't know. Seem to recall something about a reporter. She interviewed me when I was released. I can't really remember."

"Okay. Stay put. Whereabouts in Gilhurst Road?"

"The bus shelter near the traffic lights."

"Wait there, don't move. I'll come and get you. It'll be in an official car. Don't mind do you?"

"Been in enough of them not to mind," said Tony wryly.

"We'll come and get you, take you home. Right?"

Tony agreed and ended the call. Something disturbed him, something about home but he couldn't quite bring it to mind. But it would be all right. Kirsty would see to that. Everything was going to be fine. Wasn't it?

*

Rosie's stalker managed to catch the train to Birmingham with only minutes to spare. He made his way as quickly as he could to Rosie's address. He cruised slowly past her drive and looked up at the windows. Nothing. She'd obviously stopped off somewhere. Well, it would only be a matter of time. He would just have to be patient and wait. He parked his car in the grounds of the flats opposite where he could keep an eye on the place and settled down to wait. Wait he did.

The gentle purr of a Peugeot 406 came around the corner and drove straight into Rosie's drive. The photographer shifted in his seat as he watched an older woman, with her hair swept up in a French pleat get out of the car and enter the front door. He prepared himself to settle down once more when he saw the lights flood on in Rosie's apartment. Curious now and alert he sat up in his seat and watched. It appeared to be the woman who had just driven in. Was that Rosie's mother or aunt? No worries, whoever it was, was going to lead him to Rosie. That much was clear.

A tingle of excitement prickled down his spine and he was rewarded with the sight of Rosie's apartment lights being extinguished. The woman, whoever she was, emerged carrying a bag and laptop computer. She closed her boot firmly and reversed down the drive and into the road. Mary didn't hear the stalker's engine start nor did she see the car gently roll out from its parking place and follow at a discrete distance.

*

Tony was becoming agitated and confused. He wasn't thinking clearly. He knew there was a reason why he didn't want to return home but he seemed to have blocked it from his mind. In his confusion he stumbled from the shelter where Kirsty said she'd pick him up and wandered back down the road to the house where he'd seen the young reporter enter. He watched for a moment from behind the safety of a large beech tree in the leafy lined avenue. No one saw him. No one took any notice. He saw Mary returning with the car and retrieving items from the boot before going into the house. He saw another car slow at the driveway and took note of the type, model and number. He didn't know why, he just did. He watched the man at the wheel scrutinising the driveway before proceeding down Gilhurst

Road and parking in a side road. Tony watched the man, who carried a camera bag on his shoulder, venture nearer and he was filled with an unaccountable spreading fear. Tony slid down the trunk of the tree on to the grass trying to make himself as small as possible and waited.

*

"Rosie! Rosie! I've brought your things. Hope they're what you wanted. You make yourself comfortable and unpack. Take Cally's room. You know where everything is," Mary called out as she went to get her shopping bags from the kitchen.

"Right you are. Thank you." Rosie came in from the kitchen. "I've just been enjoying the view. Great garden!"

"I have to pop out for half an hour. Will you be okay? I need to get some bits and pieces for tonight. You can come with me if you like?" Mary saw the alarm register on Rosie's face. "Perhaps not. It's best you sit tight. I won't be long, I promise. Lock all the doors. Maddie is going to let us know as soon as Greg gets the message. He'll be on to it straight away, I know. Don't worry, we'll find out about Linda. I promise."

Rosie gave a feeble half smile, "Am I paranoid or what?"

"Quite understandable, I'd say," reassured Mary. "Would you rather I didn't go?"

"No, no. I'll be fine. Anyway the quicker you go..."

"The quicker I'll be back," finished Mary.

"Here, you take my phone... just in case... I couldn't bear it if he rang me again and if there's an emergency, I can ring you..."

"All right. I'm not very good with modern technology. As long as it's not too complicated."

"No. It's an easy to manage Nokia."

Mary hugged Rosie and took the phone. She grabbed her shopping bags and left. Rosie turned the dead bolt and put the chain on and checked the rest of the house. She didn't realise how important this was to prove.

Mary reversed the car from out of the drive not realising she was being watched by two people.

Rosie's stalker was oblivious to the fact that he was being

observed by Tony. He waited until the car had disappeared from view and sprinted across the road. It was daylight and he didn't seem to care. His confidence was making him careless.

Tony watched as he saw the man peer in through the downstairs' windows facing the gravel drive. He saw him try the door then rummage in his bag. He pulled out a black wallet, which he unrolled and then, selected the correct tool for the job. He made his way to the back gate, pulled at the wheelie bin and clambered on top and shinned over the gate, out of sight.

Strange things were happening in Tony's mind. The blood was rushing through his temples with such force that his veins pulsed. He knew this wasn't right. He knew there was something wrong and he felt strongly that the girl reporter was in danger. He pulled himself out of his stupor and crossed over the road just as Kirsty Beck and Gary Watson turned into Gilhurst road.

"Isn't that Tony, over there?" Kirsty pointed at the figure crossing the road and disappearing into a driveway. Gary put his foot down and screeched to a halt outside the house.

"Isn't this where the chief lives?" questioned Gary. "What's going on?"

Kirsty was afraid to even think. "Call for back-up. I'm going in." Kirsty crossed the road and walked up the gravel drive. There was no one to be seen. Her stomach was churning as if it was filled with boxing kangaroos. She was in turmoil and terrified of what she would discover. She heard running crunching steps behind her as Gary joined her.

"Help's on the way. What's the plan?"

"I'm going round the back. You ring the front door..." Kirsty didn't finish, as there was a shout and sounds of a scuffle from behind the back door. Kirsty and Gary needed no second bidding. They raced to the gate, now ajar, and fully opened it, revealing Tony and another man in a tussle.

"Stop! Police!" shouted Gary officially. Tony stopped and looked across. He was immediately slugged in the jaw by the other man. Tony fell backwards. His assailant ran around the

161

garden scrambled through the hedge and out through the garden which backed on to the house with Gary in hot pursuit.

Kirsty ran to Tony's side. "Tony! Tony! Are you all right?" she called. Tony groaned, tried to sit up and rubbed his jaw.

At that moment the back door opened and Rosie looked out.

"What's going on?" She paused when she saw Tony getting to his feet. "You!"

"I'm afraid we'll have to take you in for questioning, Tony," asserted Kirsty.

"But why? I've done nothing wrong. I was only trying to help," Tony explained.

Kirsty Beck ushered Tony to his feet and propelled him towards the waiting car.

"We'll need a statement from you, Miss...."

"Partridge. Rosie Partridge."

"I'll send someone out." She nodded her head and as she walked to the front drive, sirens were heard in Gilhurst Road. Allison and Stringer arrived in one car with Pooley and Taylor close behind. It was to this chaotic scene that Mary Allison arrived back at the house as Gary Watson came running back his face flushed and out of puff.

"I lost him," he wheezed. "Sorry."

"Did you get a good look at him?"

Gary shook his head, "Not really, only from the back."

Allison interrupted, "There's a lot of questions to be answered. I'll see you back at the station but first I want a word with Rosie."

"Sir." Gary Watson joined Kirsty Beck in the car, with Tony in the rear seat and they headed off for Steelhouse Lane Police station. Allison watched them go, his face grim.

Rosie knew something serious had happened, "Linda...!" She faltered and stopped. Her hand flew to her throat.

"Sorry, Rosie. Let's go in."

Greg Allison's lumbering frame filled the door and Mark Stringer was touched to see the Chief comforting Rosie as if she was his own daughter. Mary followed. She knew better than to ask questions. So, she busied herself in the kitchen unpacking the shopping and making some welcome cups of tea.

"Tell me... about Linda. She's hurt isn't she?"

The chief swallowed hard. He found it difficult to speak.

"She's not dead... is she? Popsie....?" pressed Rosie.

The look on Allison's face was enough. He needed no words.

"No. No. Say it's not true," insisted Rosie.

Allison cleared his throat and his usual gravel tones turned husky. "This afternoon, in the bath...."

"Was it an accident?"

The silence she received told her the awful truth before he spoke again. "No. Murder. I'm so sorry."

"It's all my fault. If I hadn't gone to stay she wouldn't have been in danger. She'd still be alive."

"We don't know that. It may have been an opportunist crime. We can't jump to conclusions. Let the Met finish their investigations. Then we'll see."

Mary entered with a tray of tea things and set them down.

"Now, what I want to know," continued Allison, "is what happened here."

Mary sat down. She wanted to know, too.

*

Back at the station Tony was in interview room 201.

"I've told you I don't remember. I was confused. It was as if I was in a fugue. When I started to come to, I rang Kirsty. She said she'd fetch me."

"Yes. But how did you end up in Gilhurst Road?"

"I don't know... I...."

"A taxi driver says he picked up a man matching your description from Birmingham New Street... The station."

"Possibly..."

"You asked him to follow a car. A Peugeot."

Tony rubbed his chin, his eyes held the look of a hunted animal. I don't know... Everything's mixed up..."

"Okay..." Pooley tried another tack. "What happened in Gilhurst Road?"

"When I came to, I rang Kirsty. I remember walking back

163

towards the house and there was something about a reporter in my mind. That's when I saw the car."

"Tell me what happened."

"I don't know. It cruised past the house really slowly and the driver stopped to look at it. He then moved on and parked in a side road."

"What about the car? Can you tell me anything about the colour or make?"

"Volkswagen, one of those new style Beetles, silver grey"

"Anything else?"

"Yes 2001 reg."

"Can you remember the number?"

"WC 51 LEX"

"You're sure?"

"Positive. I'm good with numbers. I thought it was odd someone should pick a public convenience for a number plate."

"Public convenience?"

"WC."

"I see. What happened next?"

"I saw him make his way back to the house. He had a bag on his shoulder..."

"What sort of bag?"

"Like a camera bag. One of those smart, flash ones."

"Okay, Tony. Then what?"

"He ran up the drive, looked in the windows and tried the front door then he took something out of his bag, hopped over the back gate using a wheelie bin. I knew that reporter was in the house alone and I just felt something was wrong."

"So you went after him?"

"That's when you came along and he socked me on the jaw."

"Did you get a good look at him?"

"He had a hood pulled up on his anorak, but I'd know him again. Wears that strong after-shave. Aramis. Dark crinkly hair, about five foot ten. A really lean face. I suppose you'd describe it as saturnine."

"Good. Look I'll leave you with Taylor here. I'm going to check out your number plate and see if your description tallies with Watson. Can I get you anything? Cup of tea or something?"

"That'd be good. Could I see Kirsty?"

"I'll see what I can do."

Pooley left the desk and opened the door. He did so just as Holly and Colin came walking down the corridor. Holly glanced through the glass and stopped. Colin nearly bumped into her.

"What's the matter? What's going on?"

Holly's eyes stretched wider. The breath constricted in her throat. My God. It's him."

"Who?"

"Tony...Tony Clifton, my... my... father." She pressed her hands against the glass and at that moment Tony turned around and their eyes met. Recognition dawned in those troubled dark eyes and he half rose from his seat. Taylor immediately instructed him to sit back down but not before Tony had mouthed the word, Gillian. Holly turned away, her face pale with shock, and ran down the remaining stretch of corridor straight into the arms of Greg Allison.

"Holly? What's wrong?"

"I have to get out of here...."

"Wait please..."

Colin interjected. "She's just seen Clifton. He recognised her. How I don't know?"

"Maybe this psychic thing goes deeper than you think. Holly, please. We need to talk. Come to my office."

By now Holly was convulsed in shuddering sobs and had no energy to resist. She allowed herself to be comforted by Allison and was ushered to the safety of the lift and his office.

Stringer was bemused. Greg as comforter and counsellor was a rare role for him to play. The gruff bear had much more of a soft side than he'd originally thought.

Allison sat Holly in a chair and instructed Maddie to brew some tea for them all while Colin brought the chief up to spec on everything that had happened including the boys' interrogation.

"Grace Clifton."

"What about her?"

"Can Holly get any sort of a fix on her?"

"Not at the moment, I shouldn't think. She's too upset," said Colin.

Holly nodded in agreement, "Sorry, Mr. Allison. I can't concentrate. My mind is racing."

Allison was clearly disappointed, "Fair enough." He paused, "Look would you mind waiting? Mark, here, will look after you. You never know, given time you may calm down. There's something I want to check out."

Holly turned her huge doe like eyes on Allison and attempted a smile, "Okay. I'll wait... You never know," she added quietly.

The chief left his office and lumbered towards the lift and went down into the corridor where Clifton was being interviewed. Pooley and Kirsty Beck were outside the interrogation room in deep discussion.

"Now you must see that there is something seriously wrong with him," Pooley was saying.

"I'll agree he's got problems, but you don't know him like I do. He's funny, gentle and kind. He needs help, not locking up and if it wasn't for him I think young Rosie Partridge would be in one hell of a mess," countered Beck.

"What's all this?" demanded Allison.

"Sir." Pooley straightened up and addressed the chief. "Beck is right that something was going down at Gilhurst Road and Tony intervened, but what was he doing there in the first place and what were his intentions to that reporter?"

Kirsty Beck rolled her eyes and was just about to retort when Allison stopped her. "Pooley's right. I'm going to find out and you, Miss Beck, I think it's better you are taken off this case."

"But sir, I've got his confidence. He trusts me."

"That's all very well and good, but useless if you've become enamoured with the man."

"Please, Sir. Let's just see if his story checks out."

Allison was not used to having his authority questioned. He put his hand on the doorknob of the interview room and turned to them. "I'll have no discussion on this. I'll speak to you both, later," and he entered the room.

*

Holly was beginning to feel a little calmer and was managing to drink her tea. Maddie popped her head around the door. "Mark. The Met's on the phone. Someone from Forensic."

"I'll take it." Mark answered and jotted down some notes. He had no sooner replaced the receiver and it rang again. This news was to prove even more exciting.

"Sorry. I'll have to leave you a moment. You'll be all right?"

Holly nodded and Colin replied, "Fine. We'll wait."

Mark left the office and Colin wandered to the window and peered out at the view, which had always engaged Allison.

Holly sat up straight her eyes clear once more. "He's in the building."

"Who?"

"Tough Nut. He's been released from hospital. He's scared the boys are going to talk. He's come to get them."

"Then he's a bit late. Anything else?"

"He's definitely the one who threw Ajay into the canal."

"We have to alert someone. Hang on." Colin swiftly left the chief's office and spoke with Maddie who picked up the phone and put him through to the office downstairs.

While he was gone, Holly felt a strange tranquillity possess her. She knew exactly what had happened and sympathised with young Ghita. Now she was in a dilemma. Did she reveal her knowledge to the police or keep quiet? Tough Nut had, had his just desserts. Was there any point in ruining a young girl's life? She had done as the police asked and given them the information they needed about Ajay. They hadn't asked for anything else. Holly fought a mental battle with herself. What was the right thing to do?

*

Allison was flummoxed. It certainly seemed that Tony had indeed acted out of concern, almost heroically. But he still couldn't get any satisfaction on why Tony was there in

167

the first place. It would have been easy to paint Tony as the stalker but that wasn't his style and anyway he had alibis for many of the times that Rosie had been harassed. So Allison was no further forward. There was a knock on the interrogation room's door and Mark Stringer entered. He whispered something to the chief who stood up and announced.

"Thank you Mr. Clifton. You're free to go."

Tony stood up hesitantly and made his way to the door. He was free to go home. But there was something about the thought of returning to Golden Hillock Road, which filled him with despair. Nevertheless he left the office and ventured out into the street and breathed in the traffic-fumed air with a sense of unnatural calm. Kirsty Beck ran after him to the pavement.

"Tony!"

He stopped and turned. Relief flooded him when he saw her. "Kirsty."

"I'm sorry, Tony, I'm not supposed to be talking to you, but I couldn't let you go without..." she stopped.

Tony pulled her into him and kissed her passionately. She was stunned but found herself responding all too easily. She broke away, "We have to talk. Where can we meet?"

"I have to get into work. I hope the police are going to square things with Dempseys or I could be out of a job."

"I'll do that. What about after work? I'll come to your house."

"No! Yates' Wine Lodge. Meet you at 6:30."

"I may be a little late. Hold on for me. I will be there."

Tony nodded, and turned back up the pavement in the direction of Corporation Street. Kirsty watched him go and Pooley watched Kirsty, shaking his head in disbelief.

*

"What are the facts?" asked Allison gruffly.

"The car registration number given us by Clifton belongs to Wendy Montague." exclaimed Mark.

"Who the hell's she?"

"This is where it gets interesting. Wendy Montague, middle name Christine..."

"WC."

"Yes, wife of Lex Montague."

"Photographer with the Post," affirmed Allison. "Didn't know he was married."

"No one did. But there's more," teased Mark, obviously savouring the moment, "She's in a nursing home. Some sort of incident which left her brain damaged."

"Incident?"

"After she split up from Lex, they never divorced, she was stalked and attacked."

"Why didn't we know anything about this?"

"It happened in Reading. A place called Shinfield where they used to live and here's the best part."

"Go on," prompted Allison allowing his sergeant to indulge himself.

"Guess what colour hair she's got?"

"Like Rosie's?"

"Like Rosie's." Mark confirmed. "Have we got enough to pick him up?"

"I think so because Clifton's description of his assailant closely fits...."

"Lex Montague."

"We need to know where he was today and if he travelled to London. If his DNA tallies with that imprint on Rosie's forehead. We should have enough."

"We may have even more. While you were with Clifton the Met rang. Scene of crime reported traces of semen on the bath mat in Linda's bathroom and denim fibres."

"He ejaculated in his pants?"

"He shot his cocoa plenty enough to leave a smear. That's all we need."

"Get a warrant and pick him up."

12
The night has a thousand eyes

Lex Montague was shaking. That was close, really close. Where the hell had that guy come from? He was convinced he recognised him. Someone he'd read about or done an article on. The name and story escaped him. He needed to check his files. What if the man had given out a description of him? They'd soon put two and two together.

Lex started looking through his computer files. He scrolled through news story after news story. Bingo! There he was. Well, well, well! Lex had the perfect answer now. The fellow he tussled with was none other than Tony Clifton, convicted serial killer, who'd had his sentence quashed. It would be easy enough to turn the tables on this Tony character but what reason could he give for running off? That's of course, if they tracked him down. Lex knew he had work to do. He needed to be prepared.

He carefully deleted all his computer files containing pictures of Rosie. He went to his darkroom and started gathering the evidence from off his wall, his shrine to Rosie; all the photos he'd taken over the past few months. He ripped them off his walls and stuffed them into one of his trays and took a bottle of sulphuric acid and poured them over her image. The fumes snaked up and Lex felt surprisingly good about their destruction. It was almost therapeutic.

The doorbell rang.

*

Mrs. Clifton was concerned, really concerned. She hadn't seen Tony since he'd left the house in a panic and she blamed herself for that, surprising him in that way. It must have been a shock. But now she needed to get him back, get a message to him. But how?

His direct line at work, maybe she'd give him a ring. What could she say if he wasn't there? No matter, she'd cross that bridge when she came to it. She picked up his phone book and the page fell open at Kirsty Beck. That name again, who was this woman. Grace was never faint hearted and she was cunning. She lifted the receiver and dialled 141 followed by Kirsty's phone number. The answer phone kicked in and the lilting Dublin tones sang out a message.

"Hi! You've reached Kirsty's home line. If you're hearing this message, I must be out, busy or I don't want to talk to you. No, not really, why not try me on the mobile. If you can't face that then leave me a message and I'll get back to you. Honest. Here comes the beep."

The voice was remarkably similar to Connie, the nurse from the hospital. She sounded nice. But Grace dismissed that thought. Anyone who tempted her boy couldn't be good. So, she'd got a mobile phone had she? Grace would look through the book again until she could find the number. Grace furrowed her beetle brows and turned the page again. There it was, Kirsty, mobile. With shaking hands Grace dialled prefacing it with 141.

Kirsty's phone rang she looked at the screen which said 'Private Number'. She answered, "Hello?"

A reedy voice assailed her ears, "Congratulations you have won a prize in our post code draw. Please confirm your post code for a chance of winning a superb weekend break for two."

Unthinkingly Kirsty answered, "B31 2EP."

"Thank you. You will receive a letter shortly. Be sure to follow the instructions and claim your prize." Grace quickly curtailed the call. The rest would be easy. She picked up the postal address book and fingered through it. B31 she already knew was Northfield. She traced her nail through the street names in Northfield until she found one that matched. Norman Road, this was just too easy for words. She moved on then to the telephone directory. Beck, initial K, Norman Road, Northfield. There it was. The telephone number was the same and now she had the precise address where Kirsty lived. She scribbled it on a message pad and tore out the page then went to make herself a cup of tea. She must work out what exactly she was going to do.

*

Lex Montague opened the door, "Yes, can I help you?"

"Mr. Lex Montague?"

Lex nodded.

"We have a warrant for your arrest and a search warrant for these premises."

Pooley and Taylor took Montague off in a squad car. Allison, Stringer and team proceeded to search the house.

Watson entered the darkroom and switched on the lights. He saw the line with pegs, empty of prints, saw the blue-tac covered wall devoid of pictures, noted the remnants of photos in the tray, which by now were completely unrecognisable and so turned his attention to the filing cabinet. He ploughed through the files. There was nothing of any note. But when he came to the third drawer, something was wedged in the back. He removed the drawer and tugged at the envelope and opened it. It was stuffed with an assortment of photographs ranging from children's parties to events hosted by the mayor and mayoress of Birmingham. Disappointed he replaced it but as he was closing the drawer something caught his eye. A couple of pictures had obviously fallen off the wall and fluttered down behind the filing cabinet. Gary grabbed a ruler and poked at them until he could get a grip and wrested them from their space. He whistled lightly under his breath. The chief would have to see this.

"Sir, Mr. Allison, Sir!" he called.

Allison peered into the red gloom, "What is it?"

"Take a look at these."

They were two photos of Rosie. One was grainy, obviously taken from outside at night with an infrared zoom lens. It showed Rosie wrapped in a towel drying her hair. The other was of Rosie, in her kitchen sipping a mug of tea. Again, it was clear that the picture had been taken without her knowledge.

"Bag it," ordered Allison. "And while you're about it have someone take away his computer. Who knows what that might reveal? The digital camera too, and memory cards."

"Sir."

"Good job Watson, well done."

Watson blushed with pleasure. It wasn't often the chief dished out praise.

Grace Clifton peered at herself in the mirror. A little Indian lady stared back at her. She looked the part. Now, how was she to get out without being noticed? That was the next problem. She could hear that the Singhs were in. The dog was yapping and one of the children, or someone, was playing some Bollywood type music, too loudly. She couldn't risk going out of the front door. She was more likely to be spotted especially, if there was any surveillance covering the house although she thought it unlikely. The dog was yapping inside and therefore not prowling about in the garden so now was a good opportunity. Besides, she needed to collect her bag from the shed. Grace scrawled a note to her son. She signed it 'Fluffy'. He would know who it was from and no one else would be any the wiser. Grace chose her moment and slipped out of the back, collected her bag and disappeared over the compost heap into the back alley.

*

Yates' Wine Lodge was smoky, and busy. Kirsty ventured inside; glad she had been able to change into her street clothes. She searched the bar for Tony and was pleased to see him in the corner. He had a drink waiting for her. She moved swiftly towards him, banging the arm of a longhaired drunk who was carrying a full glass of cider and teetering towards a seat. The man cursed her and began to make a fuss about his spilt drink. Tony pushed his way towards them and rescued Kirsty. He stuffed a fiver in the man's hand, apologised and told him to buy another drink. The chap was more than happy with this and Kirsty and Tony were able to safely get to their seats without further ado.

"Thanks for squaring things with my boss," said Tony.

"That's okay. Can't have you losing your job or having your pay docked when you were helping us out. Have you thought anymore about why you were there? You can see why it looked so suspicious, can't you?"

"I don't know. It's all a bit of a haze. I've got lots of images in my mind but to be truthful I don't know what's true and what's imagination."

"Try telling me. It may help you focus, work things out."

So, Tony tried to piece together his memories and sort out what was missing.

The drunk was now so far gone he started to sing in that uncontrolled way where words slid into each other and notes wandered up and down the scale. Kirsty saw the barman come over to remonstrate with the man and ask him to leave. The drunk reluctantly swayed to his feet. He reached in his pocket and pulled out an old fashioned woollen hat like a tea cosy and shoved his hair underneath it as he placed it on his head. As Tony watched him his memory came flooding back and he remembered the cause of his alarm and flight.

"My mother!"

"What?"

"My mother. She was at the house."

"Are you sure?"

"Positive. I thought I was going mad. I remember smelling baking. She'd repaired the lights around the cross in the hall and when I went in the kitchen she was there complaining that we'd got no Jaffa Cakes. She's at the house. I know she is."

"Great! I'll have to report it." Kirsty took out her mobile phone, "Damn! No reception. Hang on while I call it in. I won't be long." Kirsty rose up from her seat and went outside to call the station. She managed to get a message through and returned to the bar but when she got there Tony had gone.

*

Allison sat facing Holly. He asked again, "I know it's hard but can you get a fix on Grace Clifton?"

Holly struggled to bring the images in her head into focus. "She's back in Birmingham. I'm sure of it. I see her with an old wooden cross."

"Where? A church? Graveyard?"

"No. She's mending lights. Putting them on a wall around the cross. It feels like a house..."

"Well, I'll be... You know what she's done? She's gone home. Golden Hillock Road. Get someone round there now," asserted Allison just as the phone rang. "Yes? ...I see ....Thank you." Allison looked at her. "Holly, you're right. That was Kirsty Beck. Tony fled the house because his mother was there. That's why he was in such a confused state. The only thing is, Kirsty's lost Tony. Come on."

Allison left the office followed by Stringer. Picking up Grace Clifton was going to be a great pleasure. Colin congratulated Holly, "Damn it girl, you're good."

Holly smiled. "The sooner she's back behind bars the happier I'll be. Can we go now? Or is there something else?"

"Not unless there's something you're not telling me."

Holly blushed.

"There is, isn't there? What is it Holly? Come on."

"And if I tell you, will it be part of a patient counsellor privilege?"

"Why? What do you know?"

"Not until you tell me it's just between us."

Colin gave in, "Okay. Now give."

Holly revealed what she knew about the firebomb incident outside Darleston's.

"I see. I understand. Let's get you home. We'll discuss it on the way."

They travelled down in the lift and left the building; unaware of the fact that Tony was standing outside the main gates of the General Hospital waiting.

Colin and Holly made their way towards Colin's car and prepared to move off. Tony dashed across the road towards them to catch them, stop them, anything. He needed to talk to Holly and in his anxiety to do this he was blind to an approaching car, which hit him and tossed him over the bonnet. Several other vehicles skidded to a halt. Holly screamed and she and Colin jumped out of the car and ran to the roadside where Tony was lying. Soon there was a throng of people, either anxious to help or just plain curious surrounding Tony's still form. Doctors and paramedics from the A&E ran out of the hospital to tend to his injuries and rush him inside but not before Holly had raced to him. Tony's eyelids fluttered open and seeing Holly he smiled. She could see how handsome he was and where she had inherited some of her own good looks. He took her hand and whispered, "I'm sorry, so sorry," and lapsed into unconsciousness.

The doctors moved her aside and ferried him in through the doors of the General Hospital. Much to Colin's amazement Holly shouted, "Wait! I'm his daughter." An intern acknowledged her and beckoned her to follow. She did.

*

The curtains twitched next door to Grace Clifton's house. Lehmber and his wife Harpal watched intently as two cars with lights blazing drew up. They pounded up the path and hammered on the door. "Police. Open up or we'll be forced to break in."

Nothing. Allison gave the signal and two coppers rammed the door, splintering the wood and breaking the lock. They burst in and searched the premises.

"She's not here, Gov," called one of the men.

"Double check," growled Allison, "and look out the back."

The police looked in the garden, the shed, over the wall to the alley. Nothing. Allison mounted the stairs. He entered Tony's room and saw a note on the pillow.

"Dear Tony,

Sorry to have shocked you like that. I didn't mean to. No wonder you fled but I'm going to make everything all right again I promise. God is watching over us and he has told me what I need to do. I'm going help cleanse you by removing all temptation. When that's done I'll be in touch again. I've thought of a way we can be together forever.

Love

Fluffy."

"What's it mean, Sir? Who's Fluffy?"

"I seem to remember something about one of the earlier victims having a cat, called Fluffy. Didn't that trigger something in Tony's mind?"

"Natalie Blakeney," offered Stringer whose memory for names was always better than Allison's. "Rebecca Mills said it was Tony's father's pet name for Grace."

"That's right. Let's get back. This door must be patched up. Don't want accusations of negligence. Leave someone on duty in case she returns. Not too obvious, eh? We've got to try and figure this out. P'raps Holly can help."

176

"If she's still at the station."

"Ring through and find out."

Mark dutifully did as he was ordered. He came off the phone his face grim.

"What's the matter?"

"It's Tony Clifton. He's in hospital."

"What?" growled Allison in disbelief. As he made for the front door, Mark relayed what he knew but was stopped dead in his tracks by the chief pausing at the hall phone. Allison stared at the open pad with a page ripped out and the private address book open at Kirsty Beck's number. "I know where she's gone. It all makes sense now."

"Where? What?" exclaimed Mark helplessly.

"Grace Clifton. She's after Kirsty. That's what she meant by 'removing temptation'. Get on to Personnel. We need Kirsty's home address. If we plan it right, we may just surprise the woman."

*

Grace Clifton was waiting patiently for a bus in Navigation Street. She avoided the eyes of passer-bys. It was easy to get around in her disguise. No one gave her a second look. She checked in her Birmingham A-Z. She had to be sure where to alight. She didn't want to attract attention to herself by asking for the nearest bus stop. She replaced the book in her roomy handbag. It nestled comfortably on top of the kitchen knife hidden at the bottom.

She swivelled her head around to check the number of the approaching bus. This was it. This was the one she wanted. She pulled out her purse as it stopped and the doors folded open. Once the throng of passengers had vacated she took a deep breath and gave the driver a broad smile as she stepped onto the platform and paid her fare. With no one else in the queue she had her pick of seats and selected one at the back where she could watch the road signs and follow the map. There was no one to watch her, no one to see. In fact things were perfect. She even allowed herself to hum a little of one of her favourite hymns. After all, no one was there to listen.

*

Holly waited with Colin in the relatives' room until the doctor came through. His face was grave.

"He's not too good I'm afraid. He's sustained severe internal injuries. We've tried to halt the bleeding. We're doing all we can."

"Can I see him?"

"Normally, I'd say no, but he's asking for you and someone called, Kirsty. Follow me."

Holly gave Colin a quick hug, "Wish me luck."

"You don't have to do this you know."

"I know, but somehow I feel it's right."

She moved swiftly after the doctor, through the corridor to the Intensive Care Unit.

Tony was a mass of wires and tubes. His face was pale. Holly entered uncertainly, not at all sure what to say or what to do. Eventually she grabbed a seat and drew it alongside his bed. She tentatively reached for his hand. As she did a flood of images scurried through her mind. She shuddered and Tony's eyes fluttered open.

"Gillian," he said dryly, "You came."

Holly merely nodded.

"I wasn't any good for you or your mother. But I always loved you. We used to play a special game. I don't expect you'd remember..."

"We'd rub noses and say pobble." Holly was merely repeating what her maternal grandmother, Hilda Fisher, had told her but Tony's eyes filled with tears.

"I thought you'd have forgotten that." He smiled gently and Holly felt his years of torment and suffering. She knew he'd killed in a brutal, pitiless fashion. She also knew he was not in his right mind when he committed the murders. That belonged to another side of him, another aspect of his personality developed to deal with the years of abuse he'd endured at the hands of his mother. Yes, he had done unspeakable things but he'd also tried to control the sadistic rages, which had controlled him. Holly felt that Tony's struggle with the dark side of his nature was improving. He was beginning to conquer it. In fact, she knew he'd attempted to help a woman reporter and stopped an attack.

Tony continued, "I've done a lot of bad things, really bad things. I don't even remember some of them. It wasn't me who...." He trailed off, "... But I was trying to get my head together. Trying to start again."

"I know, I know... Ssh! Don't talk." Holly could see he was making a monumental effort.

He attempted to lift himself up. "You must stay away from her. From my mother. She's evil. She blames you... she'll try to destroy you. I know where she is. She's at the house. She must be stopped..."

He flopped back on the bed exhausted by his efforts. "Your mother, Ellie was good and sweet and kind. I didn't deserve her. You're a lot like her, the same hair, the same huge dark eyes. I pray to God you have more of your mother in you than me."

Holly squeezed his hand; tears were now raining down her cheeks. "You started to do the right thing, helping that woman."

"You know about that? The thing is I don't know if it started out like that... if that was my real intention..."

"But when the time came. You did the right thing. Now, you must rest. Get yourself well and ..."

"Will you come and see me again?"

Holly nodded, "I'll do my best." She released his hand and left the room. As she did she walked into Kirsty Beck who had just arrived.

"Is he in there?" asked Kirsty in her lilting Dublin tones.

"Yes, he'll be glad to see you... Kirsty? It is Kirsty isn't it?"

Kirsty stopped and affirmed, "Yes, it is. Why?"

"The doctor said he was asking for you. You're the reason he hasn't killed. And believe me he has killed. But you, you're the one who has the power to change all that but I don't think you'll get the chance."

Holly turned away and walked back to the relatives' waiting room to meet Colin who had now been joined by Paul. Paul wrapped her in his arms almost crushing her with a bear hug of love.

"How did it go?" he asked with his throaty resonance.

179

"All right. He's not all bad. He's not a complete monster but very sad and troubled."

"Are you going to see him again?"

"I think that decision will be taken out of my hands."

Holly released herself from Paul's grasp and walked away down the corridor. Colin and Paul looked at each other. They both knew that things were going to be tough for Holly. They started after her, but she called back, "No! I need to be alone. I'll see you in an hour. Raphael's in the Library Complex."

The two friends watched her walk away. They knew better than to follow her.

*

Kirsty Beck sat at Tony's side. His breathing was becoming more laboured. "Come on, Tony; you can hang on in there. I know it, so you can."

Tony opened his eyes and smiled at Kirsty, "Kirsty. I knew you'd come."

"Course I would. You know that. Now, what trouble have you been getting into now?"

"I don't know. I don't remember it all...."

"I read the report. You did good, so you did."

"Did I? Did I do something right?"

"Whatever reason took you to Gilhurst Road, it was meant to be. If you hadn't been there; if you hadn't tried to stop him, then it may have been a very different story. You did okay, Tony Clifton. You did okay." Kirsty's voice became choked with emotion. She fought to stop the tears cascading down her cheeks. "Now, you just concentrate on getting well. That's the number one priority."

"You really think I did okay?"

"Positive. You're quite a hero really."

"See, I'm not all bad, not all of me." The equipment monitoring his heart let out an accelerated succession of bleeps and an alarm rang. Kirsty rose as medics rushed into the room with a Crash Team. She stood back in confusion and was cleared out of the way. All she could do was watch helplessly through the window at the fevered activity, which surrounded Tony, now in cardiac arrest. The persistent flat line monotone note went on and nothing the doctors did could jump-start the heart back to life.

Kirsty watched with sadness, her face and hands pressed against the window. She saw the doctor remove his stethoscope from his ears and signal to the team with a shake of his head that the battle was lost. She was hardly aware of crying out in anger or of the arms, which went, around her propelling her away from the area. It was as if her bones had been sucked dry and her heart cut from her body. She needed to be alone, to get away, to get home. And with that thought in mind she left the ward, drifted out of the hospital and into the street.

*

Mrs. Clifton had studied the map well. She knew exactly where she was going. She stepped off the bus and scurried down the pavement, past a hotel, a parade of shops and turned a corner. She proceeded along the avenue and took the first left. There was a small Spar shop next to a garage and pub. She was about to trot by when she picked up the sound of police sirens heading in her direction. Ever cautious, she hurried into the Spar shop and immediately became engrossed in the newspaper and magazine stand, which enabled her to look out of the window to the street outside. She saw three cars zoom past in quick succession. Now, was it just a coincidence or was it something more menacing? She peeped out of the door and watched them turn round the next corner. She left the shop and carried on with her journey, ever watchful and careful. She turned the corner and took the next right. As she entered Norman Road she saw the cars' lights flashing outside the house where she felt Kirsty Beck lived.

Grace spat angrily onto the dusty road and stepped back the way she had come. Why were they here? What had happened? Did they know? No, that was impossible. All the same she needed to be prepared. She back tracked towards the pub and walked through the saloon bar and out to the ladies toilets. She slipped into a cubicle, sat on the seat and rummaged in her bag, pulling out her Bible. It fell open at Proverbs and her eyes lit on the lines,

"Come let us lie in wait for blood,
Let us ambush the innocent;
We shall fill our house with spoil" -
My son, hold back your foot from their paths.
For in vain is a net spread in the sight of any bird;
But these men set an ambush for their own lives..."

She had read enough. The Lord had warned her. It was a trap. A trap for her but she would not be caught. She was too cunning for that. She closed the book firmly and replaced it in her bag and was suddenly filled with an inexplicable melancholy. Something was wrong, seriously wrong. It was something to do with Tony, of that she was sure. She needed to get home. Kirsty Beck could wait; wait until there were no eyes watching and she would be free to wield the blade of justice. She was no fool. It wasn't safe here. They would be looking for her. Did they also know about her disguise? She couldn't be certain but that police inspector was a wily old goat. He may suspect something. He just may have put two and two together. After all, she did leave the house in Worcester in somewhat of a rush. Time for a change, perhaps? But to what? Grace was uncertain about leaving the pub by the front door. She hurried out of the back door into the beer garden, out of the side door and into the alley, which backed on to the parade of shops. She peered at the backs of them and smiled. This would do nicely, very nicely indeed.

First of all, she took out her compact and removed the red spot from her forehead. Then she took off the dark greased wig and tossed it in the bin outside the back gate of the hairdressers. She looked odd now, tanned skin, badly permed pepper and salt hair, and dressed in a sari. But that would soon change. She pulled out her plastic mac from its zip purse and unrolled it. She hitched up her sari and covered herself in the navy mac. Now she looked reasonably like any other elderly shopper. Grace scuttled down the alley to the front of the shops and entered a small, but select, ladies boutique. There were no price tags on the clothes in the window. That was always a bad sign but Grace felt instinctively that if she were going to survive then she would have to suffer the extra cost.

The shop bell rang and an elegant sales assistant in a black skirt and pristine white blouse asked if she could help.

"It's all right. I'm just looking," answered Mrs. Clifton as she headed for the sales rail.

She pulled out a cream, flower patterned suit with a pleated skirt and collarless button through jacket, an ivory lace dress and a more formal emerald linen suit in a classic style.

"Is it all right if I try these on?" she droned.

The sales woman nodded and gestured to the changing rooms.

Grace chose the suit with its rose pink flowers on a cream background. Not her usual style at all. The jacket hid her lumps and bumps, and the skirt fell softly in flattering pleats. She went back into the shop and picked up a rose pink silk trailing scarf, matching hat and gloves. She then selected a Quink blue lightweight wool coat, which she put over the outfit. Satisfied that she looked dramatically different from how she usually looked, she asked the Sales assistant, "How much for these?"

The Sales assistant checked the labels and added up the prices. "The suit is seventy pounds, the coat - one hundred and twenty, hat is thirty five, scarf fifteen and gloves ten. That's..." and she pressed the buttons on her calculator. "That's two hundred and fifty in total."

"I'll take them. Can you take the labels off I'd like to wear them now."

The assistant dutifully snipped off the tags and offered her a boutique bag for her own clothes.

"It's all right I can manage," asserted Grace stuffing her sari and plastic mac into the bag, trying not to let the woman see exactly what she had been wearing. Grace took out the credit card she'd taken from the old woman in the hospital. This was swiped. Grace signed and out she went. Phase one was completed. Next stop was the hairdressers two doors down, which advertised no appointment necessary.

When she came out two hours later it was doubtful that even Tony would have recognised her such was the dramatic change in her appearance.

Grace still carried a fake tan, but her hair had been feather cut and coloured. No longer that dark, frizzy, grey mix. Mrs. Clifton's hair was now fair with copper lights, it looked better than it had for years and the professionally applied make up, made her appear more respectable and upmarket. She purchased some high heels, which toned with her outfit and added two inches to her height. She was very pleased with result. Next stop, Windsor House Hotel where she ordered a room in her vinegar whine. The card was used again and Grace hoped she could continue to use it just a while longer. She settled into her room and switched on the television. There was a rerun of an old episode of 'Only Fools and Horses', which she settled down to watch while she waited for the comfort of the night. The night, which would mask her deeds and give her the cover she needed to fulfil her mission.

She'd be careful but she knew she'd be fine. The Lord was looking out for her.

*

Lex Montague sat in the station protesting his innocence. "For God's sake I work with Rosie. We're partners on some stories, why would I want to hurt her?"

"What were you doing in Gilhurst Road?"

"I've told you it's on my way home. I always travel that way into Lordswood Road then Lonsdale Road. It's quicker than going up the Hagley Road. The traffic flow's better."

"Why did you stop at number sixty six?"

"How many times do I have to go through this?"

"Tell me again. I just want to be certain I have all the facts right."

Lex sighed and rolled his eyes and began his story again. He'd retold it so many times that he was beginning to believe it himself. "I was coming home. I wanted to plan a follow up article on the Kumars, on little Ajay's death. The car was playing up. The engine was stuttering. I saw a man walking down the road from the bus shelter. He looked familiar and he was behaving oddly, shiftily as if he didn't want anyone to see him. It suddenly hit me that it was that fellow, Tony Clifton, the crooning killer who'd been had up for murder

184

and had his sentence quashed so I turned and parked in the next street, got out of the car and ran back to watch him. He looked about him. I ducked behind a tree and I saw him go up the drive. He tried the door and peered in the windows. It was obvious he didn't live there. Then he took something out of his pocket and clambered over the back gate. I went up to listen. I peered through a hole in the wood. He was trying to break in. I scrambled over the gate and tackled him. Next thing I know we're in the middle of a scrap. I heard more people coming. I didn't realise it was the police. I thought ... I don't know what I thought really... That it was his mates or something so I made a break for it. When I heard it was the police I got scared and kept running. I didn't really want to get involved. Look, I'm sorry I scarpered. I only did what I thought was right. Can I go now?"

"All in good time. We'll need to take a swab from your mouth. Check your DNA."

"What for?"

"If you're innocent as you say you are. You have nothing to fear."

"Don't you need a warrant for that?"

"Just waiting for it to arrive. Tell me, what are you doing with a rail ticket for London in your pocket?"

"That Tony character dropped it on the driveway. I picked it up. Why, what's the problem?"

"Can you tell me where you were on these dates and times?" Pooley passed Lex a list of dates, which coincided with, attacks and threats to Rosie.

"Can you?" retorted Lex. "I've told you I'd have to look at my diary. I can't remember. Don't expect you could either. I mean some of these dates were months ago."

"Are you into modelling, Mr. Montague?"

"Pardon?"

"Balsa wood. Do you like making models of things, boats, trains, coffins...?"

"Wait a minute..."

"Do you have a lipstick, Mr. Montague?"

"What's that got to do with anything?"

"Do you own a rat?" Pooley persisted.

185

"No, but I've got a cat, a tortoiseshell. She'll need feeding. Who's going to look after her?"

"Perhaps your wife could drop by?"

"Don't be ridiculous. What do you mean?"

"Wendy isn't it? Wendy Christine."

"I don't get it."

"You were driving her car. It's still registered in her name. After you split up she had a bit of a problem with a stalker, just like Rosie."

"Now, hold on a minute. I've got nothing to do with any of that."

"Any of what, Lex?"

"I'm saying no more till I see a lawyer."

"Fine. But I think we've got enough anyway."

The door opened and Taylor walked in with a warrant, plastic bags, gloves and a swab.

"Oh, well done. Okay, Mr. Montague. Open wide."

*

Holly sipped a vodka tonic loaded with ice. She sat opposite the entrance watching for Paul and Colin to arrive. Paul was first in. He peered around and waved when he saw her. She smiled and gestured him over while Colin went to the bar to get some drinks. He pushed his way through the thronging students from the local drama school, BSSD. They were a colourful lot. Normally, he'd be content to watch and observe them. He enjoyed listening to snippets of conversation and these students always had tantalisingly more interesting morsels than most members of the general public. He paid for his drinks and just picked up the words, "And then, of course, he got his sword stuck in the cat flap," which was followed by gales of laughter. How he wished he could follow that story through. Colin set a pint of Best in front of Paul. "No IPA. This do?"

Paul nodded and reached for the glass, he was suddenly very much in need of a drink. He took a gulp and looked expectantly at Holly. "Are you okay?"

"He's dead isn't he?"

"I don't know. Is he?" Paul looked at Colin.

"I'll check." He took out his mobile and rang the station.

Holly and Paul sipped their drinks in silence. Colin snapped it shut. "You're right. Half an hour ago."

"He wasn't a complete monster. He would have had more of a chance in life if he'd had a different mother."

"It must have been hard. Facing him like that," murmured Paul.

"Yes, but it wasn't as bad as I thought it would be. I understand so much more now. Things are much clearer. I know the real evil is Grace Clifton. The police have to get her before she kills again."

"They want your help with that," affirmed Colin.

"I know. I also know she has murder on her mind."

13
Revolution

Mrs. Clifton had settled into her room. She had intended to wait until dark but had needed to go out to purchase a few necessities. She needed to be comfortable while she waited for Kirsty Beck's return. On her last outing, she'd walked to the corner of Norman Road and noticed what she thought was an unmarked police car parked a few yards down on the opposite side of the street from Kirsty's house. It looked as if two undercover cops were keeping a look out. She had walked on and studied the houses whose gardens backed on to the ones in Norman Road. They seemed accessible enough as long as the fences weren't too high.

However, her observations were not as revealing as she thought. She had taken no notice of the workman's red striped tent over a manhole cover and the technician pretending to study telephone wires. She had taken no notice of the chap in the phone booth chatting away in an animated fashion to head quarters. But there again, neither had they noticed her, such was her transformation. They were looking for a small squat Asian lady, or someone who fitted Grace's usual description. They even kept their eyes open for a small portly gent with a toothbrush moustache; but a plump elegant woman in designer clothes didn't receive a second look. All she was missing were a couple of poodles on leads. That would certainly have completed the picture.

Grace returned to her hotel with her bag of toiletries, pencils and paper. She needed to make a plan and to wait until dark. She had made up her mind that running away to fight another day was the wrong thing to do. At least with God's advice, it seemed she must follow her instincts and eliminate her competition then she could return home. It would be easier then for her to plan her future, their future.

Grace decided that room service would be in order. It wouldn't do to eat in the main dining room, just to be on the safe side. If only she could get in touch with Tony. She'd had an uneasy feeling about him and needed to hear his voice. But what if Tony was at Kirsty Beck's place? That could cause problems. She swivelled her baleful eyes heavenward and muttered a short prayer. Oh, how she wished her abilities allowed her to see into Tony's mind but she always had difficulty reading those closest to her. Otherwise she would have stopped her husband's suicide and even prevented Tony from walking the path to damnation. She fervently prayed again,

"Oh Lord, guide my hand and heart that I may do thy will to bring righteousness where there is none and secure freedom from imprisonment."

She hoped room service would arrive soon. She was working up quite an appetite.

*

Allison rubbed his chin, "She may not have turned up as expected but I'm pretty certain she'll show. We have to keep Kirsty Beck's place staked out as unobtrusively as possible. And someone must warn her. Where is she?"

"She took Clifton's death pretty hard. I gave her the rest of the day off. I thought she'd go home," replied Pooley.

"Not the best place for her. She must be warned. I'd prefer to put a substitute in her place get her to a safe house. She's too emotionally involved."

"I'll call her. Let her know what's happening."

Greg nodded in agreement.

Pooley left the office and tried to ring the young WPC. Her mobile was switched off and he was urged to 'please try later.' He tried her home phone. Nothing. He suspected she had unplugged it. He reported back to Allison, "Can't get hold of her, Chief. Can't say I blame her. I don't think she wants to be disturbed."

"She still needs to be warned. Get the lads on surveillance to keep an eye out for her return home. We'll just have to risk one of them speaking to her."

"Sir." Pooley obediently left to carry out his instructions.

*

The dark fold of night wrapped itself around the street. Grace slipped out of the small hotel, by the back door, as unobtrusively as possible. She turned the corner of the houses, which backed onto Norman Road. Taking care to stay out of the lamplight and to walk in the shadows, Grace stepped quietly down a black tarmac drive and opened the back gate. Good, the house was in darkness. The occupants were either out or away. That made her job easier. She paused by the back fence and peered into Kirsty Beck's back yard. She looked up; a light was illuminating an upstairs room. A young woman walked past the unshaded windows, a towel wrapped around her head. So, the bitch was having a comfortable night in. Well, not for much longer, Grace just needed to wait a while longer until Ms. Beck had retired for the night and then... and then... Mrs. Clifton moistened her lips in anticipation and smothered a giggle. She tried desperately not to sing out aloud. But first, first she needed to get into the yard. She clambered on the compost bin and manoeuvred her bulk over the dilapidated wooden fence, swearing softly as she snagged her nylons as one of the fencing planks broke and splintered underneath her. She held her breath as the light went on, turned on in the landing and stairwell. A dog several doors down set up a chain reaction of barking through the line of houses in the street.

Grace pressed herself close against the crumbling brickwork and drew in her breath as the light went on downstairs. Now she could see! Now, she could see her opposition, quite a handsome woman, really, she thought begrudgingly. But wait, someone was with her, a man! Was it Tony? No, he was too tall for Tony. Maybe she'd got it wrong? Maybe, Kirsty wasn't her rival, or maybe this Kirsty was cheating on Tony? She struggled to overhear their voices. It was no good. She couldn't make out what they were saying but this Kirsty woman appeared to be crying. The man went into the kitchen and put the kettle on. It looked like he was staying. Now what? She couldn't face two of them. Her initial thoughts had been right. Time to go away and come back another day. Besides if Tony wasn't here he could be at home and then she could tell him of this woman's infidelity. Home! Grace felt the need to go home.

Throwing caution to the wind she scrambled back the way she'd come. She passed the Windsor Hotel. She could collect her things another day; after all she'd booked the room for a week.

*

Holly was trying to explain her feelings to Colin, "Look, Col, I know Ghita's responsible for the fire bomb outside Darleston's. But I haven't any proof and I'm not prepared to give the police a reason to search the kid's room to look for forensic evidence. In my mind justice has been done. The family has suffered enough. Damn it, those thugs killed her little brother."

"I must say, I agree; poetic justice, divine retribution, call it what you will. They deserved all they got," Paul concurred. "I think it's right to say nothing. Let the police find out for themselves."

"Yes, if they discover it in the course of their investigation then all well and good, but I'm not going to help them," added Holly.

"Of course, I can't force you to say anything," Colin groaned, "But check your conscience. Is saying nothing the right thing to do?"

"You can't say anything, either," said Holly forcefully. "What I have told you is in confidence, patient doctor privilege. You can't break that."

Colin was in a no win situation, "All right, all right. We'll leave it for now. But, I'm telling you now; I've not given up. Let's put it aside for the moment. I want you to turn your mind to your grandmother. The police need help in getting a fix on her. Can you do that?"

"I can try." Holly acquiesced. "Let's get home. I can't concentrate here. It's far too noisy."

"Sounds good to me, we can crack open a bottle of wine and prepare a snack," said Paul.

"Fine. I'll ring Marcie get her to join us." The three got up from the table, which was immediately occupied by a gang of students. As they walked through the complex Colin took out his mobile and began to dial.

*

Lex Montague was sitting uncomfortably under the scrutiny of DCI Allison and Mark Stringer.

"It's better for you if you come clean. It's no good denying it. We know, what you've done," growled Allison.

"We've got your photos of Rosie, photos you shouldn't have. And that neat little gadget, which alters your voice. Why would you need that in your camera bag? What's all that about?" pressed Mark.

"Someone's going through your locker at the Post as we speak. I'm sure that'll prove interesting. Why don't you save us all a lot of time and trouble and confess. The DNA evidence won't be long. I'm sure it'll match and then it'll be the worse for you."

There was a tap on the door and an officer handed Allison a sheet of paper.

"Well, what do you know? DNA is a perfect match. You're going down, Montague, for a very long time," and with that he terminated the interview and ordered Montague be taken away to the cells.

*

Grace had managed to find a mini cab office and had hired a taxi to take her to Small Heath. She was careful. She didn't go home to Spark Brook directly but made the cab drop her off by the park and once more she found herself trying to covertly enter her home via the back garden.

The Singh's house was in darkness except for the back sitting room. The children were obviously in bed and Lembher and Harpal must have settled down in front of the television for the night. Grace wondered if the dog was roaming the yard. But nothing moved, nothing stirred, so she assumed it must be safely in doors.

Her house was pitch black with no sign of life. Good, Tony wasn't home yet. He must be singing at one of the clubs. She would be able to get in and prepare. What a joyous reunion that would be. Then they could make their plans together.

She fiddled around with the back door lock and slipped in quietly. So far, so good. She closed the door quietly and went through to the parlour. There she gave thanks to God.

"Oh, Lord, thank you for all the blessings that you've heaped on my and Tony's head. I deliver myself into your hands to do with as you wish. Amen"

Fervently quoting the Scriptures, Grace set about lighting her favourite incense allowing its cleansing aroma to fill the room. She foraged in the sideboard cupboard and took out all the candles she could find. Tonight was special and she wanted the perfect atmosphere. Besides bright lights might attract attention. It was possible the police were still outside watching and waiting. But they wouldn't find her. The parlour was hidden from view and she knew God would make all blind to her activity as long as she was careful. She had God's protection, this she knew.

She covered every available surface in candles, of every colour and scent. They flickered brightly in the gloom and Grace prepared herself. She crept up the stairs and took off her expensive clothes. She rummaged through her dressing table drawers and pulled out a black lace nightdress with matching wrap. She donned the clothes of seduction and peered at herself in the mirror. She could just see in the dim light, which spilled in from the street lamp outside. Her eye make up still looked good and she was convinced her more fashionable hair made her more alluring. Smiling with pleasure she re-crimsoned those lips, which had remained naked for so long. Grace wanted to giggle, she wanted to sing but knew she had to show restraint.

She retraced her steps to the parlour and switched on the television for company. The volume was turned as high as she dared. Some variety programme was on with singing and dancing. She didn't care, Grace wanted to sing and dance and she did, softly, quietly so that no one next door would be disturbed. She felt sure things were going to be wonderful again.

The programme ended with a grand finale and parade of dancers, which neatly segued, into the late night news. Grace tiptoed out to the kitchen, made herself a cup of tea and returned to watch what was left of the news.

Grace watched how there were terror bombings in Israel and Palestine and she prayed fervently for peace in the

Middle East in between mouthfuls of muffins she'd made for Tony's return. The local Midland news came on and she was surprised to see a photo of Tony come up on screen. The food fell from her mouth as she stood up and moved closer to the television set to hear exactly what was said.

"News has just come in that the recently released Tony Clifton whose conviction for a number of slayings in Birmingham was discovered to be unsafe has died as the result of a road accident outside Steelhouse Lane Police Station earlier today. Julie Birchell reports."

Grace was uncertain whether she had heard correctly. She focused on the blonde reporter standing outside the police station detailing the facts, as they knew them.

"Nooo!" she shrieked, forgetting the Singhs were next door.

She listened to the details of the report, becoming more and more distraught. Her arms were flailing about and she tore at her clothes like a woman from a Greek chorus in an ancient tragedy. Her anguished yelps turned into the keening scream of a banshee and she fell back across the coffee table, the trailing taffeta threads of her negligee melted in strands as they made contact with the candle flames. Several candles rolled on to the floor where they spluttered and struggled to ignite the carpet and soft furnishings.

Mrs. Clifton danced the waltz of death with the devil as hell came to claim its own. She spun around the room like a whirling dervish frenziedly scattering imps of flames, which hissed and spat catching alight anything flammable that got in the way. Her skin blistered and burned as the fibres of her nightgown became molten and shrivelled onto her skin.

The old horsehair sofa had begun to smoke and soon what had been a smouldering glow developed into very real fire. The larger flames begat smaller ones and they began to spread in jigs of glee, rising and falling, engulfing everything, which came in their path.

The box of tiny scrolls, she had so carefully retrieved from the earlier debris puffed into ashes and Grace gave a mournful cry as her prophecy box began to turn to cinders. She cried and wailed and ran dementedly. The velveteen table cover gladly joined in the growing blaze. The benevolent picture of Christ became a hideous Halloween mask as the fire nibbled his nostrils and chin. The eyes, staring accusingly were the last to succumb and be eaten up by the sacrificial fire.

Poisonous fumes began to fill the room and choke her. She fled to the front room but the flames followed her like the Pied Piper.

*

"Lehmber, I can smell burning," said Harpal urgently, "And such a noise next door."

Lehmber put his hand against the wall, which adjoined the two properties. It was warm and getting hotter. The dog was snapping and barking as if warning them all of Armageddon. "Get the children and get outside. I'll call the fire brigade. Quick! Hurry. It's a fire."

Harpal rushed up the stairs and into Mohinder's room.

"Hurry! Hurry! Wake up!" she called as she shook her sleeping son. Mohinder stirred and turned over in his sleep. He had always been difficult to wake. She pulled the covers off the bed and pulled him up as Harjinder came into the room rubbing her eyes. "What's going on?"

"Quickly now, put something on your feet and a coat we have to get outside."

"Why? What's happening?" asked a drowsy Mohinder rubbing his eyes.

"Up you get and smartish."

"But I'm tired I want to sleep," he said lying down again and curling up in a foetal position.

"No! The house next door is on fire we have to get out!"

The children needed no second bidding and were immediately wide-awake. Mohinder scrambled into his dressing gown and slippers and ran down the stairs shouting for the dog. He met his father on the way up.

"Quickly now. The fire brigade and police are on their way."

"But what about my computer?" murmured Harjinder emerging from her room in her coat and school shoes, carrying an over stuffed bag of assorted odds and ends.

"Never mind that. We can always get another," shouted her father. "Hurry!"

Soon the family were outside and lights were beginning to go on in the street. The sound of a siren could be heard in the distance.

Smoke was pouring from the Clifton's house and the devilish orange glow of fire could be seen through the windows.

Harpal screamed as she saw a face at the glass. "It's Grace! She's inside! No, Lehmber! No!" she shrieked as her husband began to run up the path.

"I have to try and get her out. I can't leave her there to burn," he called as he tried the front door.

The heat from the brass knob burnt his hand and he jumped back as a pane of glass cracked and imploded.

Grace Clifton was inside wailing in a manic frenzy. Her hair was alight and her nightclothes were melting onto her skin. A back draught of flame spewed out of the gap left by the broken window and the night air fed the raging demon within. The flames licked up the brickwork and travelled to the neighbouring house fortunately empty, and fortunately, away from the Singh's home. It was lucky. There was an easterly wind that night.

Grace's image vanished from view as she ran back inside to face the flames as the first fire engine drew up.

"Hurry! There's someone inside. Grace Clifton she's trapped!" shouted Lehmber as he abandoned his attempt to effect an entry, beaten back by the heat and smoke.

"Get away!" ordered the fire chief as the hoses came out and water began to play on the burning house. Two firemen in protective suits with breathing apparatus hacked at the front door, which splintered and gave way, its paint blistering and bubbling in the searing heat.

Another fire engine joined the fray and water gushed on the neighbouring houses to prevent the spread of the flames. It was to this chaotic scene that Allison and Stringer arrived.

"Where is she?" demanded Allison.

"She's inside. Two officers have gone in to rescue her."

"There was a horrible ear-splitting crack as the timber

around the door joist tumbled to the floor and the two firemen emerged one carrying a limp Grace Clifton, so hideously burned she was scarcely recognisable.

An ambulance with its crazy flashing lights arrived to join the absolute bedlam in Golden Hillock Road. The paramedics rushed to get Grace Clifton inside and away to the nearest hospital. The fireman holding her shook his head, "You're too late. She's a goner."

The men worked tirelessly to control the hellish dance of flames and two hours later had managed to get the whole thing under control. The Singhs were removed to the Community Hall until it was decided it would be safe to return.

*

Holly raised her glass in a toast to her friends when her face turned white and the glass she was holding shattered, showering her in wine and glass splinters. The others were transfixed but Holly jumped up and laughed, "She's dead! She's dead!"

"Who? What? Holly! Who?" yelled Colin.

"Grace Clifton. She can't torment me anymore. She's gone."

"How do you know? Where is she?"

"Burning in Hell I expect. And there she'll stay."

Paul stepped forward and began to clear the mess of glass from around her. The phone rang.

Colin answered. His tone was grave and measured. "I see. Yes, I'll tell her." He replaced the receiver thoughtfully and turned to face the others. "That was DCI Allison. You're right. Grace Clifton is dead. A house fire it seems at..."

"Golden Hillock Road," completed Holly. "She died at home. She won't bother me ever again." and she started to laugh.

Paul and Marcie looked at each other. It was clear the strain and shock of the last few days had taken its toll.

Holly went into the kitchen and returned with a bottle of champagne, "Bugger the wine. Let's have a real celebration," she said, "Paul, the glasses!"

Marcie looked nervously at Colin. Holly was behaving

very oddly, but she supposed she could understand it and she resolved to be there to pick up the pieces when Holly would cry, as her friend knew she would. That act alone would herald the beginning of the healing process.

*

Lex Montague's DNA was a perfect match. It linked him to Linda's murder and it linked him to the red lipstick kiss imprinted on Rosie's forehead. Even without Tony Clifton's testimony Lex Montague was going down. It was a watertight case. Allison wanted to be the first to break the news to Rosie.

"You're safe now."

"I can go back to work."

Allison nodded, "And back to your flat."

"I wish we'd known sooner," whispered Rosie.

"I know," soothed Allison. "Linda..."

"Why did she have to get caught up in all this? It's not right. It's not fair."

"Sadly, that's a lesson we all have to learn. Life isn't fair. There's no rhyme nor reason why one person is blessed and another damned. It's all in the luck of the draw."

Rosie stuck her hand in her coat pocket and pulled out a Mars Bar, "Here, Popsie, for you. You do still like them don't you?"

"Like them? I can't work without them," and he tore off the wrapper and sunk his teeth into the melting delight that gave him clarity and peace of mind. He stepped across to the window to watch the activities of the hospital across the road. Rosie crept up behind him and twined her arms around his waist. "Thank you," she said as she hugged him and then slipped quietly out of the office door. She didn't see the stray tear roll down Allison's grizzled cheek. The job was tough and sometimes touched him when he was least expecting it.

*

The Chameleon picked up his cat and gently placed her in its travelling basket. "It's okay, Snooks. It won't be for long." He poked his finger through the metal grid and scratched the top of her nose to comfort her. Her whiskers turned down in misery and she let out a mournful mew. It was always the same when he went away. If it was just a day she could stay at home but he wasn't sure how long this job would take and he felt safer knowing she was in good hands in the cattery. He locked up his modest suburban semi and placed the cat basket on the rear passenger seat of his BMW X5. He stowed his luggage in the back and was about to get in when a cheery call assailed his ears.

"Off again, Mr. McPherson? Anywhere nice?"

"Business meeting I'm afraid, nothing more exciting than that."

"You don't have to put Snooks in the cattery, you know. I'd be happy to look after her. I'd enjoy it too," added his neighbour, a warm friendly smile spreading to her eyes.

"Thanks, but I don't know how long it will take or where they might send me. Snooks knows the cattery and she knows I'll be coming back."

"As you wish, but the offer stands, anytime."

"Thank you, Miss Hartman. Maybe next time." He gave a final wave before reversing out of the drive and heading off down the main road.

He didn't think he could take her up on her offer at least not without a thorough overhaul of his computer files and house. Maybe it was time to move again. His neighbour nice as she was, was getting too close and he didn't want to risk arousing suspicions or discovery.

He called out to the mewing cat in the back, "What do you say, Snooks? How do you fancy a life in the country? Chasing all those rodents, lots of space and no one to spy on us. Could be just the ticket."

The cat pawed at her grid. "I'll take that as a yes, then," he said. "Just a couple more jobs and we can retire in peace. I can write that book I've always wanted to do. You will be in cat heaven. I'll get on to it as soon as I get back."

He turned out into the main stream of traffic and followed the signs to Kit Hill where Pauline Dowling ran the cattery. It was a small select place and the cats had care lavished upon them by her, and her husband who ran the place between them. Snooks always came home in tiptop condition.

He pulled into the drive carefully avoiding the waddle of

ducks paddling along the path to the pond. Pauline Dowling opened the door. She was expecting him.

"Hello! Good to see you again. Hello, Snooks!"

The Chameleon smiled and handed over the cat basket. "Should be back a week Monday. If I'm delayed I'll let you know."

"No worries. We'll be fine. Won't we, Snooks?"

The cat mewed in response and James patted the cage. "You be good now. No running up the walls. Use your scratching post. Thank you. See you in a week."

He drove off and headed in the direction of the M5 and the Midlands. He had some unfinished business there. That Chrissy girl, she'd escaped but now that Vencat had been eliminated he didn't know whether it was necessary to follow through with the job after all. It would need thinking about, careful thinking. Going after her again might just blow his cover but of course he needed to be certain of his anonymity and as his next target was in Birmingham he just might be able to find out. He pulled over in a lay-by and opened the glove compartment pulling out a large manila envelope and studied the face and file of his next hit.

The grizzled features of DCI Allison stared back at him. This could be tricky. A copper, a Detective Chief Inspector no less, and by all accounts a good one. What had he done for someone to want him dead? He turned to the next photo of a dark thickset man, another detective by the name of Brand. They must have seriously pissed someone off in high places for his services didn't come cheap. In fact, you could say it was only the rich and infamous who could afford him; either that or an organisation with major financial backing. The Chameleon had very little conscience and he'd worked for terrorists before.

The call had come through his computer. Instructions and deposit through the post. 'All the more reason to pack up and leave,' he thought. Yes, now would be a good time. Go out on a high. Make this his last job then he and Snooks could retire to the country. He could readopt his own name. But for now, James McPherson would do. If not, he had plenty of other aliases and the documentation to go with them.

He shoved the material back in the envelope and continued on his way. His face creased in concentration as he worked out what he needed to do. First a trip to the Rainbow Casino. He needed to be sure that the Chrissy woman wasn't a threat. If so, then he just might let her go. He was feeling generous today.

*

Holly sat giggling with delight at Marcie's antics. She was such a good raconteur and her mimicry was hilarious. She was in the middle of an impression of Colin, shaving and in a hurry. Paul almost choked on his wine and Holly laughed until her tummy hurt. Colin adopted a pained expression of long suffering resignation, which just amused them even more.

"It's so good to hear you laugh again," said Marcie when she had finished her impersonation of Colin.

"I feel great. I really do. I believe things are on the up."

"No more Tony Clifton," mused Colin.

"Or his barmy mother," added Paul.

"No. I'm certain that now, things are getting back to normal," replied Holly.

"As normal as they can be for someone like you," remarked Paul.

Holly smiled and stood up. "My glass is empty. Anyone want a refill?"

The general consensus was that another bottle would be in order and Holly went into the kitchen and selected a Shiraz Bin 555. They all liked that. She hunted for the corkscrew and returned to the sitting room. She didn't notice the drop in temperature or the breeze, which lifted up the edge of the net curtains at the window.

*

James McPherson looked stunning in his white tuxedo. It did nothing to disguise his muscular frame. For once, he looked like himself except for the green contacts. He collected his chips from the cashier and approached the gaming tables where Philippe was operating. He placed fifty pounds on black and was rewarded with the silver ball bouncing into numero vingt huit - black. Philippe passed

201

along his winnings and James looked around at the other tables. He soon spotted her, elegant in a halter neck black evening dress, she was dealing Black Jack at table five. There was one place left. James left the roulette table and took the last seat. Chrissy hardly gave him a second glance as he joined the game. James continued, with two hands. He stayed there for the next two hours; other punters came and went. Eventually, he was left at the table alone, him against the bank. James bid on two hands and endeavoured to engage her in conversation. He was at his most charming. She was very pleasant.

James studied her. She was an attractive woman. She had a lovely smile with dimples. Chrissy's eyes didn't flicker as she chatted with the newcomer.

"Been in Birmingham long?" he asked, casually.

"All my life, born here, educated here and will probably die here."

"No ambitions to move on?"

"It's what I know. How about you?"

"Just visiting. Doing some research."

"Why? What do you do?"

"I'm a writer," he lied.

"Really? How exciting. What do you write?"

"I used to write text books, journals that type of thing but now I'm trying my hand at fiction. I've always wanted to give it a go, so I thought why not now?"

It was clear as they chatted that Chrissy had no idea or recollection of who he was. James felt safe.

"What's the book about?"

"A compulsive gambler, who gets into so much debt with a casino that its gangland boss ropes him in to do some dirty work for him. It's an action thriller. I haven't worked out all the twists and turns yet."

"That's why you're here? Research?"

"Yes and for entertainment. This is good fun."

"It is if you can afford it, but I've seen it destroy some people's lives."

"You know, you could be really helpful to me. What time do you get off?"

"I'm on till four in the morning. Sorry."

"Do you have any time off?"

"I do, but we're not allowed to fraternise with the customers. I could lose my job."

"What if I do my casino research at another club? You wouldn't be fraternising then, would you?"

"I suppose not."

"Good. When's your night off?"

Chrissy was flattered and charmed by him but she was careful. Too much had happened to her not to be. "Tell you what. Give me a number and I'll call you."

"That's easy. I'm staying at the Albany Hotel. Room 103. Name of McPherson, James McPherson. You'll ring?"

Chrissy nodded, "I will," and smiled.

She wasn't just attractive. She was beautiful. James knew she was of no threat to him. He folded his hand, picked up his chips and left the table. He winked at her. "Don't forget."

"I won't." She smiled back at him.

He walked to the door and as he turned gave her a mock salute and left. Chrissy's heart was thumping. Could it be that lady luck was going to smile on her? A writer, how fascinating!

Two more players sat at her table and she began to deal again. She had much to look forward to. Just when she thought her dreams had been shattered life was looking up again.

*

Allison had managed to clear half of his in-tray. It was time to go home. He put on his coat and hat and took a last look out of his window at The General Hospital. There was a knock on the door.

"Enter," growled the DCI.

Brand marched in, raincoat over his arm, carrying a heavy folder containing a ream of papers and placed it in Allison's tray.

"It's taken me all day to shift just half that tray, now it's full up again," groaned Allison.

"Not as bad as it looks. Some bedtime reading for you. Reports on last year's antique fraud, which is resolved. A

203

rubber stamp job," smiled Brand. "But now the whole thing seems to have started up again. I've a few possible lines of further investigation."

"Okay," sighed Allison. "Tell me about it."

"Although we've got the most of the players from the last case, we're missing the big league, the main financiers."

"I thought it was the DeVere's."

"No, just a couple in the family, Giles and Pamela DeVere. Their trial is next month. Other members of the family were duped by these two and just as much victims themselves. But there is someone else, another backer. The word on the street is that it's someone rich and powerful. No one's saying a word. They either don't know or they're too scared. Giles DeVere refuses to co-operate even for a lesser sentence. Pamela is a little more forthcoming. I've a couple of hunches and I think the Russian Mafia could be involved in all this."

"Won't the Met or MI5 think we're stepping on their toes?"

"Never thought you were one to refuse a challenge."

"I'm not. Who have you spoken to?"

"I haven't. Just wanted to run a few things by you first."

"Go on."

"I want to go under cover."

"You're too well known."

"Maybe, maybe not. I've learned a lot about art and antiques since working this case. I thought if you could spare one of the women detectives..."

"Yes?"

"We could set up in premises as a husband and wife team selling antiques. It will be easy enough to build up a profile. I'll have all the necessary expertise. But I need someone as a front person. To man the shop."

"And?"

"I can use Pamela DeVere to help me make contact to get in on the scam. It's all in there, the whole idea, which will help us, nail Mr. Big. Are you up for it?"

Allison paused and picked up the folder, "I was hoping for a nice quiet weekend."

"You will have. Just substitute that for your weekend crime novel."

"I've enough crime here, without reading about it."

"Whatever," laughed Brand.

The phone began to ring. Allison glared at it but its insistent ring demanded an answer. He waved his hand at Brand to sit down. "Yes? ...We're on our way." He replaced the receiver and turned to Brand, "Someone's saved Queen and country a job. Giles DeVere has hung himself, or so it seems. Pamela DeVere wants to see us, now." He switched on his intercom, "Maddie, can you ring Mary. Tell her to hold supper, I'll be late."

Brand opened the door to allow the chief through. They passed along the corridor and took the stairs. Allison stopped. "Darn! I've forgotten the folder. Don't really want to come back and get it. I'll meet you outside." He returned to his office to collect the file. Brand continued down the stairs to the front of the building. It had begun to rain so he donned his mackintosh just as Allison reappeared at the bottom of the stairs.

"Sir, before you go. Can I have a word?" asked young Gary Watson who'd just entered the station. Allison gestured to Brand to go on and passed him the heavy file. "Get my car. Bring it to the door," he fished in his pocket and tossed him his keys. "I'll be out in a jiffy. Brand nodded and made his exit.

It was beginning to rain quite hard. Brand scanned the deserted car park for the chief's car and made a dash for the vehicle. He unlocked it and threw the file on the back seat, sat in the front and started the car.

He glanced in the mirror and saw some sort of flyer stuck under the back wiper. He got out to remove it. The engine was still running. As he reached across to retrieve it he fell forward across the boot and lay very, very still. As fast as the blood ran from the bullet hole in his back it was washed away by the driving rain.

A figure stepped forward from the shadows, removed the file from the back seat, and slipped away anonymously.

*

Allison stared impatiently through the doors inside the building but there was no sign of Brand or his car. The desk sergeant called out, "Sir, call on line three. Sounds urgent."

Allison grunted at Gary, "Go and see what's holding him up, will you?"

Young Gary Watson stepped out into the rain and made his way to the car park. He saw Brand slumped over the bonnet and ran to him. As he lifted him up. It was clear he was dead. He went to turn off the engine before returning to the chief.

The explosion rocked the car park, police station and street. The doors shattered and both Allison and the desk sergeant were hit by flying shards of glass. Allison dropped the phone and fell to the floor. What the hell was going on?

Colin Brady's voice could be heard on the other end of the line. "Chief? Chief? But his call went unanswered.

*

Allison sat on the end of a bed whilst the Casualty nurse patched him up. Mary stood by anxiously.

Stringer's expression was grave as he entered and faced the chief. "Brand's dead, bullet in the back."

"Young Gary?"

Stringer shook his head, "Didn't make it. Both legs blown off."

"The file?"

"Not a sign. If it was in the car it'll have been cremated."

Allison looked grim. It was bad enough losing an experienced man like Brand but young Gary Watson who had his whole life before him..." he broke off and swallowed hard. He could scarcely speak. Mark had never seen his boss so chock full of emotion. Allison continued, "Anything else?"

"Giles DeVere. It wasn't suicide. He had a helping hand. He was dead before he was strung up."

Allison raised his eyebrow and winced as the action reopened a gash on his forehead. The nurse tutted as she mopped up the trickle of blood that seeped from the cut. "You can't go on chatting as usual, no more face pulling for you. Not even a smile," warned the nurse.

"But..."

"Ssh! Those are my orders. Disobey them at your peril!" she commanded.

"You better do as she says," muttered Mary. "It'll make a change for you to listen. Go on Mark," she prompted.

"DeVere was poisoned. Same way as Vencat."

Allison was about to interrupt but a warning look from the nurse and Mary stopped him.

"Pamela DeVere is screaming blue murder. She wants protection and will give us all the help she can. But she wasn't in the know about Giles' benefactor and partner. That's why he's dead. Whoever it is couldn't risk him staying alive. That's not all. Brand must have been onto something. His flat has been done over. It's a mess."

"Computer?" asked Allison and immediately felt a tap on his hand by the nurse and a glare from Mary.

"Pinched. And all his discs. Someone really thinks he had something."

Allison stood up as the nurse completed her task. "Now, all you need are a few pain killers and you can go."

"I'll get them," Mary offered and followed the nurse from the room.

Allison looked quizzically at Mark, "There's something else?"

Mark nodded; he didn't know how to say it. "Woodward's been poking about. You and Brand are on a hit list. Someone wants you dead."

14
When The Going Gets Tough

Chrissy picked up the directory and hunted through the hotel section of yellow pages. "It's no good. Vanity will not prevail," she muttered as she searched for her first grade reading glasses, which she had recently been prescribed.

She found them in her kitchen drawer and perched them on her nose. They felt alien but did the trick. "Am I doing the right thing?" she asked herself. "Blow it!" and she dialled.

"Albany Hotel. Reception. How can I help?"

"I'd like to speak to Mr. James McPherson, room 103."

"Just a moment.... I'm sorry he doesn't seem to be answering. Can I take a message?"

"Tell him Chrissy called... no, wait a minute ask him to call me." Chrissy relayed her mobile number. James wouldn't have a clue who she was; he'd never asked her name. She just hoped he'd realise the call was from her and he'd ring. She had three nights off then it was back to work for four. That was her usual routine.

She gently stroked Bonnie's head. The retriever had come up to nuzzle her while she was on the phone. Sally Johns, who had been instrumental in saving their lives, had returned the dog as soon as Chrissy had come out of hospital. Chrissy felt safer with Bonnie around, besides it was all she had left of Mike apart from photographs and memories. A small cry caught in her throat as she remembered her murdered lover. Bonnie gave a tiny bark and nuzzled her still more. The phone rang.

"Did I disturb you?"

"No, no. I'm fine," lied Chrissy wiping away a stray tear.

"James here."

"I did guess."

"Are you free tonight? How does dinner for two grab you?"

"Great! Just what I need."

"I'll pick you up."

"No need. I'll meet you. Just say where and when."

"Okay. But it's no bother really."

"It's okay. What have you got in mind?"

"What do you like? Indian? Italian? French? Chinese? Perhaps you'd like to recommend somewhere."

"I haven't had Indian for a while. There's a great restaurant in town called Rajdoot. How about there?"

"Fine. I'll get the front desk to book a table, say seven thirty for eight."

"Great."

"If you come to the hotel and meet me in the foyer about seven fifteen, we can go on from there."

"Sure thing. Catch you later. Bye." Chrissy put down her phone she was excited. "No take away and video for us tonight Bonnie. I'm going on a date. A real live date! Don't look at me like that. I'll be back before midnight. Who knows you may even get to meet him." Chrissy ruffled Bonnie's fur and set the bath running while she hunted through her wardrobe for the right thing to wear. She intended to stun him!

*

Allison looked around Brand's flat. He needed to see it for himself. Mark was right. It was a mess. He rummaged through the desk drawers. He didn't know what he was looking for or if he'd recognise something important if he saw it. He pulled at the last drawer but it was stuck. Something was caught in the back. He removed the drawer above to see what had caused it to stick. It was a padded jiffy envelope and there was something inside it. Allison tugged it free and opened it. Inside was a CD. Allison popped it in a crime of scene envelope and carried on rummaging through the pile of paper scattered on the desk. There didn't seem to be anything much. He ferreted around in the waste paper basket and smoothed out some screwed up paper. It was just a lot of names. It didn't seem to make any sense. But he took it anyway and a locker key he found hanging on the key rack. Mark looked questioningly at him.

"He had a locker at work. This looks like the key. Don't want to smash up police property, do we?"

Mark nodded, "No one's checked his desk yet. There may be something there."

"Or on his PC," added Allison. "Let's get on to it. Has anyone informed his mother?"

"Pooley, this afternoon and his ex-wife and daughter. Apparently there was talk of them getting back together."

Allison frowned, and winced. "To lose such a good man in this way...." Words couldn't describe how he felt.

"Chief?"

"Mmm?"

"Shouldn't you lie low for a while? Take a holiday? Have you told Mary?"

"And have her fussing and worrying? No way. Nobody is going to have me running scared and looking over my shoulder every five minutes. If he's going to run me down I'll be ready."

"What about CCTV footage? Has anyone checked it?"

"From the car park? Taylor should be on it. But I've heard nothing yet."

Mark took his leave and stepped out from the room. A nurse tut tutted as she saw him take out his mobile phone. He took the hint and exited the hospital before dialling Taylor's extension at the station.

"Stringer here. What have you got?"

"On the video footage?" Mark grunted. "Nothing yet. I'm just taking a break. I need a coffee. Tiring work. I'll call you as soon as I find anything. How's the Chief?"

"Doing well. Nothing serious, just a few minor cuts and bruises."

"That's a relief. Could have been worse. Look at Watson."

"What's left of him."

"Exactly."

"Right. I'll keep my phone on. Soon as you find anything, call. Day or night."

Mark flipped his phone shut. He could forsee huge problems. Greg Allison was just not the sort of man to play things cool for a while. That was the trouble. He almost invited disaster. This time they were dealing with a professional hit man, a good one.

Mark made his way to his car a worried expression on his face.

*

The date was going well. Chrissy was relaxed in James' company. And she was enjoying herself.

"So, how come a beautiful girl like you isn't attached?"

"I was, but not anymore."

"More fool him, to dump a woman like you."

"He didn't dump me..."

"Didn't like commitment then?"

"It's not that. It's just," Chrissy hesitated. "I find it very difficult to talk about it."

"Sorry, I didn't mean to pry. I just couldn't understand how anyone could let you go."

"It's okay. One day, when I'm ready I'll tell you about it."

"Fair enough."

"What about you? Why isn't there a Mrs. Mcpherson?"

"Maybe there is..."

"What?"

"Only kidding. No, I've been married to my work for too long. That and my cat."

"You have a cat?"

"For my sins. She's been my companion. I haven't missed someone being in my life... until now."

Chrissy lowered her eyes. She was flattered but didn't quite know what to say. She was saved by the waiter approaching the table and offering them a choice of desserts.

"Right! What are you going to have? Remember the Titanic."

"Pardon?"

"I wonder how many women refused a sweet the night it sank preferring to take a walk on the deck. In reality they should have scoffed everything they liked."

"I expect it was more a case of the corsets restricting their food intake not will power."

"Maybe... maybe..." James laughed, "What can I tempt you with?"

*

Taylor rubbed his eyes and yawned. He'd still got two

hours of tape left to study the coming and goings in the police car park. Damn it! There had to be something. Unless he'd missed it. He didn't fancy studying the whole lot again. Suddenly, he became alert as he watched a figure carrying a bag and holding a bottle in a brown paper bag, who seemed to be lurching across the car park. The character appeared to be some sort of down and out in clothes, which had seen better days. He was wearing an anorak type tracksuit top with a hood, which shielded his face. It looked like he had long straggly hair. The tramp slouched down by the chief's car and appeared to be swigging from his bottle, and then he deftly rolled under the vehicle taking the bag with him. Taylor watched as minutes later the man reappeared. He took another slurp from his bottle and lurched off back across the car park. He stopped to rewind the tape and watched the episode again. Then he called Stringer.

*

"That was great. It really was but I'm absolutely pogged."

"Pogged? That's a new one on me."

"Stuffed to the gills! A great Midland and Northern expression."

"I see. I can't tempt you to a night cap at my hotel?"

Chrissy hesitated. "Er no... thanks. Another time?"

"Do you want there to be another time?"

She blushed, "I didn't mean... only if you want to."

"I'm teasing. Of course, I want there to be another time. What are you doing tomorrow?"

"Can I call you? Or you can ring me. You've got my number."

"Okay, I'll settle the bill and get them to call us a cab, if that's all right with you?"

Chrissy nodded her head and smiled. It had been a pleasant evening but she would be glad to get home.

James rose from the table and approached the receptionist who nodded and picked up the phone. He returned to the table where the bill was waiting.

"Let's share," said Chrissy.

"No." James replied firmly. "I invited you out. It's my treat." He tossed a credit card from his bulging wallet onto the plate, which was whisked away by the imposing Indian waiter complete with turban and scimitar at his side.

He dutifully signed his receipt and added a twenty-pound note to the plate, which was more than eagerly removed.

A cab driver entered the reception area and spoke to the receptionist who came across to the table. "Mr. McPherson your cab has arrived."

James thanked her and he and Chrissy left arm in arm.

"Albany hotel first, Gov?"

"Yes, please."

"Then on to the Bristol Road? What number?"

"I'll show you," smiled Chrissy as she ducked her head to get into the cab.

They settled comfortably in the back sharing pleasantries and a few jokes until they reached the Hotel.

James alighted and handed the cabbie twenty five pounds. "That should cover it. Keep the change." He leaned across and kissed her lightly on the cheek. "I'll call you tomorrow, okay?"

"Tomorrow," acknowledged Chrissy. She waved goodbye as the cab moved off and then settled back in her seat with a happy little sigh as her mind replayed the evening like a video in her head.

It wasn't long before they reached the Bristol Road. "Here!" she called out, "The next house on the right."

The cabbie turned into the next road and returned along the road on the right side. "Don't want you getting run over now do we?" he twinkled.

Chrissy laughed and thanked him and made her way up her drive. As she was putting the key in the lock, a thought struck her. How did James know she lived in Bristol Road? Had she mentioned it? She was almost certain she'd never said anything.

*

The Chameleon lay back on his bed in his hotel room browsing through the evening paper. The front page was full of the death of Brand and the explosion in Steelhouse Lane car park. So Allison had escaped, had he? Some poor bloke called Gary Watson had taken the hit. He had to do some more planning and then... then there was Chrissy. There was no doubt she was a lovely lady. It seemed right he should get to know her a little better. It was exhilarating to feel he held life and death in his hands. He picked up the phone and dialled her number.

"It's me."

"Oh, hello." Chrissy was surprised but pleased.

"I'm lying here thinking about you and just wanted to hear your voice, to say good night. It sounds daft but it will give me a great kick if I think I'm the last person you spoke to before you went to sleep... Chrissy?"

"I'm flattered..."

"I don't want you to be flattered. I want you to have enjoyed yourself tonight as much as I did."

"I did..." Her voice softened, "I had a great time."

"Good. I couldn't wait until tomorrow to call. Can we fix something up now?"

"Sure," Chrissy smiled. Things were definitely looking up.

"How about I pick you up around ten?"

"Great."

"We'll go for a drive. Find somewhere nice for lunch. Then take it from there."

"What about your research?"

"I can talk to you. Then when you go back to work I'll go to the Midland Wheel or one of the other casinos and soak up the atmosphere there."

"I see. That sounds cool."

"Fine, so where do I pick you up?"

"Bristol Road."

"Yes, what number?"

"Tell you what. I'll wait outside the park by the crossing. Then I'll be on the right side of the road."

"... Yes?" he hesitated, "Don't you want me to know where you live?"

Chrissy laughed, "It's not that. It'll be easier. It's such a busy road, you can wait for ages to turn across the traffic and then we'd be facing back into town!"

"Oh, I see. Right. Outside the park, you say?"

"I'll be there by the crossing and I'll be on time. You'll see me."

"Good. Till tomorrow. And Chrissy... I really did have a great time tonight."

"Me too. Goodnight." She replaced the phone and a warm glow spread through her.

Bonnie clambered on the bed next to her mistress. She sensed her owner's happiness and looked soulfully at her, wagging her tail.

"Okay. Okay. You'll get to meet him. Maybe tomorrow. You'll like him Bonnie. I know you will."

*

No matter how much they tried to enhance the CCTV footage, even with specialised computer software help, the images were indistinct and fuzzy. The assassin was an expert. He made certain there was nothing given away. Identification was impossible.

"I still think you ought to take precautions, Chief," pressed Stringer.

"I've told you," argued Allison, "I'm not letting this fellow intimidate me and have me running. The next time he tries I'll be ready."

Stringer sighed in exasperation. Allison could be belligerent but this he considered was foolhardy.

"I know what you're thinking, Mark. But it's the principle. If we let terrorists and the like, dictate how we live. It's the end of freedom and democracy. When your number's up, it's up." Allison was a fatalist.

"At least let me put a watch on your house."

Allison grunted, "That's all. No favours. I've sent Mary to visit her sister, under protest of course, they're not the closest of siblings."

Mark was forced to shut up on the subject. But, he was worried. It wasn't just the chief's safety that was compromised but everybody who came into contact with him.

*

Chrissy sighed in contentment. She had had the most blissfully delightful day. They had walked on the Lickey Hills found an 'old world pub' in mock Tudor style, which served amazing food. This was followed by another walk and now they were on their way back.

Chrissy wanted to shower and change before their evening date. James had booked tickets for the theatre and a late supper at the Celebrity restaurant. Lost in her reverie she almost missed her house. In fact, if it hadn't been for James slowing down for the lights.

"Stop! It's the next drive on the left."

James signalled and neatly turned into the drive and parked the car.

"Do you want to come in?"

"Just for a minute. Remember I have to get back and pretty myself up too. I've got a hot date tonight."

"Have you indeed? I may just have something to say about that." Chrissy responded.

James caught her completely by surprise as she was fumbling for her keys. He grabbed her around the waist and kissed her with a fierce passion, which left her breathless and giddy.

"Sorry. I couldn't help myself. I've been wanting to do that since I first laid eyes on you." James whispered tenderly. "Perhaps I'd better not come in. I don't know if I can trust myself."

"I don't know if I can trust myself either," Chrissy replied. "But there is someone I want you to meet..." she said as she opened the main door and started for the stairs.

James followed questioningly, "I didn't know you had a flat mate."

"I don't, not anymore," said Chrissy as she inserted the key in the lock on her front door. "It's my dog."

There was a scrabbling and whining on the other side of the door.

"That's funny. It's not like her," said Chrissy.

"You have a dog...?" James hesitated. "I'm not good with dogs. I have a cat myself."

"Oh, you'll love Bonnie. She's exceptional. We've been through a lot together. I'll tell you about it one day." Small short barks could be heard getting louder and more urgent as they talked.

216

"How long have you had her?"

"Just over a year now."

"I see." James' stance and demeanour visibly altered much to Chrissy's puzzlement. "Actually, I'd better get on." He moved back to the stairs as she opened the door. "See you to..." He didn't finish the sentence as Bonnie bounded out from the apartment and dived down the stairs after James, snarling in fury.

Chrissy screamed at her dog who returned reluctantly, still baring her teeth, hackles raised and growling threateningly at the figure in the stairwell. "I'm sorry. I don't know what's the matter with her. She's usually so good."

"Lucky for me she's so obedient. I did warn you, I'm not good with dogs. See you later."

Chrissy nodded and yanked Bonnie inside. She closed the door and Bonnie returned to her loving, playful self. "What was all that about?" She ruffled the retriever's fur. Bonnie lovingly licked her mistress's face. But the incident had set her thinking.

What had upset Bonnie so much about James? She'd never seen her dog act this way before with anyone else. Chrissy began to wonder and worry.

James McPherson returned to his car and started the engine. That was a blow. The dog recognised him. Of that much he was sure. And that changed everything, unless he could get rid of the dog. The Chameleon cruised out into the traffic. He was going to be busy over the next few days if his plans were to come together.

Chrissy picked up the picture of Mike adorning her bedside table and gazed lovingly at his smiling reflection. "Is it right, Mike? Is it? Tell me what to do."

*

Holly stood at the chopping board in the kitchen peeling onions when she began to feel queasy. For no apparent reason at all she lurched to the back door and was violently sick. She began to tremble uncontrollably and felt freezing cold. She shuddered, not again. Moments later she was sitting on the kitchen stool desperately trying to understand what was happening to her.

"Paul!" she called weakly. "Paul!" she cried again, more insistently.

"What's the matter? What is it?" he asked as he came to her side.

"I don't know. It's just a feeling."

"What? Tell me."

"It's not like the other times. I think... I think something is going to happen."

"Come on Holly. Talk it through. Think it through. What's this about?"

She struggled to put the jumbled thoughts into some sort of order and focus. "It's that same house."

"What house? Golden Hillock Road?"

"No. The one on the Bristol Road."

"What? With the dog?"

"Mm. The dog. Someone's after the dog."

"But why?"

"It's too dangerous for the dog to live. And the Inspector."

"What inspector? Christ, Holly you're not making a lot of sense."

"It's not making much sense to me. What do I do?"

"Ring Colin."

"For God's sake, Paul. We can't keep ringing Colin every time I have a psychic moment. He's got his own life to live. Take me there."

"Where?"

"Bristol Road. I want to see the person who lives there. I have to warn her."

"She'll think you're off your trolley."

"And then again, maybe she won't. Please Paul." Holly turned her huge dark eyes on him pleadingly, in a way that he'd never been able to resist.

"I hope you know what you're doing."

"I do. Then we can grab a bite to eat in town. That's if I'm up to it."

"If this is your way of getting out of doing the cooking tonight. It's not very funny."

"Come on. I'm sure I could be more inventive if that was the case. Hurry up. I've a feeling this is really important."

Paul switched on the answer phone and grabbed their coats and the mobile.

"Have you got your wallet?"

"Yes. But there's not a lot in it, better bring your purse."

Holly picked up her bag and credit cards and together they dashed out of the house. Again an errant breeze lifted the net curtains by the kitchen window and seemed to sigh back into place.

*

Chrissy showered and towel dried her hair. She applied fresh make up and styled her still damp hair before changing into a smart linen dress. She paused as she gave herself the once over in the mirror. Something didn't feel right. What was it? Why? She should be elated. Another chance of happiness ... but ... but ... She had no time to consider things further. The doorbell rang.

Chrissy ran to her sitting room window and peered out. There was a man and woman on the doorstep, neither of whom she recognised. Probably Jehovah witnesses. She could do without that right now, and yet... Chrissy opened the window and shouted down. "Yes?"

"It's about your dog. Can we talk?"

"I'll buzz you in. First floor, flat three."

"You go on up," said Paul. "I'll join you in a mo. Like it or not I'm calling Colin."

The door buzzed and Holly entered the hallway. As she mounted the stairs she was getting more powerful impressions of Mike's death, the attempt on Chrissy's life and the bravery of the dog.

Colin's line was engaged. The call waiting facility asked him to leave a message. Paul explained the situation as best he could and hoped his friend would be in touch soon. Paul had a peculiar feeling of dread creep over him. He wasn't used to this.

*

James McPherson examined his options. Getting rid of the dog would be the thing to do. But how and when? He'd wait until Chrissy was back dealing Black Jack at the casino. That would be the time to strike. He rubbed at his eyes; the city's dust and grit had got behind his green contact lenses. He had to take them out. He needed to soothe his sore eyes before reinserting them for his evening's date. He was just engaging with the eye bath when there was a tap at the door.

"Room Service."

"Just a minute." James hurriedly wiped his eyes. He stuffed on a pair of sunglasses and peered through the spy hole in the door Holly was waiting with fresh towels and soap. He opened the door to admit her. As he did, Chrissy stepped into view from the corridor.

"Chrissy! What are you doing here? I thought we were meeting at the theatre?"

"We were, we are. I was just so upset with Bonnie. I'm really sorry. She's never done anything like it before. I had to apologise."

Holly returned from the bathroom where she had deposited the towels and toiletries. She lingered as James fished in his pocket for some change. He handed her a two-pound coin. Holly nodded and left the room, leaving the door wide open. She heard James say, "No harm done. Just don't think I'm ready to get to know her just yet. Like I said I'm not a dog person."

"She didn't hurt you did she?"

"No why?"

"The dark glasses..."

"Oh, it's nothing. Bit of grit in my eye. Nothing that good old Optrex won't cure."

"Let me see," persisted Chrissy, taking his glasses off. James blinked his eyes closed and turned away from her. "Look, I still have to get ready. I'll meet you at the theatre as planned. Okay?"

"Okay," said Chrissy more subdued. She left quickly and closed the door behind her.

Holly and Paul were waiting. "Well?" Holly demanded.

"I can't be sure, it was very quick. But James McPherson has green eyes. Mike's killer's eyes were cold and empty. That awful glassy watery blue colour. Eyes that I've never forgotten. I didn't get a proper chance to see."

"There were green contacts in the bathroom," said Holly.

"He's a killer, I know it. Not just Mike's death on his hands but a lot more."

"Now what?" asked Paul who had waited by the lifts.

"If he's innocent. He'll turn up at the theatre as planned," said Chrissy. "I'll get across there. What about Bonnie?"

"She'll be safe in the car with me," replied Paul. "And I'm calling the police. Better safe than sorry."

*

James McPherson grimaced as he looked around his room. It was far too late to do anything now. He needed to get away. Too many people had seen him. He grabbed his bag and strapped on some stomach padding and a serge wool suit, which looked too tight. He sprayed his hair with some silver spray, donned a hat and thick glasses. Using spirit gum he attached a small drooping moustache. James looked around the room. It was a mess. No time to fix things here. He hunched his shoulders; stooped over and adopted the gait of someone more middle aged and stepped out of his room.

No one gave him a second glance as he walked out of the lobby past Holly and Paul waiting for the police to arrive. He saw Chrissy climbing into a black cab, and sighed. It could have been good. But not now. Now he *had* to take her out. But first he needed to get reorganised. James made his way to New Street Station.

Colin was the first to arrive on the scene, full of questions, which Holly did her best to answer. Five minutes later Allison and Stringer were in the lobby, with a team of men. The manager on reception gave them the key to one-o-three.

The police burst into the abandoned room. There was plenty to interest them, photographs, details of Allison's home address and house floor plan. There was information on Brand, the newspaper cutting of the attack at the police station and even more on Chrissy Stephens. But there was no sign of James McPherson. He had vanished into the evening air.

The police impounded McPherson's car. Of course, it had false plates but it did contain some petrol receipts, which could prove to be useful and some more white hairs. Allison was positive they'd prove to be cat hairs. The dirt from the

221

wheels was extracted for analysis. He thought it may just pinpoint the Chameleon's home location.

A disappointed Allison barked out his orders before returning to the lobby and instructing Pooley, "Get along to the Rep and pick up Miss Stephens. She'll need protective custody. We have to get her to a place of safety."

"Are we talking witness protection, Chief?" asked Mark.

"I'm afraid we are. She's the only one who could really recognise him."

"Don't forget I've seen him too," said Holly.

"Yes, but with a bit of luck he may not realise you're a threat. But you'd best be careful. And," he took Holly by the hand, "Thank you. You really have made a difference."

"Not so sceptical now, eh?" observed Colin.

"No. I'm not. One more thing, Holly."

"Yes?"

"This character has a cat. Important?"

"Very. The only thing he cares about."

"In that case, he wouldn't leave the animal to fend for itself."

"He may have someone going in to feed it," offered Mark.

"Or," said Allison, "He may have boarded the animal. I want notices sent out to every cattery in the country that has taken in a white cat this week or a cat with a predominance of white in its coat."

"That'll take forever," grumbled Mark.

"I don't care who does it. Just see it gets done," commanded Allison.

*

James McPherson sat on the train. It was a pity, such a pity that his last job should go so dramatically wrong. And Chrissy. He really had developed a soft spot for Chrissy. But he was no fool. He hadn't lasted this long in the business without detection. But now, he needed to return home albeit for a short time before selling up and moving on. He thought he might move somewhere near Birmingham. He'd gotten to know it quite well. He'd done enough jobs here. And he needed to retrieve Snooks.

Then, when the time was right. He'd be back.